Sentenced

to

Shakespeare

Iris Dorbian

MILFORD
HOUSE

Milford House Press
Mechanicsburg, Pennsylvania

MILFORD HOUSE

an imprint of Sunbury Press, Inc.
Mechanicsburg, PA USA

For information about special discounts for bulk purchases, please contact Sunbury Press Orders Dept. at (855) 338-8359 or orders@sunburypress.com.

To request one of our authors for speaking engagements or book signings, please contact Sunbury Press Publicity Dept. at publicity@sunburypress.com.

ISBN: 978-1-62006-150-3 (Trade paperback)

Library of Congress Control Number:

FIRST MILFORD HOUSE PRESS EDITION: June 2019

Product of the United States of America
0 1 1 2 3 5 8 13 21 34 55

Set in Bookman Old Style
Designed by Chris Fenwick
Cover by Chris Fenwick
Edited by Chris Fenwick

Continue the Enlightenment!

To the freaks and the misfits, the unloved and unlovable,
the mocked and the marginalized, this is for you.

Preface

When I first heard 18 years ago that Shakespeare & Company, the critically acclaimed classical theater troupe based in the Berkshires, had launched a unique program in which juvenile offenders in their local court system were being sentenced to participate in one of their Shakespeare workshops or else face the dire consequences—I was transfixed. The premise that at-risk youths could find their salvation in iambic pentameter was a strangely perverse yet fascinating proposition. Could it really work? Would kids used to resorting to violence be swayed to adopting a more pacifist lifestyle after experiencing a brief dalliance with Shakespeare?

As someone who is neither a sociologist nor therapist, I was stumped for answers. But as a journalist trained and groomed to be a professional—and inquisitive—cynic, my mind reeled with myriad scenarios about these kids and the complicated emotional journeys they must undertake when they go through this program.

In early 2002, after receiving a press release on the then nascent Shakespeare in the Courts program, I decided I wanted to write a story about it for *Stage Directions*, a national theater trade publication for which I was then editor-in-chief. Phoning Shakespeare & Company's publicist, Elizabeth Aspenlieder, I was soon granted interviews with some of the program's key players: Judge Paul Perachi, the program's co-creator and muse; Mary Hartman, Shakespeare & Company's then director of education programs; and Jenna Ware, then teaching artist for Shakespeare & Company.

As Perachi, Hartman and Ware freely discussed their thoughts on the program and its future, which seemed very precarious back then, I was struck by a commonality: All shared an unmistakably sincere passion for the program and a deeply felt belief, detractors aside, that what they were doing would benefit troubled teens, instilling in them the lost confidence that might help them direct their lives back on track and never break the law again.

Through the framework of a contemporary young adult novel (with crossover components), I've constructed "Sentenced to Shakespeare" to be my homage to this program as well as a statement on the ramifications of bullying and juvenile justice. Of course, there is no Garden State Bard, the fictional New Jersey-based program in which the teen protagonist Leah is sentenced to complete as a condition of probation after she's charged with assault and battery of a classmate who had bullied her for months. Similarly, there is no Highland Hills Junior High, the school attended by Leah in the story nor is there a Lee Downey, the director of both Garden State Bard and Palisades Shakespeare (or a Palisades Shakespeare for that matter). All of the characters in the story are works of fiction and any resemblance to real-life people are purely coincidental.

This beggars the question: Why fiction and not non-fiction? Originally, I did intend to write a nonfiction book on the program ten years ago; but personal circumstances and the recession derailed the project. Some time later, I attempted to revive the dormant book proposal; unfortunately, for reasons only a psychiatrist or mental health professional could fathom, I found I lacked the impetus needed to drive it forward. Maybe too much time had elapsed in the interval and, to invoke an old cliché, my heart wasn't in it anymore. Or was it?

Then several years ago, after writing a lightly fictionalized novel inspired by my father's experiences as a 14-year-old Holocaust survivor in a displaced person's camp in Germany after World War II, my thoughts drifted back to my old idea. This time, fiction was the inspiration and "Sentenced to Shakespeare" the end result. With bullying remaining an omnipresent problem that continues to plague teens and stymy adults when it comes to resolving this issue, I think the novel's relevance is as potent and pertinent today as it was nearly 20 years ago when the Shakespeare in the Courts initiative launched.

Iris Dorbian
May 2019

"The law hath not been dead, though it hath slept."

—*Measure for Measure*, Act II, Scene 2

Chapter 1

It was a beautiful sight.

PWOCK!

A strike.

Leah's face broke out with infectious glee. She was smiling so hard that for once, she was not self-conscious about the braces on her teeth.

"Yeah, you go killer Leah!" yelled one girl while another patted Leah on the back, "Nice job."

The junior league bowling group was hardly professional as everyone, including Leah, was in the sixth grade, yet the girl couldn't help but revel in the sweetness of victory.

She wasn't always a good bowler. The first month Leah started with the league, she only bowled gutters. Anxiety would consume her every time it was her turn to get up and bowl. She'd shove her skinny fingers into the holes of the ball, contemplate the 10 pins standing in repose; then when she felt confident enough to let go and roll the ball, she'd swallow a deep breath and hope for a miracle.

Gutter. Again.

Avoiding Leah's mournful gaze, the other girls on her team would let out a deep sigh, while some looked downright sullen.

"Sorry," Leah would mutter, dejected.

Until one day, her fortune took a turn for the better when an adult bowler in an adjoining lane took pity on the hapless girl and showed her the tricks of the trade.

"Make sure your arm is straight like this," he demonstrated while holding the ball, "and when you roll the ball, always make sure it's over this dot," he said pointing to a tiny black spot in the center of the lane's starting point.

Leah followed his advice and for the first time ever, she didn't get a gutter. Except for a stubborn pin left standing in the extreme right corner, most of the pins fell in a single swoop.

Clenching her fist in the air, Leah squealed with delight. The other girls, shocked and impressed by the sudden improvement in Leah's game, clapped. A few roared their approval, "Go Leah!"

Since then, her game kept getting better and better and so did her standing with her teammates.

Most of them were from her school, Whittier Elementary. Before she joined the league, she only knew a few by name or had seen them in the school hallway as none of them were in her classes.

The only girl her age she knew well was Evelyn, her BFF. Her parents liked Evelyn, who had been a fixture in Leah's life since they met in Ms. Klein's class three years earlier. Bonding over books, Taylor Swift and bad reality TV, the two became inseparable. As far as friends went, Evelyn was it. That concerned her parents who both agreed that their shy daughter needed to expand her circle of friends. Without Leah's knowledge, her mother had signed her up for the league.

At first, Leah protested.

"I'm not going! I don't know anyone. And I suck at bowling."

"You'll get better," insisted mom.

"I don't want to go," Leah pouted, crossing her arms. "You can't make me!"

"This will be good for you, honey. You'll meet other girls. Evelyn is wonderful. We love her, but you need to talk to more girls your age."

Soon after her bowling improved and she developed more confidence around her teammates, Leah was invited to one girl's birthday party and then another.

She would never be the most popular girl in school or in class, but she was building a life that stretched beyond Evelyn, her parents and older brother Stu.

Then eighth grade happened, and everything went downhill. The cause was a 5'4, 102-pound blonde cyclone named Dede. She was everything Leah was not: charismatic, extroverted, openly rebellious and unrelievedly vicious. Feeding on the hidden and not-so-hidden animosities of her fellow teens, Dede gathered a posse around her and began to torment the powerless and the vulnerable: a girl with a stutter, an over-weight boy, a skinny, geeky kid with borderline autism, anyone who was different: It was all comic fodder for Dede and her pack of feral she-wolves.

When Leah was in the seventh grade, she had heard a little bit about Dede's antics through classmates but had never witnessed them herself as she wasn't in any of Dede's classes. A year later, that changed, and the nightmare began.

At this point, it was hard not to miss Leah in a crowd. In addition to her braces, her long thick curly hair, which had once been one of her proudest traits as it would cascade down to her shoulders and back in a leonine mane, became the scourge of her existence--a wild, unruly mess, resistant to countless straightening treatments. And, her cute oval face was now overrun with blemishes. The combined effect was awkward, to put it mildly.

Still, she was startled the first time she got pelted with one of Dede's insults. It happened in Mr. Harrison's social studies class. Dede was assigned to sit behind Leah. Immediately, Dede began chattering with the boy seated next to her.

"Miss Lawrence, please be quiet!" ordered the teacher. When Dede refused to comply, he gave her an ultimatum: silence or the principal's office.

Like everyone in the class, Leah was curious to see Dede's reaction. No sooner did she spin around in her seat to steal a glimpse at Dede did the latter spit out, rage blazing in her icy blue eyes, "Who are you looking at, you ugly freak?"

A mantle of silence enveloped the room.

Horrified and embarrassed, Leah turned around.

"Yeah, that's right," Dede chortled. "Turn around. Pizza face. Loser!"

Tears welled at the corner of Leah's eyes. She wiped them away, but it was no use as one tear, then another trickled down her face.

"Aww, now the baby's crying," mocked Dede, hearing Leah's sniffling.

"That's enough," said Mr. Harrison, raising his voice. "Miss Lawrence, please leave and go to Ms. Sanchez's office. Now!"

"But—"

"Don't make this worse for yourself, young lady."

Her face flushed, Dede stormed out of the classroom but not before glowering at Leah, who was wiping her face with a tissue from her purse.

From then on, it was a full-out war on Leah.

"Ugly freak."

"Brillo head."

"Puke face"

"Your mother should have gotten an abortion!"

With each insult, Leah felt like she was shrinking more into herself until there was nothing left but a shell of a person.

Then, there were the prank phone calls: the stupid breathing, the hang-ups, and the taunting texts, each a deeper stab in the heart.

"Hey, hottie! How many boyfriends do you have?"

"Don't you vomit when you look at yourself in a mirror?"

"You really are a joke. I'd kill myself if I were you."

It got to a point where Leah couldn't cry anymore. Either her tear ducts were worn out from crying so much or she was numb. And, even if she did cry, that would only make Dede and her followers ridicule her even more.

Sometimes, if the weather was permitting, Leah would hide near the local VFW hall rather than go to school, which was within walking distance to her house. It was safe to play truant there as usually, no one was around on the weekdays. Within the bowels of a staircase that'd slope into the subterranean entrance of the building, she'd seek refuge. Her legs splayed out on the concrete, Leah would huddle in the corner, staring at her watch, waiting for each minute to pass into the oblivion of another minute until she knew her parents were out of the house and on their way to work. Then she'd return to the safety of her home, away from Dede and the harassment. Free and happy.

But it was a temporary solution. Worried that her parents and the school would find out and that her grades would slide from the absences, she stopped.

Leah tried to devise other ways she could avoid Dede but how? They were in several classes together and had a similar schedule. She was trapped.

She tried waiting in a bathroom stall, rushing to class a minute before it would start, thinking that would spare Dede the extra time she'd needed to pick on Leah. Only it never did. Save for that one time with Mr. Harrison, who from then on ignored Dede rather than deal with her outbursts probably because nothing seemed to get done about her despite the complaints, the teachers did diddly-squat.

What made it even more crushing was how her classmates either encouraged the mocking with their uproarious laughter or gaped at Leah with a mixture of curiosity and detachment, as if she were some specimen they were about to dissect in biology class.

Even the girls Leah bowled with from the sixth grade no longer greeted or chatted with her. Although they all pretty much stopped hanging out with each other after the league ended, Leah was still on good terms with them or at least she thought she was.

Evelyn's rejection hurt her the most.

Leah remembered the day Evelyn had first snubbed her. They were in the cafeteria; Dede and her crew were nowhere in sight. Leah was carrying a tray holding her lunch when she spied Evelyn at a table by herself.

Spooning soup into her mouth, her black horn-rimmed glasses hovering over her short, wide nose, Evelyn was engrossed in a novel.

"Hey there!" Leah chirped as she placed the tray opposite her friend and sat down.

Without missing a beat, Evelyn picked up the book and her tray, tossed back her shiny black hair that crimped inward at the ends and shimmied to another table. Once she sat down, she didn't even bother to look over at Leah; instead, she adjusted her glasses, licked her chapped lips, and resumed lapping up her soup, her concentration redirected back to her book.

"Evelyn!" pleaded Leah, her voice choking with emotion.

"Why are you ignoring me? Say something. Evelyn!"

Silence.

"Evelyn! Why?"

Her now ex-friend said nothing, her concentration riveted by the novel.

"They got to you too, didn't they?" seethed Leah. "They can all go to hell. And you, too."

Amid a giggling undercurrent of whispers and snickers, Leah had grabbed her food and sprinted out of the cafeteria.

Later, when Leah was unloading her books at her locker, her iPhone vibrated in her pocket. Pulling it out, she saw a text message from Evelyn: "I'm sorry."

Leah deleted the message and turned off her phone.

That evening, Evelyn had besieged her with several voice mail messages. Leah erased them all.

There was only one way out—she'd kill herself. Everyone would be better off, and this nightmare of a life would be over.

Leah thought about her father's painkiller meds, which he had used to help him sleep when he was ill. Unfortunately, she was thwarted when she couldn't find the refills in the medicine cabinet.

When that fell through, Leah had prowled the Internet looking to score sleeping pills. She was skeptical about the dodgy Ambien copycats on various pharmaceutical sites. They were also too expensive: one hundred dollars for a few pills. She couldn't afford that on her minuscule monthly allowance. Her father gave her only enough to buy a decent lunch and anything else she might need for school, like pens, pencils, and notebooks.

She'd mulled over the brand-new steak knives her mom had bought dad for Father's Day. Pulling one out of its rack, she glanced at the steel blade, holding it in her hand, feeling the sharpness.

I can stick this into my stomach right now and that would be it. I wouldn't have to worry about Dede or anybody. It would be over.

She hesitated, balking at self-mutilation; it would emit too much blood. That was gross. She couldn't stand seeing a lot of blood. Besides, her dad loved those knives, flaunting them every time they managed to congregate for dinner. Even if they weren't eating steak, her father would still come up with an excuse to use them.

Foiled, Leah had decided suicide was not an option. Besides she couldn't do that to her parents. Yet she couldn't tell them about Dede, either. It was too embarrassing and humiliating.

They were also never around. Her father Irv was always working, doing people's taxes, while her mother Dana was at an office that got so busy at certain times of the year that Leah often had to make dinner for herself—a can of Campbell's soup and a piece of bread with peanut butter.

Stu was rarely around either. He would slip away to his girlfriend Julie's house for dinner and then stay to, supposedly, study with her.

My problems will only inconvenience them.

So, she said nothing.

Maybe it'll go away. Maybe the bullying will stop.

It was only after another incident that Leah resolved to do something about her situation.

* * *

It was an unseasonably balmy day in mid-March. Leah was in gym class and she and the rest of the students, all girls, were outside on the field. Their teacher, Ms. Evers, had ordered them to do jumping jacks and squats, followed by a lap around the track.

"Come on, you lazy bones," yelled Ms. Evers, her ubiquitous whistle wedged in her mouth. "Pick up the pace. You're moving like old ladies!"

The class fell into formation with three lines in front of each other. Leah kept herself in the front. She wanted to be as far away as possible from Dede, who was loitering in the back.

Panting from the vigorous exercises, Leah spun around and saw Dede, who unlike everyone else was standing defiant, her arms crossed over her chest, smirking.

Their eyes locked.

"Who are you looking at, puke face?" barked Dede.

Flushed, Leah whirled around, wishing she could make herself invisible.

Ms. Evers shouted, "What is this rest hour, Dede? Ten jumping jacks and ten squats. Now!"

"I wasn't doing anything! She started it," she protested, pointing to Leah.

"Keep it up, Dede, and I'll throw you out."

"But..."

"Do it now!"

Annoyed, Dede began the calisthenic jumps.

"Faster! That's too slow. Legs apart, arms over your head!"

Dede's breathing accelerated in line with her movements. She mumbled something—probably an insult—while glaring at Ms. Evers.

"Did you say something? You keep this up, young lady, and I'm sending you to the principal's office. I've had enough of your crap. Now do the squats!"

Standing with her head facing forward and legs apart, Dede grudgingly lowered her body and then brought it up, her snarl giving way to an enraged scowl.

"Up and down, that's right. Put your chest out. Head up. Don't hunch your shoulders! Put your weight on your heels. Good, there you go."

Done with the squats, Dede was panting. Sweat glistened on her milky white skin. She rubbed her face, wiping away the beads of perspiration.

A whistle screeched.

"Okay, girls. Now let's see those feet run."

Leah, along with her class, groaned. Audible in the murmur of discontent was Dede's voice: "I'm going to get that little bitch for this."

Leah's heart pounded. She knew who Dede was referring to.

"Did you say something, Dede?" asked a stern Ms. Evers, her jaw tightening.

Tense silence crept in.

"No," whispered Dede, sulking, her eyes cast to the ground.

"I didn't hear you."

"I said no," Dede roared back.

"Good."

The gym teacher blew the whistle. "On your mark, go!"

To stay away from Dede, Leah forced herself out in the front of the pack. Because she was a fast sprinter, Leah was confident she could outrun her straggling tormentor. Still, that didn't mean she wasn't worried about Dede's threat. There was an ominous tone in her words that made Leah tremble.

Her feet beating the asphalt, Leah pulled away from the others as if she was a marathoner in the race of her life.

Her eyes ahead, she inhaled and exhaled.

I have to keep ahead of Dede. I have to. No one else will help me but me.

Then it happened.

She was only halfway done with the lap when her foot tripped over a rock, making her stumble and hit the ground. This was a part of the track where an overgrown row of hedges and shrubs, resistant to regular trimming, jutted into view.

Apart from a tiny scrape on her knee, the spill wasn't nasty. She was shaken, a bit fuzzy in the head, but not injured beyond her pride. For a moment, she forgot about Dede as she picked herself off the ground. Then she heard the jeering. And felt a push so forceful she nearly lost her balance.

Flanked by her cult egging her on, Dede, flashing a brash smile, had pushed her into the bushes. Ms. Evers stopped and shrieked at them both.

"I'll have you two suspended if you don't quit playing around and do your laps like everyone else."

"Leah started it," butted in one of Dede's underlings.

"It was her fault," sniped another one.

"Do two extra laps around the track," demanded Ms. Evers, "And if you girls want to join them, you can."

As soon as Ms. Evers turned her back and advanced toward the rest of the class, Dede again shoved Leah. "You *bitch!* It's because of you I'm in trouble."

Petrified that this violent gesture would unleash a storm of punches, Leah recoiled.

Dede chuckled. "Ha-ha! Did you think I'd hit you?" she chortled. "That would be like hitting an insect."

She then dashed around the track, as did Leah.

When they were done, Dede bid her farewell, snickering.

Walking home from school a little while later, Leah felt something sticky in her hair. It was gum.

The gum Dede had been chewing.

Inside her mother's garden, Leah found a large rock and pocketed it with shaky hands.

The next day, Dede homed in on Leah during lunch break.

Not wanting to sit in the cafeteria and be subjected to the mocking that would inevitably follow if Dede and her crew traipsed in and saw her, Leah bought a tuna-fish sandwich and sauntered outside for solitude and escape. Spring was on the cusp of blooming. Unlike the day before, the temperature was a bit nippy—fifty-five degrees—and because of that, Leah was wearing a light-blue windbreaker. Tucked in her right pocket was the rock and an old, small penknife Stu had used when he was in the Boy Scouts. Leah had filched it from her brother's desk while he was at Julie's the previous night.

Now she knew no one else would protect her, she had to defend herself. Just in case.

In the distance—beyond the track and the adjoining tennis court surrounded by large swathes of freshly mown fields— was a forest. By the clearing, a tan-and-white-coated fawn emerged in all its splendor.

Leah smiled at the sight. She had always loved animals, remembering how her father used to bring her to a local petting zoo when she was a child.

As Leah eyed the deer, her lips folded into a half-crescent smile. Carefully, she walked slowly toward the deer, practically tiptoeing, as to avoid scaring it away.

Staring at the looming form of the young human female, the deer dilated its opaque black pupils, as if assessing the situation, then fled back into the thicket of trees.

"Stupid animal. It figures a retard like you would like it."

Leah groaned and turned around. That's when she noticed

Dede was without her little army of flunkies—and their absence emboldened Leah.

"Leave me alone!" Leah yelled back to the girl who had made her life so joyless the last few months.

Dede's blue eyes flickered in astonishment. For a moment, her heart-shaped face lost its color, casting a pall over her alabaster skin. But not for long; Dede recovered her bravado. With arms akimbo, she shook her hair back, exuding a menacing air as she inched closer to her mark, like a gunfighter in a Western movie. Clad in her trademark black leather jacket, black T-shirt, and low-slung blue jeans, Dede was the personification of teenage rebellion, a cliché stolen from every iconic movie or book depicting disaffected adolescence.

"What did you say?" she fumed, her alto voice reduced to a low timbre.

"You heard me," Leah countered, returning Dede's scowl. But her newfound courage was belied by a tiny quiver in her upper lip.

Dede clenched her right hand into a fist, but just as she was about to throw the first punch, Leah yanked out the rock from her pocket and smacked her fair-haired bully with it.

Dede's face registered paralyzing shock as blood spurted from her nostrils.

"Help—someone help me! She's crazy!" she squealed so loudly her throat became hoarse.

Dede weaved and wobbled around Leah, but Queen Bee could not escape.

Who's the loser now, bitch?

Because of the distance from the school grounds to the woods, it was near impossible for anyone else to hear Dede's screams.

Where are your buddies? You coward.

The blows, dealt in a steady rhythm, smashed into Dede's elfin features. In minutes, her face became a mess of red welts, contusions, and gushing rivulets of blood.

Then it stopped. The blood-dappled rock slid from Leah's slender fingers, falling from her viselike grip. The reality of what she'd done was sinking in, and her eyes widened in panic.

What am I doing?

The break in retribution elapsed for what seemed like an eternity and yet was only seconds. Though somewhat incapacitated by the pain of her wounds, Dede gained the upper hand with a mighty punch that sent Leah to the ground.

She climbed on top of Leah, who was now sprawled out in a daze. Dede was maimed but wore a triumphant sneer that ripped across the lower part of her bruised, bleeding face. She raised a fist, about to finish Leah off...when something poked at her denim-sheathed thigh, then at the right side of her waist and her stomach. Stupid, loser, weakling Leah, whom everyone hated, was stabbing her.

Dede's screams escalated into caterwauling, the kind you hear from a dying, scared animal.

With Stu's penknife still clutched in her right hand, Leah got up from the ground and looked down at an ashen Dede. Her tormentor looked more like a pitiful ragamuffin and less like the bully who had terrorized her for months. Leah felt detached from her body too. It was as if she had died and was now floating over her corpse, watching the earthly proceedings unfold beneath her.

Did I do that?

On one hand, Leah was stupefied and in shock over what she had done; yet she also felt a perverse sense of pride. *They're never going to mess with me again.*

Chapter 2

"Name?"

"Leah Friedman," the girl mumbled.

"Will the defendant please speak up?"

"*Leah Friedman,*" she responded, the resonance of her increased volume gusting through her throat and nostrils.

"Are you aware of the gravity of the charges filed against you?"

Furrowing her thick eyebrows, Leah studied the face of her lawyer, Jerry Adamson, for reassurance.

A tall, wiry man in his late forties, Adamson was an old college friend her dad had called pronto after Leah was arrested for aggravated assault and battery.

As the judge spoke to Leah, Adamson nervously adjusted his tie. Both he and Leah were standing at the Highland Hills Juvenile Court in front of Judge Dennis O'Reilly, a grizzled, balding, no-nonsense man in his late sixties. They had spent the last hour in the gallery waiting for their case to be called. The session, the second of the day, commenced at six p.m. It was now eight thirty.

"She is, Your Honor."

"I would like to hear it from your client, Mr. Adamson."

"Yes," Leah blurted out in a modulated voice softer than her last response to the judge.

The whole thing felt so unreal to Leah. Like she, the real Leah, was watching the proceedings from the sidelines while a hologram or a robot who looked exactly like her was sitting in the defendant's chair. It was a numbness like what had overcome her during the fight with Dede.

"I would like to remind the judge that this is the defendant's first offense. She has never been in trouble before. Based on the affidavits I've gathered from firsthand witnesses, which include teachers and classmates, Ms. Friedman was provoked into an uncharacteristic act of violence against Ms. Lawrence as self-defense."

Producing a sheaf of documents, Adamson handed it over to the judge, who perused the paperwork as the lawyer continued to speak.

While Judge O'Reilly read over the affidavits—Ms. Evers and Evelyn were among those who'd offered their testimony on Leah's behalf as to what had transpired—Adamson resumed.

"For a period of six months, Ms. Lawrence had targeted Ms. Friedman for a regular campaign of bullying, harassment, derision, and name-calling. The attacks were verbal until Ms. Lawrence shoved Ms. Friedman in gym class. This was seen by a number of witnesses.

"There were also character attacks on social media. Ms. Lawrence created a Facebook page whose purpose was to further debase and embarrass Ms. Friedman. She invited others to participate. Until Facebook canceled the account, which only happened after charges were leveled against Ms. Friedman, the page had two hundred active followers." Pointing to the paperwork, Adamson added, "I have a copy of that infamous Facebook page in the documentation for the record."

With his face burrowed deep in the affidavits, the judge nodded as he sifted through the paperwork and found the copy of the Facebook page in question.

The judge contemplated the page. A sardonic harrumph erupted from his closed mouth.

After a moment of examination, O'Reilly looked up and asked, "Was this the only social media platform that hosted this puerile maliciousness aimed at Ms. Friedman? Were there others?"

Bobbing his head up and down, Adamson again gestured at the paperwork. "Yes, there was a nascent Instagram account created by..."

"Instagram?" asked O'Reilly, knitting his brows.

"It's a photo messaging app. Very popular with teenagers."

O'Reilly deadpanned, "Never heard of it. But that means nothing. I'll take your word for it. Is there a copy of it in here?"

"Yes."

"Good. How active was this account, and was it directed against Ms. Friedman as well?"

As her lawyer and judge jabbered on, Leah thought about her parents sitting in the back, gnarled with anxiety. They had glued themselves to her like an appendage since this ordeal had begun.

Part of her regretted what she did to Dede while the other part felt it was true justice. She wasn't a monster, but she became one because of Dede. That gnawed at her. If it had been the reverse and Leah was injured in the fight, would Dede feel any remorse? Probably not.

Worse than the regret was the guilt that tugged at her when she contemplated how her arrest and journey through the labyrinth of the juvenile court system was affecting her parents.

Her eyes watered.

A cough erupted from Adamson, bringing Leah's distracted attention back to her case.

She saw him make a slight grimace. He and the judge were still prattling on about Dede's social media accounts.

"Not as much as the Facebook account. It had about seventy-five followers, and it was a mix of photos of Ms. Lawrence, her friends, scenes from the school, shopping at the mall..."

"What about Ms. Friedman?"

"Yes, there were a few candid shots of Ms. Friedman in class, sitting alone in the cafeteria, as well as outside the school grounds..."

Leah remembered when she'd first learned about that Facebook account. A few kids had been snickering about it in English class. Even though she knew checking out that page would cause her untold pain, her curiosity was piqued. She had to see what was on it and how many followers there were. When she found it on her iPhone while on a bathroom break, she wasn't shocked at the viciously infantile posts all from Dede—that was a given—but at the number of followers it had amassed.

She'd expected a couple of Dede's mindless puppets, but *two hundred?* These were kids she'd grown up with—two were even from that old bowling league.

And that Instagram page, teeming with a photo montage of Leah taken without her knowledge and cruel comments, had churned the insides of her stomach. She nearly missed her social studies class because she thought she'd puke her guts out. Kneeling before the toilet, nothing had come except dry heaves.

Her attention reverted to the judge, who was still grilling her lawyer about that nasty Instagram page.

"I assume these photos were framed in a derogatory context?"

"Yes, each of them had a caption that poked fun at the defendant. One of them said, 'The class joke in all her...'"

"Spare me, counselor," interrupted O'Reilly. "I think the court understands the gist. We don't need to enumerate the sordid particulars."

"Your Honor, the aggregate effect of the harassment in school and on social media left Ms. Friedman so humiliated and afraid of Ms. Lawrence that she even resorted to truancy several times to avoid Ms. Lawrence. And Ms. Friedman is an excellent student with a spotless record. The abuse was relentless and played a role in making Ms. Friedman feel she had no other recourse than to take matters into her own hands and protect herself."

"With a rock and a penknife?" interjected the judge, raising his brows.

Adamson was about to respond when O'Reilly cut him off.

"Why didn't the teachers intervene when they saw Ms. Friedman being persecuted by a classmate?"

Leah stifled the urge to laugh. She wondered if any of them had children and, if they did, how they would feel if their child was being targeted by someone like Dede?

Adamson let out a weary-sounding sigh. "Several teachers I spoke to became aware of the situation, but they thought it would 'blow over.'" He over-enunciated the trite phrase and used his fingers to create air quotes.

"Initially, they regarded it as harmless teasing. I also spoke to Mr. Thomas, the school psychologist. Ms. Friedman had been in his office several times before the physical altercation with Ms. Lawrence. According to this gentleman, he tried offering her advice on how to reason with Ms. Lawrence."

"Which was, counselor?"

"He suggested Ms. Friedman ask Ms. Lawrence calmly why she was attacking her. Or, if that didn't work, then the defendant should indulge in reverse psychology and laugh with Ms. Lawrence and the others, thinking the attacks would stop once they saw they weren't getting to Ms. Friedman."

"Yes, I'm sure these tactics, had they been employed, would have been hugely successful on teenage girls," snorted the judge.

Leah smiled wanly.

I like this old guy.

"Mr. Thomas feels very guilty about what later transpired, as he told me the defendant is a 'very nice, sweet girl.'"

O'Reilly made a sound of disgust.

There was silence for a long moment before the judge spoke again.

"Mr. Giraldi," said the judge addressing Dede's lawyer, a balding middle-aged man of average height and build," what was the nature of Ms. Lawrence's injuries? You told the court earlier she was hospitalized after the altercation with Ms. Lawrence."

Grimacing, Leah shut her eyes and remembered.

* * *

After Ms. Evers and a few girls from class had found her and Dede, what occurred next was like something out of a B horror movie...

Still conscious, Dede was slumped on the ground, her blood-smeared hands grasping her stomach where the penknife had made shallow wounds. She tried lifting herself up before collapsing in a swoon.

Leah's first impulse was to run.

What's the point? Dede will blame me for this. And, it's not like I didn't do it.

"Oh my god!" Ms. Evers gasped. "What happened?" she bellowed at Leah, whose immobile face showed not a scintilla of emotion.

Staring at the gory penknife in Leah's hand, Ms. Evers ordered, "Drop it!"

Leah gaped dumbstruck at Ms. Evers.

"Drop the penknife, Leah! Do it now!" repeated Ms. Evers with a militaristic harshness that cast into sharp relief the striking plainness of her features, which in a certain light were akin to those of the actress Frances McDormand.

Leah relaxed the fist that was holding the penknife. It dropped to the ground with a barely audible thud.

"Good," said Ms. Evers, forcing an air of unnerving calm.

Leah noted the teacher wasn't picking up the knife.

Oh yeah, it has my fingerprints on it, I get it.

She thanked years of watching TV's *Law & Order* and other procedural dramas for this insight into criminal forensics.

Dede's clique morphed into bug-eyed silence. Leah could feel their fear almost as much as she could imagine smelling or tasting the blood on the penknife.

"Fucking bitch," yowled Dede, her hands gripping the superficial nicks in her stomach while glaring at Leah. "Lunatic! She stabbed me! Are you going to let her get away with it? Look at her standing there!"

"Calm down, Dede, we'll sort this out," said Ms. Evers.

"I want you to do something! Have that freak arrested."

Ms. Evers took an elongated breath. She beckoned over one of her favorite students, Marianne, a rosy-cheeked athletic redhead who never bothered Leah nor was part of Dede's cheering section. She whispered into the girl's ear.

"So, I should call 911?" repeated Marianne to a nodding Ms. Evers.

Leah watched as if this weren't happening to her but to someone else.

Let them send me away. Anything is better than spending another minute being Dede's chump.

"Yes," responded Ms. Evers in a hushed tone. She pulled the key from the string-like pendant hanging perpetually around her neck, the same one holding the now idle whistle, and handed it to Marianne, who nodded to the teacher before racing back to the school.

"Why are you being so nice to her? I'm the one she attacked," Dede squealed.

Little Miss Innocent. Shut your big, fat mouth! Look at what you made me do, what you made me become because I wanted to defend myself.

Leah wanted to scream that aloud until she became hoarse, but she wasn't sure if she could form intelligible sounds, let alone words.

"The police are coming, and paramedics will attend to you, Dede," answered Ms. Evers in an icy tone. Jerking her head around to face Leah, she said in a softer voice, "I'm sorry, Leah, but you can't go. You have to stay here." She trod gingerly over to Leah and gently rubbed her right arm. "You understand what I'm saying?"

"Yes."

Leah's face was still expressionless.

Taking another breath, Ms. Evers whirled around and narrowed her eyes. She approached the wounded girl, who was now sitting upright on the ground, her hands still fastened around her stomach.

"Let me see. Take your hand away."

Bending her knees, Ms. Evers squatted down to Dede's eye level. She flicked Dede's blood-grimed hands away from the origin of the wounds, then scrutinized the cuts.

"They look very superficial...you'll live," she monotoned.

"I'm bleeding a lot—look," cried Dede. "You're a piece of shit, the worst teacher in the world. I can't wait to report you."

Standing up, Ms. Evers straightened her posture and eyeballed Dede.

"Go ahead!" she snorted. "Who do you think the school board and police will believe? A respectable, well-meaning teacher with multiple awards under her belt, years of service, someone who is ethical, compassionate, and upholds a high set of standards—or a vicious child, a bully who picks on innocent kids for her own sick amusement?"

"Like you cared! You never did anything." Dede scoffed.

"Oh, I cared. I cared," repeated Ms. Evers. "But I have a school board to deal with, rules I have to obey, and a burden of proof I have to build up and maintain if I'm going to lodge accusations against a student. And, missy, I have tons against you..."

Emerging from her stupor, Leah broke into a faint grin as she heard her gym teacher tell off her enemy. Then terror gripped her as the truth of her situation dawned on her.

What's going to happen to me?

* * *

"...Excuse me, Ms. Friedman?" the judge prodded.

The question jolted Leah back to reality. "What?"

"Do you have anything to say?"

Leah was about to shake her head when a stream of thoughts flooded her mind.

"Yes, I would like to say something."

"Please do, young lady," said the judge.

Leah turned around to cast a sweeping glance at her parents. They were poised on the edge of their seats, their faces lined with distress and worry. Seeing their daughter acknowledge them, they both nodded back in unison.

Reassured, Leah swiveled back to face the judge.

"First, I'm sorry for having to put my parents through this. I'm also sorry that the situation at school got so out of hand. I'm not a violent person. I can't even step on ants. But you see, sir, Dede, um, Ms. Lawrence, made my life so miserable, the way she constantly picked on me, wouldn't leave me alone, with the insults and the name-calling, the way she always made me look like a fool and no one at school seemed to care..."

Her voice cracked. She took a breath and resumed.

"I knew I had to protect myself from Ms. Lawrence. Because if I didn't, she would have physically hurt me, badly. She was already hurting me mentally..."

"Why didn't you tell your parents about what was going on at school?" asked O'Reilly in a low tone.

Leah bit her lip. A tear welled up in her eye, which she brushed away with her hand. She drew a long breath, then answered.

"I didn't want to bother them. They already work so hard as it is, and...I was also ashamed, sir. I didn't want them to know what a sad, pathetic loser their daughter was, how everyone hated her. I didn't want them to know. I mean, they know I don't have a lot of friends, but they don't know what an outcast I am..."

Hearing the tremor in her own voice, Leah stopped.

"I understand," responded the judge. "Do you regret your actions?"

Yes and no. I should have kicked her ass earlier but without the rock and penknife.

She paused and thought of her parents and lawyer. Her tongue licking the lower part of her mouth, she answered. "Yes, sir."

"Your Honor, my client has great remorse over her actions. She has never been in a situation that required her presence in a court of law before. We believe Ms. Friedman acted in self-defense, and her behavior toward Ms. Lawrence was the result of months of wanton mental abuse and anguish that the plaintiff put the defendant through."

"Duly noted, counselor. Now before I issue a judgment, let the record show that Ms. Lawrence, at the advice of her counsel, Mr. Giraldi, has declined to testify in court. Instead, she has chosen to present written testimony as to what transpired between her and Ms. Friedman prior to and during the physical altercation in question."

The judge held up a document, then put it down. "Ms. Lawrence denies culpability and other than a preliminary report we have no substantive medical information on her injuries. Mr. Giraldi, can you please enlighten the court?"

"Your honor, my client did not stay overnight in the hospital. She was discharged after being attended to by a physician. However, she lost a little blood and was weak afterward."

"The injuries were not serious then?" queried the judge.

"No. Although she was out of school for the remainder of the week."

Leah fidgeted again. She felt her palms sweat.

Poker-faced, O'Reilly cast another glance at the paperwork before him, the nexus of legal documents chronicling the chain of events leading to Leah's attack on Dede.

"The court will recess for fifteen minutes before I render judgment. Counselors, I would like to see you both in my chamber."

He pounded the gavel and strode away to his official sanctum.

Nudging Leah by her left arm, Adamson reassured her, "It's okay, Leah. We'll talk about the case and come up with a legal remedy that should be fair for you and the court. It'll be okay."

Leah turned around to see her parents sitting flustered and impatient in the back of the court. Adamson raised his hands in a partial wave to his old college buddy, who mirrored the motion.

"Go talk to them," Adamson urged his client before exiting to the judge's chamber.

As the other juvenile offenders and their lawyers decamped from the courtroom, some bumming cigarettes from one another, Leah teetered nervously toward her parents.

Shaking his head, her dad threw his hands in the air while her mom, smartly garbed in a light blue-and-white suit, exuded pre-rehearsed poise that crumbled as her daughter approached.

"Leah," said Irv, seizing his daughter's right shoulder, "why did the judge recess? I thought your case was going to be settled. I still don't understand why you're being punished while that nasty little brat gets off scot-free."

He wiped his forehead, bathed in sweat, and undid the black-tie hanging stiffly from his neck, one of an interchangeable set that lined his closet.

"This whole thing isn't fair. Leah is a good girl," he insisted, his callused fingers scratching at the salt-and-pepper-flecked five-o'clock shadow that stubbed his face, an aberration for the normally clean-shaven Irv. Since her legal troubles began, Leah had noticed her dad's need to shave fell by the wayside.

"Now, honey," her mom chimed in, "Jerry told us this whole thing is just a formality. Everyone knows it was self-defense. Leah snapped—"

"Snapped? Yes, she should have snapped that demon seed's neck months ago when she started in on Leah," Irv fumed to his wife.

"Maybe we should have taken Leah out of that school and sent her to a private one, like that nice man..." Dana faced her husband, creasing her eyebrows. "What was his name? He had red hair and a slight beard."

Leah's eyes nearly exploded out of her head. "Mr. Thomas? You saw Mr. Thomas?"

Her parents nodded.

"When was this?" asked Leah, flabbergasted.

"It was about two months ago," said her mom, her trim fingers stroking Leah's right shoulder. "He called us in because he wanted to talk to us about the problems you were having in school with the other kids."

Leah shook her head at the adult deception. "What did he say?"

Her mother's voice dropped a pitch as she focused her eyes on her daughter. "Mr. Thomas told us that the kids were picking on you. At first, we thought it was just teasing, but he said they were being...relentless about it."

"It was really only one girl, Ma."

"Yes, the girl you hit with the rock—"

"The girl she *defended herself from*, Dana!" Her father interrupted, correcting his wife.

"Yes, yes. The ringleader."

"Dede," Leah broke in. "Yeah. The other kids just kind of followed her cue...by laughing at me and mocking me."

Irv and Dana stared at each other, their faces shaded in guilt. Silence reigned until Irv broke the lull.

"Mr. Thomas suggested to us we send you to a private school where you could be with kids on your level, kids like you. Smart kids, special kids..."

"'Special'? What's that supposed to mean?" Leah reacted testily. "Like there's something wrong with me? That I need to be locked up in a rubber room?"

"Absolutely not," Irv declared unequivocally. "He didn't mean that. And I think you know that, Leah. The teachers always told us how smart you are, how gifted...but we don't have the money right now to send you to a private school."

Ever since her father was treated for prostate cancer a year before—he was now in remission—they rarely went out as much as they did before, and the vacations the family used to take had ceased.

"It's okay," a dispirited Leah offered. "I understand."

"No, it's not okay!" countered her father; then, seeming to realize he needed to calm down, he took a deep breath before proceeding. "It's not okay, honey," he said as he gently tapped Leah's left shoulder. "We spoke to the Meyer School about giving you a scholarship, but they only offered you a partial one. A *partial* one!" He grunted in disgust. "My daughter is a straight-A student!

Leah didn't know much about the Meyer School other than it was a fancy Jewish private school for kids from the seventh to twelfth grades. In terms of the quality of education, it had a reputation of being far superior to many public schools, including Highland Hills Junior High, where Leah was a student.

"Irv, you're upsetting Leah," her mom pointed out, attempting to defuse the situation.

Irv opened his mouth, about to respond, but he stopped when he seemed to notice someone behind Leah. "I think he's looking for you," he murmured.

Leah whirled around and saw the bailiff had returned to the courtroom. The slim and short African American man, who appeared to be in his early thirties, caught sight of her and flagged her over.

"I've got to go back, I guess." She looked back at her parents, her hands shaking.

To stop the tremors, Dana held Leah's hands between hers. "It'll be okay."

Leah nodded tentatively as her mother kissed her on her cheek and mussed the top of her dark-brown hair where it was pulled back with a gold barrette.

Her father embraced her. "Just remember. You were *defending yourself.* You did nothing wrong."

"Thanks, Dad," said Leah, pulling herself from the clinch before approaching the bailiff.

"Please wait here," the bailiff told her. "The judge will be out in a minute. He's ready to render a verdict."

His purple robe billowing, Judge O'Reilly reentered the courtroom with Adamson in tow.

"Court attention, all rise," announced the bailiff.

Leah noticed a freckle-faced boy with a small shock of curly light-brown hair. He was sitting in the front with an older balding man. On the boy's straight ski-slope nose were bifocals, through which limpid green eyes peered curiously at Leah.

As Leah made her way alongside Adamson to the judge's bench, she hastily exchanged glances with the boy and could have sworn (unless it was her heated adolescent delusions or hormones acting up) he winked at her.

No, you're imagining things, Leah.

Leah stole one last look at Adamson. He nodded his head to her.

"In the case of Leah Dorit Friedman, a minor, accused of aggravated assault and battery against Deidre Lawrence, a minor, how does the defendant plead?"

"Guilty, Your Honor," replied a carefully coached Leah, sneaking a furtive glimpse at her lawyer, whose eyes were planted on the judge.

"It is the court's judgment that Ms. Friedman be released into the custody of her parents, Irving and Dana Friedman, and sentenced to one year of probation. During this time, she will be required to check in regularly with an officer of the court. Ms. Friedman will continue to attend school, but she will be required to participate in the Garden State Bard Program. Satisfactory completion of this program is a mandatory condition of Ms. Friedman's probation. If the defendant fails to complete the program, she will be remanded back into the custody of this court to face further sentencing, which could involve incarceration to a reformatory facility for an indefinite timespan decided by the court. Case dismissed."

Leah registered a baffled expression.

Garden State what?

O'Reilly slammed his gavel.

"Will the bailiff please call the next case?"

"Miller versus the Summerhill Board of Education," the bailiff intoned in a deep voice that resounded throughout the courtroom.

Adamson pulled a confused Leah away from the bench, escorting her back to her parents. While passing the bespectacled teen who'd piqued her interest earlier, Leah caught him beaming at her as he rose with the older gentleman, whom Leah presumed was his attorney. Both solemnly approached the bench.

Her thoughts were a jumble. She was intrigued to learn more about this strange boy and his case. But the terms of her probation mystified her.

What was that? "Garden State Bard?" She racked her brain.

Wait, does that have something to do with...Shakespeare?

She remembered last year when she was studying *Romeo and Juliet* for her English class; her teacher had referred to Shakespeare as "the Bard."

Nah. That can't be. It doesn't make sense.

Before she could press her lawyer, Leah's parents descended on her.

"Thank god it's all over," Dana rejoiced as she grabbed Leah, hugging her in the hallway where Adamson led the trio after they reunited in court. "But she still has to go back to that school where that horrible girl is?"

"Deirdre Lawrence was expelled. It happened this morning," interrupted Adamson.

Leah's mouth fell open. She was about to speak, but again her lawyer broke in.

"It wasn't just you," he told her pointedly. "There were other things that girl did. At least you don't have to worry about her anymore." Adamson turned to her mother. "She'll be okay, Dana. The school is on notice. The board wasn't appreciative of all the publicity this case has generated. And other parents have complained about the school's inaction."

Irv's face flushed. Biting his lower lip, he extended his hand to his old college buddy. "Thanks, Jerry, from the bottom of our hearts. You did a real mitzvah for us," he said, hugging Leah and caressing her left arm.

Wrinkling her forehead, Leah broke in, impatient.

"Mr. Adamson, I want to ask you—"

"Jerry," her lawyer corrected.

Flustered, Leah tried not to roll her eyes.

"Jerry." She sighed, adding, "Um, I'm sorry, but...I don't understand. What is the Garden State Bard Program?"

"You've been sentenced to Shakespeare."

Chapter 3

Leah's heart was beating at a locomotive pace. It was beating so loudly, she wondered if the other kids in the room or the strange older woman standing in the front center of the space where they were meeting could hear it.

She had been like this ever since her father had left work early that day to pick Leah up from school and drive her to Shakespeare rehab. They were alone when he gave her a pep talk.

"Leah, just do what they tell you to do. Listen to them," he'd pleaded. "And, if anyone gives you grief, let me know and I'll call Jerry."

"I should have told you and Mom about Dede months ago..." Leah had replied glumly.

"Well, it happened. We can't go back, Leah. The only thing you can do now is move on and get through this program. Focus on that, and it should be a breeze." He'd leaned over and kissed Leah on the cheek. "Remember what I said about anyone bothering you."

To get her nerves under control—she was now shaking—Leah scoured her surroundings. Except for several old-fashioned conjoining desks and chairs, the space was sparsely furnished. Judging from the posters on the wall, the room looked like it had been borrowed from the Boy's Club of America.

The lady in the front coughed, then introduced herself as Gina Tully, the program's chief probation officer. She was short and stocky, with a dark shoulder-length pageboy haircut. Leah couldn't figure out her age. Maybe she was in her forties or fifties. She wasn't sure. It was hard for Leah to approximate the ages of grown-ups. Often, she would use her own parents as a metric: If the grown-up had more wrinkles than Irv and Dana, who were in their mid-forties, then they were older. If not, they were younger.

"Listen closely. Here are the rules, which you must obey or

else. First, there are no absences, no excuses, even if you're at death's door. And if that's the case, you *still* need to come in before you go home and drop dead," began Tully.

"Second, you must respect the other kids in the group, even if someone does something embarrassing like mispronounce a word. There is to be no mocking, no catcalling, no snickering, or any other disrespectful actions. What happens in the group stays in the group.

"Third, no bullying—no one is to be intimidated by anyone. And fourth, no texting. *Absolutely no texting.* All phones must be turned off. We mean it. If you feel an overpowering need to text or you must make a call, do it during a break. And if we catch you doing it during the session, we'll give you one warning and that's it. You'll be out of the program."

Leah's heart continued to race. She could feel her throat constricting with anxiety.

"Oh, I forgot," added Tully, the features in her pudgy face growing sterner, her posture more defiant as she tightly held her left arm with the elbow turned outward on her hip and the other arm draped down the right side of her frame. "There's a fifth rule. It's a new one, but just as important. No dating, no touching, no kissing."

She waited a moment for that to sink in, her cheeks pinched and her eyes roaming Leah and the other kids like she thought they were nothing more than adolescent thugs before stealing a glance at an older guy leaning against a wall on the left side of the room.

It was clear from this man's body language—the interlocked arms, the stony, no-nonsense bearing—that he'd heard this spiel an infinite number of times and agreed with it.

"The only time touching, or kissing is allowed is if you're cast in scenes where that's required. That's acting," Tully qualified, "and here, we allow acting."

Leah wondered if she would have to kiss a boy for this program. She felt her bottom lip quivering at the prospect. Unlike most girls her age, she'd never kissed a boy.

She touched her trembling lip as nonchalantly as possible, willing it to stop. It wouldn't.

Ugh, I am hopeless.

She glanced at the other kids in the room, hoping they wouldn't see her spazzing out. She didn't need to embarrass herself on the first day.

Relax, Leah. Do those breathing exercises that Mom does when she gets nervous. Breathe in, breathe out...

She was about to inhale and exhale but stopped, afraid she'd draw too much attention to herself.

"Are there any questions?" asked Tully. Her manner reminded Leah of that drill sergeant character in that old but pretty funny movie she'd watched on TV with her mother a while back, the one that starred that old blonde actress who used to be big in the eighties. Her parents were fans of hers. Leah racked her brain to remember the actress's name; nothing was coming up other than she was Kate Hudson's mom.

Tense silence ensued as Tully waited. Her warrior posture—back erect, chest protruding forward, lower abdomen also elevated—made it appear she was ready to defend herself with an artillery of prefabricated responses should the teens go on the offensive.

Leah's eyes flitted to the other teens, all of whom were gazing at each other. She wondered who would break rank first and say something. Finally, a few of the kids, including Leah, shook their heads.

"Good," Tully piped back, quickly directing her line of vision to the other guy.

As he marched to the front of the room to address the latest crop of errant youths, Tully said, "I'll leave you all here in Mr. Downey's capable hands. He's a wonderful and caring instructor. I don't know where this program would be without him."

She winked at Downey, then scurried out. There was a beeping coming from the smartphone tucked into her navy-blue blazer pocket.

"I guess she had somewhere to go," Downey said in a flat, near-monotone voice. "Usually, Ms. Tully is here for the 'getting to know you' phase that begins orientation. But that's fine. We can do this without her."

Leah was struck by Downey's appearance. Wearing a light-blue gingham shirt and jeans, he exuded an unruffled calm that meshed perfectly with his casual dress code. From his thinning sandy hair to his neatly trimmed beard to his regular, unassuming features, Downey possessed a look and demeanor that made Leah think of those Silicon Valley guys, like Mark Zuckerberg, nerdy and super smart.

Downey was obviously much older than Zuckerberg, probably around fifty. He had a lot of wrinkles around his eyes, and very dark shadows, making him look like he hadn't slept the last few weeks. Maybe he was too busy coding.

He introduced himself as the artistic director of the Palisades Shakespeare Festival, which he said he formed almost twenty years ago after working in the city as an actor. Five years later, he conceived the Garden State Bard Program with Judge O'Reilly, after the latter reached out to him with an idea he had "gestating" in his head.

At the mention of the judge's name, the teens emitted murmurs of discontent, interspersed with a few indecipherable profanities. Leah joined in the displeasure with an exaggerated roll of her eyes, even though she felt her reaction was a total scam. She liked the judge, thought he was nice and fair. Most importantly, she was grateful to him for not sending her to jail like he could have done, for giving her this chance.

"The judge told me he had an idea for a new program he wanted to discuss with me," continued Downey, ignoring the boos. "I brought two of my colleagues, the first being Michelle Markson, our director of education and another former New York actor. You'll become familiar with her because she will be teaching your speech class and helping with rehearsals. The other was Frank Kingston, my old college friend, and a theater colleague. He'll be teaching your movement and stage combat class."

"Cool!" exclaimed a boy sitting in front of Leah. "Like with swords?" His face lit up with excitement.

"Like *Game of Thrones* or *Lord of the Rings*?" another chimed in, squealing with delight.

Downey roared with laughter, as did the rest of his teen audience.

"Um. Not quite. There certainly won't be any casualties in Frank's class."

"Too bad," grumbled the first boy, slumping into his chair.

Downey kept talking. "We all met with Judge O'Reilly. We knew him through his wife, Nancy, the principal at Townsquare High in Ho-Ho-Kus—"

"Oh, Mrs. O'Reilly. I know her," a girl blurted out, her mouth contorting into a lopsided grin. "She's nice."

"Yes, very nice. And she's a very passionate advocate of arts education and a big fan of Palisades Shakespeare and our outreach program. We've toured her school many times. Are you"—he craned his neck, scouring a sheet of paper on the lectern— "Tiffany?"

"I'm Tiffany," said another girl, who was seated behind Leah, as she raised her hand.

Swiveling her head and body around, Leah saw a beautiful African American female with creamy mocha skin. She was a drop-dead stunner, with a haughtiness that intimidated Leah, who felt like such a hideous troll next to this goddess.

Hmm. I wonder what she did to get here.

"I don't go to Townsquare," Tiffany offered, a tinge of contempt oozing into her clear alto voice. "I'm a sophomore at James Madison in *Mahwah.*" She deliberately over-enunciated the syllables of her town as if she wanted to ridicule it for some reason.

"Okay," Downey coolly responded, his fingers strumming the fastidious beard coating his chin. His eyes flipped back to the paper on the lectern before he pointed to the girl who knew Nancy O'Reilly. "And you are...Kelly?"

The husky blue-eyed brunette sighed impatiently. "Yeah, that's me."

"So, you've seen what we do?"

"Yeah," Kelly answered, uninterested and fidgety. "It was...okay."

"You sound like a tough critic," Downey teased.

"I don't know," she snapped, shrugging her shoulders. "I think this whole thing is so fucking stupid." Her eyes glazing over, Kelly used her hand to prop up her right cheek.

This girl made Leah think of Dede, who had the same tough-girl act.

I bet she beat someone up. That's why she's here.

She contemplated the irony of her theorizing over Kelly.

Like I'm one to talk.

"No profanities, please," rebuked Downey. "Unless, of course, they're Shakespearean profanities," he added with a smile.

Save for sullen Kelly and the condescending and reticent Tiffany, most of the kids, including Leah, chortled at Downey's joke. Leah didn't especially find Downey funny—she didn't understand what Downey was referring to—but she didn't want to let on, so she forced a chuckle.

Better to get on his good side.

"To continue, the judge had seen some of our productions. Nancy invited him to check a few out at her school, which he did. He also checked out a few workshops we did the week we were in residence at the school. Kelly, maybe we came to your English class?"

"I don't remember," Kelly mumbled. She averted her gaze from Downey, then pulled out her phone to scan for texts.

"Put that away!" he ordered, his voice high-pitched and strident. Its volume and tone caused Leah to recoil in her seat, a reaction that was shared by everyone in the room. It forced them all to pay attention to the ostensibly mild-mannered Downey.

"Do it *now!*" His smile from a few moments ago was nowhere to be found.

Her breath quickening, Kelly obeyed, shoving the phone back into her overstuffed purse.

His tongue pressed behind his teeth, Downey waited until Kelly's offending phone was hidden from view. He then composed himself; his voice returned to its regular honeyed baritone.

"You do that again, young lady, and you're out of the program. And that applies to anyone else here. We have rules, rules we take seriously, and so should you. Phones should be put away at all times during the session."

Leah grabbed her satchel lying on the ground and covertly checked her iPhone tucked into one of the inner pockets. It was on vibrate. *Thank god.*

Her heartbeat, previously pounding out of control, was ebbing now that she knew her pet electronic device would not get her into trouble.

Downey forged on, picking up the broken thread.

"The judge observed something remarkable when he checked out our workshops with the kids: Shakespeare seemed to have this harmonizing effect on all the students, whether they were the class valedictorians, the football players, or those in danger of dropping out. He couldn't believe how all these different students worked so well together when studying and working on Shakespeare. It amazed him.

"The judge—he'll be the first to tell you this—he's not a theater guy. He's a sports guy. Loves his Giants and Knicks. And don't even get him started on his beloved Mets."

A couple of the boys clapped at Downey's mention of these sports teams as a few booed. Leah cupped her mouth with her right hand, concealing a yawn.

"So, he decided he wanted to start a rehabilitation program for the young adults he saw every day in court, in particular, those kids who were in and out of the system and seemed to have problems getting out of this...cycle. The judge wanted to do something that used Shakespeare as an anchor. By that time, my colleagues and I had already been running Palisades Shakespeare for a few years. So, when the judge approached us about his idea, we were game.

"We launched almost fifteen years ago, and let me tell you, it was very touch-and-go that first year. But you know something? The judge was right. We saw up close how even kids who were veterans of detention facilities—very hardened types, with numerous arrests—would become transformed through working with Shakespeare. And many of them have never been in trouble again. Yes, performing in front of an audience of judges, probation officers, and the legal community, which is what you're all going to do at the end of this, is nerve-racking, but—"

A chorus of deafening groans and protests ensued.

Leah joined in, frowning until she contemplated the alternative. *I guess it's better than being in jail. It could be fun. Maybe.*

"Okay, okay," said Downey, his hands up, "pipe down everybody."

When the uproar subsided, Downey resumed.

"We don't expect or want you to become the next Denzel Washington or Meryl Streep. That's not our mission. But as Ms. Tully explained to you, we expect you to obey the rules, come to every class, and do the work."

Leah felt an overpowering urge to check the time on her iPhone. She couldn't help it; she was feeling restless. Afraid she'd set off Downey, who'd throw her out if she did this and then she'd get sent to a reform school, Leah resisted the impulse. Instead, she perused the faces of her fellow juvies.

Most of their expressions were blank, borderline frowns or, in the case of Kelly, an undisguised scowl.

Then Downey did something she had seen adults, like her father, do so many times, that always made her gape in disbelief because it was so weird and so stupid: he cracked his knuckles. It was a gesture that never ceased to elicit a mix of horror and consternation from Leah because she never understood the motivation behind popping the joints in one's knuckles.

Do they have what Grandma had —arthritis? Why do they do that?

It relieves anxiety, her mother had told her once when Leah asked.

In Downey's case, that was probably his cue to shut up. But sure enough, he jabbered again. Leah inwardly griped. *Can we get on with this already?*

In his smoothest, most actory baritone, Downey said, "That's my story and the story of how the program got started. Now we will go around the room and learn your stories one by one."

That intrigued Leah, as she was very curious about how the other kids had ended up here.

Downey leaned over the lectern to read over a sheet. Peering up, he said a name.

"Rob?"

Screwing up his face, the program's chief instructor and director skimmed the room. His eyes fell on the pale platinum-haired boy sitting on the left side of Leah. This kid hadn't stopped coughing and shuffling since Downey had announced his name. The boy was also sweating profusely.

"Me?" the teen croaked out amid the onrush of tics.

"Yes," responded the older man. "This is part of our getting-to-know-you phase of orientation. Everyone in the room will introduce themselves and tell us why they're here and what they hope to gain from this program. Why don't we get started with your age, where you are from, and what school you go to?"

Flushed and hyperventilating, Rob succumbed into contractions of anxiety, verging on what psychiatrists would term a panic attack.

"Um—I—I'm sixteen," he stammered, each word seeming like a Herculean undertaking for him to get out. "And"—he reached into the pocket of his jeans and took out a red bandana to wipe the droplets of sweat off his face— "I'm a sophomore at Pascack Tech." His plaintive voice sunk to an anguished whimper as his blue eyes toured the maple-brown linoleum floor.

Leah twisted her mouth a little, feeling concern for the boy's mental health, a sentiment that was echoed on the faces of the other teens, and Downey.

Even glowering Kelly looked worried. "Is he okay?" she asked Downey before turning back to Rob. "Are you okay?"

Downey put his hand up to Kelly to desist. He would handle this situation.

"Rob...do you need a minute? It's all right. I can get you some water if you like. It's fine. We're all—"

"Fuck you! I'm *not* doing this," Rob bellowed at the top of his lungs.

He jumped from his chair and overturned it with a violent velocity that shook the equilibrium of all in the room. Using one of his blue-and-white Reebok sneakers as a weapon, Rob kicked the chair to the farthest end, where it crashed into the wall with such a powerful thud it was a wonder the impact didn't cause any damage. "You can't make me do this!" he screamed, his hands flailing wildly in the air. "It's stupid. I'm not going to be acting. Send me to jail!"

Rob flashed the bird sign at Downey before he ran out of the room, slamming the door shut so forcefully behind him it nearly came off its hinges.

On the edge of her seat, like everyone else, Leah and the others waited to see what Downey would do next. Would he go after the recalcitrant teen?

Strangely enough, he didn't.

"At least he didn't hit anyone or destroy property," Downey remarked with a composed sternness, his eyes not locking with any of the teens. "Welcome to day one of the Garden State Bard Program."

Chapter 4

"Why are you avoiding me?"

Leah was putting her algebra book back into her locker when she heard a familiar voice.

I guess now it's okay to talk to me again?

Since Leah's arrest and subsequent trek through the juvenile court system, she had been inundated with e-mails and texts from Evelyn asking her how she was doing and telling her how much she wanted to get together with her for lunch.

"I want us to be friends again!" she said now. "I want us to go shopping and hang out. I miss you."

The wound was still too raw for Leah, though. She snatched her American history textbook and notebook for Mr. Harrison's class and flounced away.

"Leah! Don't act like this. I had no choice!" Evelyn shrieked defensively as Leah hurried down the hallway.

Even with the din of the clanging bells announcing the end of one session and the start of the next, combined with the conversations overflowing from the open doors of the classrooms, Evelyn's piercing cries resounded above the student hubbub.

As she ascended the stairs to the second floor, Leah could have sworn she heard a hush of strained silence trail after her. *Or, maybe not...?*

Ever since she'd returned to school following her arrest and sentencing, and Dede's expulsion, Leah noticed that everywhere she went she seemed to evoke a mixture of apprehension and perverse interest from the other students. Even Dede's old pack of worshippers, the cackling herd, was no longer on her case, or at least not directly.

Instead, whenever Leah filed past them to get to class or in the cafeteria, she'd hear them whisper to each other as they glared at her: "Who does she think she is? She has the nerve to come back here after what she did to Dede?"

The only problem Leah had now that she was back in

school was that no one, with the exception of Evelyn—who didn't count, considering she was persona non grata—would talk to her. Before, she was the class joke; now everyone seemed to be *too* intimidated by her.

The firsthand and hearsay accounts of Leah's victory over the class bully, courtesy of a rock and a penknife, had circulated throughout the school. As a result, Leah was being ostracized yet again. The only difference was, this time, it was fear, tempered with grudging respect, that was at the root of her isolation.

In the cafeteria, she observed how, after paying the cashier, the other students suddenly parted like the Red Sea for her as she searched for a place to sit as if she were Moses leading the Israelites to freedom.

Still, this didn't stop a few outliers from spewing their bilious mutterings.

Hoisting her tray of food, Leah confronted these lily-livered adversaries. "Did you say something?" she asked, narrowing her deep-set brown eyes into thin black incisions.

"No," one girl gulped, her face an almost immutable mask, save for the slight tremor developing around the corner of her mouth. "Nothing. I said nothing."

This was the usual cue for Leah to utter no response before spinning her body around in a 360-degree revolution to search for a table and eat in solitude. Invariably, as she walked away from these passive-aggressive harassers, Leah would hear their snickering, leading her to believe the same girl who'd spoken shit about her had either waved an obscene gesture or made a ridiculous face behind Leah's back.

Leah's tormentors were always girls, never boys. Oddly enough, the latter never bothered her. Yet they wouldn't speak to her either. There *were* a few instances, though, when she thought she detected a sliver of admiration emanating from a few boys in class or in the hallway.

Earlier that day, for instance, a group of boys—which included George, a short, brawny, blond jock who used to sit next to her in seventh-grade homeroom and playfully tease her way back when—had immediately fallen silent when Leah strode past them.

Seconds later, when the boys had thought Leah was out of earshot, George had broken the lull, insisting to the others, "Leah's a good kid. Dede got what she deserved."

Elated to see Evelyn nowhere in sight in the cafeteria, Leah spotted an empty table by a window that offered a panoramic view of spring unfolding outside. She deposited her tray on it and sat down. Ignoring the racket around her, she diverted her eyes from her plate and directed them to nature: the flowers in bloom and the trees dried up from winter regaining their leaves. The luminous sunlight that no longer cast the day in a pall of darkness by four p.m. was now spreading its rays of seasonal rebirth everywhere on the East Coast.

If it weren't so aggressively windy out there, she'd be basking in the glow of the dazzling April sun while chomping down her lunch al fresco. But the blasts had been horribly brisk that morning when Stu had dropped her off. Since her legal troubles began, her family made a pact that one of them would either drive her to school or pick her up. Leah worried that if she ventured outside, her books and notebook would fly pell-mell out of her hands. Rather than risk it, she simply eyed the swaying trees, her ears taking in the swooshing sound of the wind.

"How are you doing, kid?"

Feeling a tap on her shoulder, Leah twirled around to see Ms. Evers. She was in her usual gym attire, replete with her trademark whistle dangling from a chain around her neck.

"Ms. Evers?" Leah questioned, startled at the appearance of a teacher she hadn't seen since the fracas with Dede.

That incident had occurred almost three weeks ago, and yet, to Leah, it could have been an eternity. Through her lawyer's connections and long-standing friendship with Judge O'Reilly, he'd been able to fast-track her case so she wouldn't be stuck in a bureaucratic backlog. Leah had been absent from school over a week and wasn't scheduled for her gym class until the end of the week.

"I'm just checking in," Ms. Evers chirped. Her hair was cut shorter than usual, giving her a more austere look, like she was a nun making one final round as a civilian before donning the veil. "Everything going okay?"

Leah gestured to her empty table and then waved to the teeming horde of invisible people clamoring for her attention.

Ms. Evers let out a sigh. "They're scared. Listen, if anybody acts up or is giving you a hard time, you let me know, okay?"

Ms. Evers clasped Leah on the shoulders before she zoomed away.

Done with her sandwich, Leah pulled out her phone from her purse and took it off vibrate. The device was humming with a flurry of voice mail messages and texts. Scanning them, she saw most were from her family, including Stu, who'd sent her a text saying he couldn't pick her up after school as he had track practice and that Dad would pick her up. That was uncharacteristic for Leah's father; it was tax season, a time when he was at his office burrowed deep in other people's returns and working all hours of the day and night filing before the deadline.

Maybe he needed a break, Leah mused to herself.

Scrolling down, her eyes fell on another text. She groaned.

"Leah, I don't think it's fair you're blowing me off like this. I told you I'm sorry. I'm not another Sarah. You're not being fair."

She deleted the message and then blocked Evelyn from texting her again.

I should have done this weeks ago.

She put her phone back on vibrate and tossed it into her purse.

But she couldn't ignore what Evelyn had said. *I'm not another Sarah.* Was that a dig? Leah contemplated that with narrowed eyes as she bussed her tray on the conveyor belt and trotted out of the cafeteria.

Sarah was a touchy subject for Leah. Evelyn knew that, and damn her for bringing up her former good friend.

Leah and Sarah had met and bonded in the seventh grade. Sarah had just moved to town, down the block from Evelyn. Her father had remarried a local woman who, like him, had lost her spouse a few years before, also to cancer. Sarah's stepmom had two young sons, making Sarah, an only child, an instant stepsister. Having stepbrothers lifted Sarah's spirits, as the boys were surprisingly receptive to her, yet she was disoriented by the cataclysmic changes that led her father to uproot their lives and relocate to a different town, one no longer associated with her beloved mother.

That entire year, Evelyn, Sarah, and Leah had been an inseparable threesome, always having sleepovers, hanging out at local malls, and constantly on the phone exchanging cathartic confessionals and pubescent yearnings.

The big thing that year for them was getting their period. Leah was the last one in the trio to menstruate—it happened when she was in a Young Men's and Young Women's Hebrew Association sleepaway camp when she was thirteen. She went to that camp because of Sarah, who had been going for several years. When Sarah found out that Leah's mom and dad wanted to send Leah to camp that summer so she would have something to do, Sarah eagerly suggested her summer camp.

"You'll be so popular there, Leah," Sarah gushed. "You're going to have so many boyfriends."

Leah was thrilled. The way Sarah effused about this camp, it had seemed like a real-life fantasy come true. Her excitement about this nirvana in the Poconos was infectious. She had to go there!

And so, after hearing Leah sing this camp's virtues ad nauseam, her parents had sent her there. Leah had never been to a sleepaway camp, only day camps, but her parents' worries were eased knowing that Sarah would be there too. However, unlike Sarah, Leah would only be there for one month—August—while Sarah would be there for the entire summer.

In the end, that one month had been enough to destroy their friendship. Unbeknownst to Leah, Sarah ran around with a group of "fast" girls whose sole distinguishing trait was to get to third base with as many boys as possible. In hindsight, Leah wasn't sure if any of them, including Sarah, had actual intercourse. But based on the number of boys they'd "dated" that summer, coupled with the multiple hickeys they sported on their necks like Dracula's underage brides, they certainly got very close.

Leah had been a virgin—she still was—and except for the air-kisses she once blew at a boy during a silly game of spin the bottle when she was ten, she had never been kissed. Sarah had to have known Leah was inexperienced, but perhaps she'd thought her new friend's trip to this Valhalla, which morphed her own gawky self into a popular swan every summer, would do the same for Leah.

Unfortunately for Sarah, Leah wasn't anywhere near becoming an early-adolescent Anaïs Nin, and this became clear as soon as she arrived at camp. Sarah, delighted to see Leah, began introducing the girl to all her cool friends. The result was less than auspicious.

"Hey Larry. Come meet my good friend Leah. We go to school together."

Sarah flagged down a lanky black-haired boy who appeared the same age as the two girls. With a saucy twinkle in his eyes and a wry smile that resembled a smirk, Larry wrapped his long and bony right arm around Leah's right shoulder.

"Welcome to Camp Nahjeewah!" he said, his smile contorting into a leer. "You're going to have fun here. Right, Sarah?" Larry winked at Sarah.

Immediately, Leah could feel the heat in her cheeks aflame. She was blushing, and she couldn't help it. This was the first time that a boy—her father and brother didn't count--had touched her—and it was a palpable touch that lingered, not a superficial graze on the arm. The sensation both tickled and frightened her.

Sarah nodded to Larry, the joyous glint in her eyes fading as they locked with Leah's. Sarah's features, previously transfigured with joy at her hometown pal's appearance in camp, were now crestfallen and colored with disappointment

"We got to go," she murmured, motioning Leah to follow her as she escorted her pal away from Larry. "See you later."

"Good to meet you, Leah," replied Larry, the leer now frozen on his face.

"Um, you too," Leah whispered.

Real smooth, Leah. You really did it! Dummy!

Cursing herself, Leah prayed as she and Sarah walked back to their bunks, that her pal would forgive this lapse in coolness. Silence ensued until Sarah broke the tension.

"Leah, if you want to have a boyfriend, you'll have to get used to that. You know, having a guy put his arm around you and stuff like that. You can't blush like that."

Leah's humiliation was now complete.

"I'm sorry," Leah responded, deflated and penitent. "I didn't mean to do that, but I didn't know he'd---I didn't expect it."

"Okay, but it's no big thing."

Only, it was to Sarah. Soon after the incident with Larry, Sarah stopped introducing Leah to her camp buddies and ignored her.

One night, after most of the campers were roasting marshmallows at a campfire and the junior counselor sang a few songs on the guitar, Leah ran back to the bunk to grab a sweater. Still wearing a tank top and shorts from the morning when it was hot and humid, she was feeling cold due to a brisk wind. She hadn't seen Sarah all night and didn't expect to see her as Leah figured she was no doubt preoccupied with her usual nocturnal activities.

The door to the cabin was locked.

That's strange. It's always open. They said they don't lock the cabin until we turn in—not before.

She heard a girl's voice, then a boy's.

Leah's ears perked up with recognition.

Is that Sarah?

She knocked on the door.

"Sarah, are you in there? It's me, Leah. Can you please open the door! I want to get a sweater."

She heard a flustered voice say, not realizing Leah could hear, "Shit. What does she want? Go away. Go back to Highland Hills."

Leah gritted her teeth. It *was* Sarah.

Nice friend.

She waited a few minutes, then knocked again.

Unbelievable. She's not coming, is she?

Undeterred, Leah banged on the door.

"Please open the door, Sarah. I know you're in there. It's not fair having me wait out here like this. I just want to get a sweater. Please."

She heard the boy's voice plead with Sarah. "Go and open the door. Come on. Let her get her sweater."

"Coming," yelled Sarah. The latch to the cabin opened.

"Enter," she said. With an exaggerated wave of her hand, Sarah ushered Leah inside the cabin before adjusting her halter top. Leah noticed her hair was disheveled.

"Sorry," mumbled Leah, as she rushed to her dresser to retrieve the sweater. Her eyes darted to the boy, whose name she didn't know but had seen around the camp.

Saying nothing, the boy acknowledged Leah with a slight shake of his light brown shaggy hair.

"We're out of here," said Sarah after dapping lip gloss on. "See ya." The boy followed.

Waiting until the two left, Leah changed to jeans and a long-sleeved cotton shirt. Grabbing the sweater, she was about to run back to the campfire with the others when she thought about putting on her favorite pendant. It was a small gold heart inscribed with "I love you." Leah wore it all the time, even when she was swimming or taking a shower. Except that morning, she took it off. Rather than put it in her jewelry case above the dresser, Leah placed it underneath the pillow on her bottom bunk.

That's weird.

She noticed her bed was messed up: the pillow was askew, and the blanket had a slight cavity, which it would get after someone would sit or lay on it.

Sarah and that boy must have been on my bed!

Leah peered up at Sarah's upper bunk. Unlike Leah's, it looked undisturbed.

Maybe she thought a bottom bunk was more convenient for her and this boy to get busy. Couldn't they have chosen someone else's bunk?

Snorting with disgust, Leah straightened the blanket and turned over the pillow to get the pendant. The trinket was a gift from her parents for her 12th birthday. It was one of her most treasured possessions. Fortunately, it was still there; but it was now cracked.

She ached at the sight. Holding the damaged pendant, Leah examined the fissure. It was between the words "love" and "you." Tears rushed to her eyes as fury raced through her.

She knew this wasn't a deliberate act of sabotage on Sarah's part. No doubt she and the boy didn't see or know the pendant was underneath the pillow before they got it on.

This is my fault. I shouldn't have left it here. But Sarah shouldn't have used my bed as a make-out pad either.

The following day, Leah confronted her now ex-pal in the cabin. It was after dinner. Sarah's squad was nowhere in sight. She was changing her clothes, preparing for another night out, which naturally excluded Leah.

"Do you see this?" Leah was holding the ruined pendant close to Sarah's face.

Sarah registered alarm. She stopped brushing her hair.

"What happened? You always wear that."

"I'm glad you remember," answered Leah, sarcastic. "What happened is you."

"What are you talking about?" Sarah snapped. She resumed brushing her hair.

"You and that boy happened. I took it off yesterday and put it under my pillow for safe-keeping. And then you and that boy went on my bed and did...whatever."

"I'm sorry. It was an accident."

"Like this summer has been an accident. My being here at the camp is an accident."

"I already told you it was an accident," Sarah barked, her voice becoming strident. "What do you want me to do? Listen, we'll talk about this later. Darren is waiting for me."

"Who's Darren? Is that the boy you were with yesterday?"

"No, that was Mike. This is someone else."

Leah rolled her eyes.

"Hey, that's not my fault." Sarah scowled.

"Not my fault, what? That I don't want to go through guys like someone going through potato chips? Like you and your friends here. I told you...I've never had a boyfriend. I've never gone out with anyone."

"Well, you could have changed that."

Leah shook her head in disbelief. All the accumulated anger that had been boiling up within her the past two weeks since Sarah's rejection of her exploded.

"Sarah, what is wrong with you? You convinced me to come here. Remember that? We were good friends. We saw each other all the time. You came to my Bas Mitzvah. We hung out with Evelyn. We were the three musketeers. That's what you called us. And now you're treating me like something you scraped off your shoe because...of what? Because I blushed when Larry put his arm around me? Because I wasn't going to be popular with the boys?"

Frowning, an irritated Sarah threw on a jean jacket over a T-shirt.

"Leah, I see you all the time at school. I want to spend time with my friends here. I never see them except when I'm here. That's all. Later."

She hurried out of the cabin, escaping further interrogation.

The next day, Leah saw Sarah had accidentally left her phone on her bed. Leah loitered in the bunk, waiting until two campers and a counselor left. When she knew it was safe, Leah crept over and picked up Sarah's phone. She knew it was wrong, but she was curious whether Sarah was in contact with Evelyn, complaining about her. Sure enough, her hunch had been correct.

There, in a time stamp from an hour earlier, Sarah had sent a fresh text to Evelyn, griping to her about Leah.

"I should have never convinced Leah to come here. What a loser. She's hopeless. Maybe you can call Mrs. Friedman and ask her to pick Leah up and get her out of here. My friends can't stand her. Guess what? We were thinking of short-sheeting her bed but decided not to. LOL."

To Evelyn's credit, there was no response.

Leah recalled when her parents and Stu came to visit on family day. They were all smiles that sweltering afternoon, carrying a bag of goodies earmarked for Leah's discerning adolescent tastes: peanut butter cookies, pita chips, and the latest issue of *Girls' Life* magazine with Taylor Swift on the cover.

First, Leah had hugged her dad, then her mom, who also kissed her on the forehead. "How are you doing? We missed you," she whispered into Leah's ear as they embraced.

Then Stu engulfed her in a quick bear hug. "Hope you're having a good time."

I'm not. I'm miserable. Sarah isn't talking to me because I'm not a slut. And, she ruined the pendant mom and dad gave me. I want to go home. I made a mistake. Please take me back.

"It's great," Leah lied, forcing a wide grin. "Last night we had a pizza and pool party. And tonight, we're going to a movie!"

"That's wonderful. How's Sarah?" asked Dana.

"She's fine, Ma," Leah piped back, still affecting fake glee and trying not to wince from her disingenuousness. *If only I could tell you all the truth. I shouldn't have listened to Sarah.*

Not wishing to disappoint her parents by exposing her humiliation, Leah kept up the pretense. "Sarah says hello to you and Dad."

By the time eighth grade came along, Leah's friendship with Sarah was a memory. They hadn't been in the same classes anymore, but because Sarah was still friendly with Evelyn, Leah would run into her at the cafeteria or at Evelyn's locker, where they'd both be engaged in chatter about school and other trivialities.

"How are you, Leah?" Sarah would ask, her features tightening and reddening with embarrassment at the charade. Evelyn had heard both sides of what had happened, and rather than express a bias, she opted to be the neutral party to remain friends with both girls.

"Fine," Leah would harrumph, storming away in chagrin and not even bothering to hide her displeasure at Evelyn's ongoing association with the poster child of a false friend.

Leah had never told her parents what happened at camp that summer. But she had a feeling her parents guessed, thanks to Sarah's disappearance, that something had gone awry. They never pressed her about it, but Stu did one day when they were out buying an Amazon gift card for Mom's birthday at the local CVS.

"Hey, sis, what went on at camp?" Stu had asked in an undertone after he paid the cashier.

Leah had waited until they'd walked out of the store so no prying ears could hear.

"Sarah is a slut, and she was upset with me because I didn't want to put out like her and her camp friends."

Barely flexing a facial muscle, Stu responded coolly, "Sarah's a bitch. And ugly too. Those guys must have been desperate and blind. You're better off."

"Don't tell Mom and Dad, please," Leah entreated her big brother.

"I won't," he answered.

Now, in the corridor after lunch, Leah opened her locker and pulled out her math book. In an odd moment of synchronicity, Leah saw Sarah traipse down the hallway clutching her books. A wary gleam in her eyes, Sarah acknowledged her ex-friend with a half-hearted shake of the head, her lips pursed.

Leah glared, slammed her locker shut, and stalked away.

Chapter 5

Leah knew Rob looked different. It wasn't just the buzz cut; she couldn't pinpoint it. Or at least not right away. Until a gawking Kelly, wearing her perpetual surly expression, exclaimed, "He shaved his eyebrows!"

"What did I say were the rules for this program, Ms.—" said Tully, who was back at the session, before pausing to glance over the attendance list on the podium in front of her— "Turner?"

"I didn't do anything," protested Kelly.

"There will be no attacks on other participants in this program. Do you understand? We won't tolerate these kinds of outbursts."

Flinging her arms in the air, Kelly continued to protest. "But he has no eyebrows, and he looks weird!"

The last time they were at the session, there'd been scuttlebutt among the other kids during the break that Rob was coming back to the program. Supposedly, his lawyer had worked out a deal with the judge. That's what some people were hearing. It was either that or send Rob to a detention facility for selling OxyContin to other kids—which would probably kill him.

As Leah surveyed Rob, who was quiet, glassy-eyed, and downcast, she wondered how much Xanax he was on.

"I think he looks cool. Very sci-fi," interjected a male voice.

Everyone's attention turned to the kid who'd made the remark.

He was sitting in the back of the room, a row behind Leah but to the extreme left. His right thumb was elevated upward in a gesture of support to Rob for his new quasi-alien exterior.

He was a last-minute addition to the group, and Leah instantly recognized him as the boy who had been in court the same day as her—the one who'd winked at her, although she still wasn't sure if that had happened or if she'd only imagined it.

"Thank you, Jake," said Tully, "but we don't need any more commentary on this subject." Her eyes reverted to the culprit who'd started this, and she dropped her voice to a lower, foreboding octave. "And, Kelly, this is a warning. Understand?"

Kelly rolled her eyes and folded her arms. The sneer was gone from her face, replaced by a pout. When she finally deigned to answer Tully, she mumbled, "Okay," punctuating the utterance with a lengthy sigh.

Pivoting her head, Tully nodded to Downey. A changing of the guard was afoot. Tully proceeded to the outer margin of the room as Downey took over and eyeballed the sheet on the podium.

"Jake, you're a newcomer here," he said, looking up. Why don't we continue the getting-to-know-you phase of orientation with you? How old are you, and where are you from?"

Jake perked up as soon as Downey called on him. Unlike Rob, who collapsed at the mere notion of revealing anything about himself, Jake seemed to bask in the limelight.

The bifocals, resting on his curved beak of a nose, illuminated his translucent green eyes, the same penetrating orbs that had shimmered at Leah in the courtroom. His mouth, indented by a pearly white smile, was a dentist's dream. Straightening his posture, Jake took in his small, seemingly rapt crowd with an excited "here goes" attitude before answering.

"I'm Jake Miller. I'm sixteen. I live in Mahwah, and I'm a sophomore at James Madison."

As he mentioned the school, Jake motioned to Tiffany. "Hi, Tiffany," he greeted, his eyes flickering with delight as they alighted on a familiar face from school.

Refusing to take the bait, Tiffany averted her eyes from Jake, focusing instead on her long and lacquered nails painted a light fuchsia. "Hello, Jake," she murmured, her demeanor shaded by a tinge of hauteur.

Tiffany's beauty and style intimidated Leah so much so she wasn't surprised to hear at the last session that Tiffany wanted to be a model. That made sense, given how gorgeous and tall Tiffany was, although Leah had been shocked to hear how she'd ended up in the program: she had been arrested twice for shoplifting at Nordstrom's. The first time they'd let her off with a warning; the second time, after she'd pocketed jewelry and stuffed a scarf and blouse into her bag, she got booked.

That offense, combined with Tiffany's unmitigated arrogance, brought her down to mortal level, a footing equal to Leah and the others. She could pretend she was better than them, but she was just another juvie like they all were, stuck in the same program. The realization buoyed Leah's spirits every time she saw Tiffany put on her untouchable snob act.

"You two know each other from school?" asked Downey.

They bobbed their heads up and down.

Downey frowned. "Are you in the same classes?"

Before he finished voicing the last syllable of the question, Tiffany replied with a curt and clipped, "No."

"So, you and Jake just see each other in the hallway," Downey deduced, trying to gain clarity on a potentially dicey situation.

"Yeah, we've never hooked up," Tiffany responded impassively, scrutinizing her nails. "I don't know him personally, but it's hard not to know who he is, considering..."

Leah's eyes dilated as she leaned closer to Tiffany, who was sitting to the right of her, to hear the juicy details.

Tiffany compressed her full lips, giving Jake an accusatory once-over before becoming transfixed with her manicure yet again.

"That's enough," Tully cut in sharply. "What did I say about the need to respect each other? Tiffany...*Tiffany?*"

The girl was now filing her nails with an emery board she'd yanked out of her purse.

"Oh, for god's sake," snapped Tully, snatching the accessory away from Tiffany, whose eyes widened in horror and incredulity.

Leah's mouth fell open. She almost let out a giggle, but seeing how irked Tully was, she instead raised a cupped hand to her mouth to quash any sounds that would resemble amusement.

"*Hey!*" the girl cried, glaring at Tully.

"You will get it back *after* the session. What is this? The spa?"

Defiantly protruding her upper lip, a speechless Tiffany gawked at her shoes.

Leah's eyes followed Tiffany's to her shoes, gold Stuart Weitzman ballet flats.

I wonder if she shoplifted them.

"Excuse me, young lady," Tully shrilled at Tiffany, whose eyes were now glued to the court officer. "I'm sorry I'm taking you away from salon time."

She marched to the center of the room and vented the full scope of her wrath. "Do you *all* think this is a *joke*? That this is *playtime*? I hate to break this to you, but you are not angels. You all are juvenile offenders in the eyes of the law." She paused like she wanted the impact of her words to sink in. "You know, I can go into the judge's chambers tomorrow and say everyone in this specific session is beyond hope of rehabilitation and recommend it be terminated at once. And he can do it."

Leah's heart pounded again. Her face turned ashen with fear.

Can she do that? She has to be bluffing. Oh god, if she is telling the truth, I'm screwed. Hello, reform school.

A tense stillness followed, which Downey shattered by quietly saying, "Let's resume. The spotlight is back on you, Jake. How did you end up here?"

"Excuse me, Mr. Downey?" Jake coughed, surprised at Downey's bluntness.

"What were you arrested for? Everyone will have to go through this," he reassured the teen.

Leah felt empathy for Jake as she, too, was not looking forward to relating the circumstances that had led to her arrest. Then again, none of them were innocents.

"But," said the puzzled teen, "I thought you and Ms. Tully knew..."

"Yes, you're correct. Ms. Tully, as your probation officer, and I are well aware of how all of you got here, but the others don't know. So please, tell them."

Leah's ears perked up.

Jake threw his eyes downward and mumbled something unintelligible.

The kids in the room stared quizzically at one another before looking to Downey for help.

"Please speak up...and clearly," said Downey.

Once again, Jake's response was garbled and incomprehensible.

Downey was about to repeat his request until an impatient Tiffany said in a roar, "He made a bomb and threatened to blow the school up!"

Leah gasped while a few others like Kelly cheered and clapped. Even Rob was impressed, giving Jake the high-five sign.

"Takes all kinds, I guess," muttered a grimacing Tiffany as she fiddled with her nails again.

"Sorry, everyone, but Jake's offense is not unusual," noted Downey. "We've had quite a few people in the program over the last decade who've been convicted for the same thing. What happened to push you over the edge like that, Jake?"

"I wanted to blow up the entire school," Jake boiled, his face reddening with rage. "I wanted to destroy it! See it gone, reduced to rubble and ash."

"What happened that was so egregious that would cause you to do something so drastic and destructive?" asked Downey.

"Erg—what?" answered a befuddled Jake.

"Sorry. What happened to you that was so awful?" corrected Downey.

"I was fed up."

"With whom?" Downey inquired.

"I was never going to use it. I just wanted to scare them. I doubt it worked."

"The bomb?"

"Yeah. I tried to order a gun over Amazon, but I had problems doing that. Instead, I found a website that showed the best quick ways to make a bomb."

"What happened to make you so upset you'd do that?" pressed Downey.

"I don't have any friends there," related Jake, wincing. "Everyone calls me 'four-eyed freak' or 'freckle freak,' which I guess is better than when I was called 'freckle pig.' That was in the seventh grade when I weighed more.

"But even after I lost weight, some kids wouldn't leave me alone. One tried to push me into my locker and then shut it. If it wasn't for a teacher walking by, he would have gotten away with it. My parents have complained about these assholes for years, and the school always says they're going to do something about it—keep a closer eye on me and all that bullshit. Sorry," he said sheepishly, apologizing for his profane language.

"It's okay." Downey smiled. "You're not in school. If you want to curse to help you express emotion while you're in here, that's fine. But within reason, and not all the time or every other word."

He paused for the teens to absorb that disclaimer, then cued Jake to continue his account.

"They did diddly about it," recalled Jake. "Then the star jock, Scott," he snorted with disgust, "a brownnosing two-faced prick, started picking on me too, and that was it. I knew I wouldn't get any justice. Jocks are gods at my school. They can do anything and get away with it. And look at me!" He pointed to his unmuscular and slim frame. "How am I going to beat up the hulk? That's when I thought about buying a gun. To protect myself. When that fell through, I researched how to make a bomb."

Leah stared at Jake, riveted by his account of being bullied. Although the details differed from her own—she had never entertained any idea of detonating anything; that was creepy and sinister, not to mention terrorist-like—she could easily relate to Jake's story. His telling of it had engrossed her so much she was practically falling off her chair, her face and body completely turned toward Jake's direction—but she quickly corrected her position.

Still, she found Jake to be unsettling and quite the oddball.

Not counting the time in the courtroom, she had only been in his presence for an hour, but in that time, his moods had wildly fluctuated between strange joviality and abject despair. Between the borderline behavior, he'd cast myriad flirtatious glances toward all the girls in the room, not just her. Only Tully seemed to be immune to the optical come-ons.

So, I guess I wasn't imagining the wink in court.

"Bullying always seems to be a common theme at our sessions, right?" said Downey, exchanging knowing glances with Tully. "Either we get kids who have been bullies or, more frequently, kids who just got tired of being pushed around and snapped."

He perused the room.

"A raise of hands. Who here has been bullied? It doesn't have to be connected to why you're here."

Except for Kelly and an excessively buff boy wearing a New York Giants cap sitting to the left of Jake, everyone put their hand up.

Downey nodded. "You see how common it is?" His eyes homed in on Kelly and the burly teen. "Kelly, you've never been bullied?"

"Nope. Not me. Someone messes with me, I break their face," she answered through gritted teeth, her arms crossed.

Ignoring her bravado, Downey moved on to the other teen. "And you are?" He looked at the sheet on the podium. "Derek?"

"Yeah, that's me," the boy uttered in a deep, throat-hugging baritone.

"Is it because you're relatively big, and you seem strong and menacing?" asked a tongue-in-cheek Downey.

Clad in jeans that snugly fit his well-defined legs and a short-sleeved white T-shirt with the name of a local gym embossed on it in gold lettering, Derek exuded confidence when it came to displaying his sinewy biceps.

Downey's jibe was lost on the boy.

"Probably. I lift weights at my dad's gym and work out every night to make sure I won't get picked on."

"That figures," muttered Jake.

"What did you say?" Derek asked, cocking his eyebrows

and acting like he was ready to lunge at Jake.

Tully stopped him. "That's enough. You're a tough guy; we get it," she said sardonically. "By the way, if you or anyone else smacks another person in the program or intimidates them in any way—I don't care if it was provoked—you're out of here. And you know what the next stop is?" she asked rhetorically, her eyes ping-ponging between Derek and Kelly.

"Let me explain something," said Downey, breaking in. "Ms. Tully and I are *not* psychoanalysts. We're not here to diagnose you and treat you. We're only here to help navigate you through this program. Hopefully, you'll come away with the tools you'll need to get your lives back on track, so you won't commit any more crimes. This process we're doing now—getting to know you—is just that. It's also a great way for us to zero in on who you are, which will aid us when we cast you in scenes and monologues. So, it's not a waste of time. It's necessary.

"Contrary to what many of you might think, it's not meant to be a painful or a traumatizing exercise. Although for many kids, it is; for others, it's not. They find it liberating to finally be able to speak truthfully to others just like them."

He turned, walking to the podium and poring over the sheet for a moment until his eyes settled on a certain name. Lifting his head, he peered at Leah while scratching his whiskered chin.

"Leah, you had your hand up before when I asked who has been bullied. Why don't you tell us a bit about your experiences? How old are you, and what school are you attending?"

Leah's throat knotted. "I'm Leah Friedman," she said in a croak, then cleared her throat. "I'm fifteen, and in the ninth grade at Highland Hills Junior High." The pervading quiet was unsettling. "What else do you need to know?"

"What brings you here?"

Drawing a breath, in the most detached manner she could muster, Leah described the last year of hell that had culminated in her taking matters into her own hands.

"Was this the first time you were picked on?"

"No, I've always been picked on, but it was never so..." Leah scrambled for the right word.

"Consistent?" Downey chimed in.

"Yes." She paused, then resumed. "Before, it was a couple of stupid comments here and there. But it wasn't so...malicious."

"You were never in trouble before, correct?"

"No, this was the first time."

"How did your parents react?"

Leah flashbacked to the memory of her sitting in the police station where she had been driven after the cops told her they needed to speak to her to find out what happened between her and Dede. They also had to call her parents.

With the ambulance in tow, two police officers, a young man and an older one, had arrived minutes after Marianne phoned 911. Even placed on a stretcher, Dede wouldn't shut up.

"She should be locked up," she shrieked. "I didn't do anything!"

As Leah was led away into the police car, she watched Ms. Evers attempt to corral the students, most of whom were too transfixed to move, back to the school.

"Come on, everyone. It's over. The police are now taking care of this. Let's go inside. Time to get back to class."

"What's going to happen to Leah?" she heard one classmate ask. "Is she going to get arrested?"

"The police will handle this. It'll be okay," she heard Ms. Evers say before the door of the police car closed and the vehicle sped away.

Both her parents had been dumbstruck. Their sweet, gentle, smart daughter was being charged with beating up a classmate, and with two weapons, no less. Something was not right.

"Are you sure *Leah* is the person you're looking for? This isn't a case of mistaken identity?" asked a shell-shocked Irv.

"That's the only thing that makes sense, honey," Dana panicked. "This can't be Leah."

"I'm sorry, ma'am, but I'm afraid it is," remonstrated the officer.

After being booked for aggravated assault and battery, Leah had felt discombobulated as her fingerprints and mug shots were being taken. Yet there was a certain order about it she found oddly comforting, unlike the months before when she'd never been sure if this would be the day when Dede would do something drastic and dire to her.

As she recounted her parents' astonishment at her arrest, silence enveloped the session room, and Leah was stung with a pang of regret and embarrassment. *I should have kept it short and simple. Even that cranky girl, Kelly, is looking at me with pity.*

"Your parents never knew what you were going through at school?" asked Downey, breaking the lull that seemed excruciating to Leah.

"No."

"Why didn't you tell them? Were you afraid of their reaction?"

Leah bowed her head, her eyes on the ground. "I didn't want to bother them. And I didn't want to tell my brother because I knew he would tell them."

"So, you said nothing?"

Leah nodded her head in assent. After a minute elapsed—a minute that seemed like an eternity—she conceded, "I thought this was my problem, and I needed to think of ways to solve it. But it wouldn't end. It still hasn't. I'm still treated like an outcast, although no one picks on me anymore. At least not directly."

"That's a shame," answered Downey.

And judging by the bobbing of the heads of a few of the teens, including Rob, Tiffany, and Jake, the rest of those in the room roundly echoed Downey's sentiment.

"I'm glad you smacked the hell out of that bitch," said Kelly in commiseration, her glower yielding to a more congenial bearing.

Leah mouthed back, "Thanks," to her.

"And how about you, Kelly?" asked Downey in a measured voice. "What's your story?"

"What do you mean?" she retorted, kneading her forehead.

"How did you end up here?"

"Okay, I'll be easy," she allowed. "I'm Kelly Turner. I'm seventeen and a junior at Townsquare High. I live with my mother and younger sister. My older sister is married and out of the house. Has been for years. Good riddance, Miss Know-It-All. Oh yeah, my father split when I was eight." She said all this in a singsong voice as if she were reciting the dullest Sunday school religious catechism learned by rote. But as she continued, she became animated, proud, and unapologetic. "And I'm here because I got arrested for beating the crap out of this little whore who slept with my boyfriend; if it weren't for these guys pulling me off her, I would have finished her off."

Hearing that, Leah resolved not to get on Kelly's bad side.

Frowning, Downey rubbed at his eyes. "We only have about five minutes left, so let's adjourn until next time."

No sooner did the last word issue from Downey's tongue than Kelly stormed out in a huff. "What a fucking waste of time. This is such a joke," she snarked.

Chapter 6

"It's for you."

Stu handed the landline phone to Leah. She frowned.

"Who is it?" she whispered to her brother, who shrugged.

A phone call for her, and on the family landline, no less. Very few people, save ancient relatives and telemarketers, ever dialed it—everyone else preferred cell phones—so it was downright weird. And no way would Evelyn call her on the landline.

"Hello," said Leah stiffly, as if she expected an alien or the president to be on the other end.

"Leah?"

It was a girl's voice. She sounded young and about Leah's age.

"Yeah?"

"I'm sorry to be calling you at home, but I'm at the Westfair Mall, in the parking lot. I just pulled in and I was wondering about you, whether you want to hang out. You must be close by because you go to Highland Hills. That's about five minutes away, right?"

Instead of waiting for Leah's response, the stranger prattled on.

"So, I called Information and I got a couple of Friedmans. I called everyone asking for Leah." She let out a throaty laugh. "Then...bull's-eye!"

The stranger's guffaw was so infectious it caused Leah's lips to fold into a very reluctant grin. "Who is this?" she asked.

"Yeah, I should tell you who I am. This is Kelly."

"Who?"

"Kelly. Kelly Turner from the Garden State Bard Program. I'm in your session."

Her? That grouchy girl who always looked like she'd swallowed a lemon? *Is this a joke? Some nasty prank?*

Leah almost choked. "Are you kidding me?" she coughed out, stunned.

The mirth in Kelly's voice faded. "I don't blame you for being on guard, Leah. I would be, too, if I were you. A strange girl from this weird-as-shit rehab program."

She paused. "Listen, I'm here by myself, so if you're not doing anything, how about I pick you up? We'll come back here and maybe get some grub at the food court?"

"Why do you want to hang out with me?" Leah asked, candor and social clumsiness getting the best of her.

"Good question," countered Kelly. "I don't like the others. That girl from James Madison seems stuck up. Way too into herself. Can't stand girls like that. My school is filled with them. Besides, you seem nice."

Although Leah was softening, a legitimate worry entered her brain. "Are we allowed to hang out? Maybe that goes against the rules Tully was talking about."

"No, that applies to dating. A friend of mine got in trouble a few years ago for stealing. She went through this program, so I know all about it. To be safe, let's not say anything?"

"You're on."

As soon as Leah spoke, she berated herself. Her mom and dad were eating out, and they would be furious with her for going out at night without them knowing beforehand, especially in the company of someone they'd never heard of. But it was a Friday, Stu was leaving for Julie's shortly, and Leah did not know when her parents would be home. Besides, it had been eons since anyone other than Evelyn or Sarah had invited her to go anywhere. Although she was uncertain of Kelly's intentions—the girl was so different from her former friends—Leah was starved for attention, no matter how dubious the source. *I need to have fun.*

After giving Kelly her address, Leah knocked on the bathroom door, asking Stu how long he would be in there. She could smell the fumes of aftershave her brother was rubbing on his neck and his immaculately shaved cheeks. The pungency of the odor was so strong that, even with the barrier of the locked door between them, Leah's eyes watered from the acidity.

Stu opened the door, almost hitting Leah in the face. Leah was so anxious to use the facility she hadn't realized how close she was.

"Hey, I could have taken your nose off!"

"Sorry." Leah fidgeted. She pulled her phone out of her black jeans' pocket. Kelly would be coming for her in five minutes. "I've got to get ready quick."

Stu paused and looked at her more closely. "Where are you off to?"

"This girl from the program I'm in just called me from the mall asking if I want to hang out with her. So..."

Like a bolt of lightning, Leah flashed past him into the bathroom and locked the door.

"Do Mom and Dad know?" Stu yelled through the door, lingering in the hallway.

"No," Leah yelled back, furiously brushing out the knots in her long and unruly dark hair. With a silver barrette, she clipped her overgrown bangs to the back of her thick tresses and dabbed a smattering of makeup on her face, including the cheap mascara and eyeshadow she'd bought at the dollar store a month ago. She did all this while Stu was giving her the third degree from the other side of the closed door.

After applying her favorite pink rose lip gloss, she threw the cosmetics into a red sack and shunted them haphazardly to their regular resting place, the bottom tier of the yellow cabinet. Above it was the sink, faucet, and a three-way mirror that showed Leah at various angles. She cringed at the ninety-degree view exposing the bump in her nose, a facial flaw she hated and sometimes obsessed about. Unlike her, Dana's nose was small, thin, and straight.

Her mother was an unequivocal beauty. Leah didn't begrudge her mom her blessed DNA, inherited from her maternal grandmother, who'd died five years ago of a stroke. Yet sometimes Leah couldn't help but wish she saw traces of her mother's prepossessing image staring back at her in the mirror, instead of her father's. As much as Leah adored him, his features, although not ugly, were nowhere comparable to her mother's exquisite physiognomy.

At least her braces were off—finally—her face was clearing up and the gawkiness that made her catnip to bullies like

Dede was dwindling, but Leah's appearance still bothered her.

"I'm only going to be out for an hour," Leah told her brother, who, rather than run off to meet Julie, had remained waiting to get the 411 from his sister over the mysterious person picking her up.

Even with a two-year difference between them, Stu was naturally protective toward Leah, a quality that her recent troubles had only magnified in him. Leah sensed that, like with her parents, guilt was the underlying factor. They had all been too self-absorbed in their work and commitments to detect anything awry in Leah's life.

"Who is this girl?" he probed.

"Someone from the program."

Stu tilted his eyebrows.

"It's okay," Leah assured him. "She's cool."

"Are you sure? Is this allowed...fraternizing with the other...?" Stu seemed hesitant to utter the term.

"Juvenile delinquents?" Leah finished his sentence. "Oh no, excuse me, it's 'juvenile offenders,'" she enunciated the term with bitter sarcasm. "They didn't say anything about not hanging out with the others outside of the sessions. Only that dating is not allowed."

Leah paused to ponder that disclaimer. "I don't think this girl's a lesbian. She was arrested for beating up this chick who slept with her boyfriend."

Stu chuckled, then reined himself in, like he thought he should adopt a more mature attitude for his wayward sister to emulate. "She hit the girl! What about the guy?"

"Boys always get away with everything."

"Only because the girls let them."

Dressed in his finest denim and a starched white collared shirt, Stu appraised his sister and the situation she was about to enter with a sigh. "I hope you know what you're doing."

"I'm tired of being alone all the time. I want to be like everyone else. I want to go out and have fun."

"Okay," said Stu, resigned. "Have fun, then."

He waved at her and turned to leave, but then halted, turning around. "But if things get. . . dodgy, text me and Julie and I will pick you up. See you, kid."

* * *

She almost didn't recognize the friendly, happy girl behind the wheel. When Kelly greeted Leah on the driveway in an old Ford sedan, the former's face contracted in an ebullient smile. Leah was struck by how different Kelly was in the car: relaxed and affable, a far cry from her rebellious, surly persona at the session.

Does she have an evil doppelganger? Is she schizophrenic?

"So, you're familiar with this town?" Leah asked as she settled into her seat.

"Yeah. I used to have a pal a few years older who lived here, and we'd hang out a lot. We'd always cruise the mall. She was a lot of fun. She's in Colorado now."

"Oh...that's nice."

Truthfully, Leah was indifferent about it, but she didn't know what else to say.

"Yeah, I suppose. We used to e-mail and text each other a lot when she first moved. Her parents thought she was partying too much...with the *wrong crowd*." Kelly punched up the last two words for sarcastic effect. "So, they shipped her off to Grandma. She hated it at first. But then when she started attending this community college nearby, I stopped hearing from her. I called, left a few messages, texted. Nothing."

"Sorry about that."

"It's okay. She has her life and I have mine."

After Kelly found a parking spot near Nordstrom's, she and Leah set off for H&M, where they browsed the racks, chattering about a slew of topics even Emily Post would deem acceptable in polite company—the early April weather, the classes they were taking, music and TV shows.

Leah's stomach growled. Hearing it, Kelly chuckled. "Yeah, I'm hungry too. Let's go get something to eat."

Riding the escalator to the lower level where the food court was, Leah and Kelly strolled around the cluster of fast-food chain counters before deciding on Chipotle. That was the easy part; finding two unfilled seats was another matter.

The Friday-night crowds were a fact. Unless the weather was insanely bad, like a blizzard or a hurricane (tornadoes rarely happened in Jersey), every person in the vicinity with a pulse, from age zero to near death, would flock to this complex of department stores and retail outlets for bargains or choice items they didn't need but would buy anyway just to while away the time in a county that had limited cultural prospects other than shopping.

Toting their trays filled with diet sodas, burritos, tortilla chips, and guacamole, Leah and Kelly looped through the chomping multitudes until they spotted two empty seats opposite one another, near the Dunkin' Donuts kiosk.

"Let's grab those seats before somebody else does," commanded Kelly.

Above the babel of tongues, silence reigned between the two. After swallowing a generous bite of the pseudo-Mexican concoction, Kelly disrupted the conversational respite with a question.

"So, what do you do when you're not at school or *in session?*"

Her sarcastic pronunciation was not lost on Leah.

"Not much these days." Leah tore through her burrito, tackling it with a gastronomic gusto that was a combination of hunger and deflection.

"Hmm." Nodding, Kelly took a sip of her soda. Raising her lips from the straw, she said, "That sucks. But I bet those kids who picked on you have stopped now, huh? They're probably too afraid after what you did to that girl. I would have pulverized her a long time ago. When you were telling that story, I kept thinking, *why did you wait so long?*"

"I guess I don't go around beating people up." Leah immediately regretted the comment when she remembered she was talking to Kelly. "I'm sorry. I didn't mean it that way."

"No, that's fine," pooh-poohed Kelly with a wave of her hand. "I don't either, believe it or not. I know that must shock you, but I don't go around punching everyone. Only those who deserve it, like that little slut I thought was my friend."

Kelly put her lips back onto the straw sticking out of her Diet Coke and sucked on it, drinking until there was nothing left in the plastic cup.

Leah waited until Kelly finished before asking, "How did you find out about it?"

Kelly's eyes glazed over at the memory.

"He left his phone out one time when he was over at my house. I already had my suspicions, but he said I was just crazy and jealous. That nothing was going on between them. So, when he went to the bathroom, I looked at his phone and saw a few texts from her that day asking him when they were going to get together. She told him she missed him and sent him a photo of her wearing a stupid teddy. Then she wrote below that photo, 'Come see what you're missing and not getting from Kelly!' And this was someone I thought was a good friend of mine! I knew her since the fifth fucking grade. And now she's going after my boyfriend behind my back?"

Kelly snorted with disgust, shaking her head. "When he came out of the can, I showed him the texts and the photo from her and asked him what the hell was going on. We really got into it. I'm so glad my mom and sister were out shopping," she said, grimacing. "We were screaming so hard at each other, Leah, I lost my voice for a few days. Swear to god.

"Anyway, I got him to admit that he and my sweet old childhood friend, the girl I trusted like a sister and felt closer to than any of my actual sisters, were screwing and had been for a few months. He told me she'd started it."

"Don't they all say that?"

"Yeah, they do," admitted Kelly, fiddling with the straw sticking out from her now-empty plastic cup. "Men are pigs, and I know that. My mother always told me. My dad split when I was eight. He cheated on her for years. She knew about it, but he would always come back home to her. Then one day, he didn't. He left her for his secretary, and they moved to Florida. Now I have two stepbrothers and a stepsister I've never met. I've spoken to my dad three times on the phone since he got hitched, and that's it. He used to tell me how much he missed me and my sisters, you know. What a joke."

Recalling her absent father, Kelly's eyes, a stunning turquoise, grew glassy for a second until she shrugged. "But...but I expected more from *her*. Girls shouldn't do that to other girls. I confronted Gail—that's my friend. *Was* my friend. It was lunchtime, and we were in school. She was sitting in the cafeteria with a bunch of people at a table. I walked up to her and as calm as I could be, asked her if she could speak to me outside. She was surprised. Didn't have a clue what I wanted to talk to her about, which pissed me off even more.

"She denied it at first, then later admitted it, telling me my boyfriend was the one who had started it. I told her it made no difference who had started it—she was my friend. She was supposed to be loyal to *me*. Then she opened her shriveled, ugly-ass mouth at me, told me how much better my boyfriend liked her body and how much hotter he thought she was in bed. Leah, I tell you, I lost it. I kicked her ass so hard, my knuckles hurt for a week. And her cute little face wasn't so cute afterward. I beat her so bad she went to the hospital. So, I got arrested."

Leah nodded her head in recognition. "That's like what happened to me too. Except Dede was not my friend, and she didn't sleep with my boyfriend. She just made my life hell, and I...snapped, I guess."

At that remark, the corners of Kelly's mouth crinkled into a half smile. She glanced at her phone. "We should go. I bet your parents will get worried about you hanging out with an offender from the program."

As they gathered their things and tossed out the remnants of their dinner into the nearby garbage bin, the conversation reverted to the realm of the superficial: the weather forecast for the weekend, movies both girls wanted to see, and TV shows they enjoyed. It continued when Kelly was driving Leah home until a thought entered the latter's head.

"I have to ask you this question, and I hope you don't mind," Leah ventured.

Her hands cemented on the steering wheel, Kelly shot a

speedy glimpse at her new friend before shifting her focus back to the road. "Yeah, sure. Fire away."

"Well, you seem cool and I'm glad you invited me to hang out with you. I enjoyed it."

"I did too."

"But...you're going to hate me for bringing this up. I'm sorry, but why do you have such an attitude at the session? It doesn't seem to be too bad. I'd rather learn and perform Shakespeare than be in jail."

Leah was apprehensive of Kelly's reaction, but Kelly surprised her by giving an honest and nonhostile reply.

"You're right. But I can't stand that probation officer. I want to wipe off that puss that's always on her face. And that guy, Downey...he's a weasel."

Despite her better instincts, Leah giggled. Kelly joined in as she pulled into the Friedmans' driveway on the right side.

Leah worried when she noticed her dad's blue Toyota Corolla on the left. Right away, she took out her phone, which she'd placed on vibrate when she and Kelly had entered the mall. She saw several voice mail messages from her parents, including a text from her mom: "Where r u???"

Noting the distress on Leah's face, Kelly's titters abated, her blue eyes turning slate with concern. "What's wrong?"

"My parents. They sent me a bunch of voice mail messages and texts. I should have let them know I was out. I forgot."

"It's okay. Tell them your new friend led you..." Kelly seemed to be groping for the right word; her eyes lit up when she found it. "Led you astray! That's it. I'm guilty. I led you astray."

Leah tried to smile, but her lips twisted into a forty-five-degree angle, making her appear more like a stroke victim and less like a teenager who'd just returned from a lighthearted night at the mall.

"It'll be okay," Kelly said, but the attempt to reassure Leah failed. "And if not, you can always sleep in my sister's old room."

Leah responded to her crack with a pained expression before she bolted out of the car and trotted up the driveway.

No sooner did Leah open the door with her key than she looked up and saw her mother standing by the head of the stairs.

"Where were you?"

"Out," replied Leah.

"I know. But where?"

"At the mall. Didn't you get my text?" she lied.

"No. But your brother texted your father telling him you went out with a new friend. Someone from that Shakespeare program? Leah, is it smart to associate with someone like that?"

Leah ignored the question. "Weren't you supposed to be out the rest of the night? How come you're home early?"

"Your father had a headache. So, we called it a night. He told me I should leave you alone when you come home, that it's good you have a new friend." Her mom bit her sculpted lips, covered with the shiniest patina of ruby red, then reopened them to ask Leah the all-consuming zinger. "What did she do?"

Her hand at the knob of her bedroom door, Leah stopped and turned to face her mother.

"Assault and battery. Just like me."

Leah resumed the act of opening the door to her bedroom. Again, her mother stopped her.

"Who did she hurt?"

Leah exhaled. "A friend." She corrected herself. "A former friend who went to bed with her boyfriend."

Her mom let out a gasp. "She should have hit the boyfriend."

"She told him off," added Leah. "Not sure if she hit him, but she beat up her friend when she found out how she was sleeping with her boyfriend and badmouthing her behind her back and talking all kinds of shit—"

"Watch your mouth!" Dana scolded. "We didn't raise you to speak like a lowlife."

Leah rolled her eyes. When they relaxed back in their sockets, she saw that her parents' bedroom door at the end of the hall was closed.

"Is Dad okay?"

Dana dismissed the question with a flourish of her lithe hands.

"He's fine. Just tired."

Leah nodded, but her throat constricted. Ever since Irv had his illness, Leah couldn't help but worry whenever her father was indisposed. Even if it was a minor ailment, like a cold, Leah's fears would reappear. She knew a few people at school who'd lost their fathers over the last year, from either cancer or a heart attack, and she blanched at the thought of Irv joining the ranks and becoming a premature death statistic.

"Ma, she's okay," Leah returned to the previous topic. "Really."

Leah wasn't sure if that reassurance was for her mother or herself.

"You should be careful around her. I mean, she was arrested."

"So was I! I'm no angel."

"Yes, you are. You're a good girl who was pushed to the brink by that vicious—" Dana stopped abruptly, and Leah sensed she'd been about to say "bitch" but had censored herself in time.

Rather than continue this futile argument, Leah capitulated. "Okay, Ma."

"Good." Her mother kissed her on her cheek.

Leah was about to open the door to her room, but once again, Dana stopped her. Her hazel eyes shone with a glimmering resplendence that only occurred when an idea had crystallized in her head.

"Honey...this girl....is she Jewish?"

Chapter 7

Leah stared quizzically at the sides, which in theater lingo meant short excerpts from a script that actors performed at auditions. In this instance, they were a monologue from *A Midsummer Night's Dream* and a scene from *Hamlet*. In putrid lime-green highlighter on top of the *Midsummer* side, "HELENA" was scrawled in blaring caps; on the other side, "GERTRUDE" was written in a similar fashion.

Leah scanned the monologue first before flipping through the five-page scene. *Hey, wait a minute.* She raised her hand.

"Um, um, Mister Downey," Leah stammered, her eyes ricocheting to the scene from *Hamlet*.

"Yes?" Downey responded, a knowing gleam in his eyes. "What is it?"

Downey seemed so receptive to Leah's befuddlement she wondered if he was telepathic. He was far more relaxed today than in the previous sessions. Leah surmised that Tully's absence was the probable reason for this bubbly tranquility, along with the presence of two colleagues of his from Palisades Shakespeare whom he'd referenced on the first day.

Michelle, on his right, was the speech instructor. She was an attractive, unassuming tawny blonde dressed in a plain yellow blouse and khaki pants. To Downey's left was Frank, who taught movement and stage combat. Tall and curly-haired, Frank's features were an anatomical study in homeliness: a large, bulbous nose, squinting brown eyes, acne-scarred skin, and jutting ears. In some angles, he resembled a rodent. But even with these less-than-appealing traits, Frank emitted physical magnetism from every pore.

"Isn't Gertrude Hamlet's mother?" asked Leah. "I saw the movie on TV. She's an old lady. Like fifty. I'm fifteen."

A chorus of titters burst from the other kids in the room, and Kelly playfully tapped Leah on the back of her neck.

The gesture prompted Leah to pivot her body around and

ask Kelly, "What did you get?"

"Kate from *Taming of the Shrew* and Regan from *King Lear*." Her stubby fingers rifled through the sides, her face riven by an ear-splitting smile.

Tiffany, seated to Leah's right, spun around to Kelly. "I have *King Lear* too. Goneril." She showed the pages to Kelly, who nodded her head in recognition.

Jake, seated at the back, yelled out to Leah, "I have *Hamlet* too—it's a scene with him and Gertrude."

Great.

Kelly howled and tapped Leah again, this time on the shoulder. Tiffany also broke into fits of laughter while clapping her hands.

Yes, that's right. Laugh. Go ahead.

The hilarity at Leah's expense wasn't so much Schaden-freude—Kelly had just befriended her, and Tiffany was too indifferent to entertain the notion—but an emotional cathar-sis of merriment that soon swept through the room like a contagion. Frank and Michelle, who'd been stoic and poker-faced since their introduction, were now brandishing scintil-lating smiles. Only Downey and Leah, growing increasingly irritated, were holdouts.

"Okay, okay, pipe down," declared Downey, trying to curtail the mini pandemonium engulfing the room.

When the final gasp of guffaws tapered off, Downey re-sponded to Leah's earlier question.

"Yes, Gertrude is Hamlet's mother. That is correct."

"But—but—" Leah slipped back to stammering. "Won't that—that loo-look weird?"

"No, not really. Well, let me take that back. Yes, chronolog-ically, it's impossible for you to play the mother of a twenty-year-old, considering you're fifteen. However, Gertrude most likely married Hamlet's father very young and had Hamlet around your age. So, she's maybe about thirty-four or thirty-five during the play. So, she's not old, and there's not a huge age difference between her and Hamlet."

His cogent explanation did not convince Leah.

"Doesn't Hamlet have a girlfriend?" Leah protested.

"Yes, Ophelia. But..." His voice trailed off, and he looked at Michelle and Frank, clearly hoping they would chime in with a plausible rationale for the age-inappropriate casting.

Michelle stepped up to the challenge. "Ophelia is...a bit of a doormat. Very meek, docile, does what her father and brother want her to do. She's easily controllable. A delicate flower. Not a character who projects sensuality and strength."

Whaaaaaaatttt? I can't do that! Leah's bewilderment gave way to astonishment, tempered with abashment at the flattery.

She opened her mouth, preparing to speak, but nothing came out. The grandiosity of Michelle's implicit suggestion, that Leah possessed those two traits she never thought anyone would discern in her, rendered her speechless.

Seeing her unease, Michelle glanced back at Downey, who took over.

"I don't know if 'strength' is the right word to describe Gertrude. She definitely is a pawn in her brother-in-law's scheme to become king of Denmark, very much the way Ophelia is a pawn in the intrigue with her father and brother against Hamlet. But she is not as fragile as Ophelia."

There were confused looks around the room, and Leah's face scrunched up too. It wasn't like they were all as well versed in the Bard as Downey and his colleagues. Downey seemed to realize this after a moment, and swiftly altered his tactics.

"Why don't you try it and we'll see? If it doesn't work out, we'll choose another scene— and this applies to everyone else. But if we do change, we'll have to do it soon. Now, for the next half hour, I want you all to meet with your scene partners and read your scene together. Then I want you to figure out what the scene is about. We will go around to see how you're doing and answer questions."

Leah glanced over at Jake on the other side of the room. In addition to the scene with Leah from *Hamlet*, Jake had also been given a scene from the same play between Hamlet and the First Clown. Rob, the alien with no eyebrows, had been assigned to play that part. He immediately rotated his chair around to face Jake after Downey instructed the teens to work on their scenes.

"We're going to work on this scene first," Jake yelled over to Leah. "Then we'll do our scene."

What am I supposed to do, then?

"Hello, everyone!" Downey waved his hands just then like an air traffic controller, until the noise temporarily ceased. "If your scene partner is otherwise engaged and you only have one scene with other actors, then what I want you to do is read your assigned monologue. Think about the language and the meaning behind it."

The din resumed. Again, Downey interrupted the collective clatter. A rush of silence overtook the space.

"Folks. If you want to go out in the hallway, where the sound buffers are much better than in this room, I would highly recommend you do so. I'd suggest outdoors too, but it's a little windy outside, so maybe not."

As soon as Downey voiced the last syllable of his last word, the teens were back reading and yakking about their scenes. Leah gazed down at the sheet in front of her and read through the opening lines of her Helena monologue, trying to ignore the voices around her:

How happy some o'er other some can be!
Through Athens, I am thought as fair as she.
But what of that? Demetrius thinks not so.
He will not know what all but he do know.
And as he errs, doting on Hermia's eyes,
So I, admiring of his qualities...

Helena's lovelorn plight reminded her of when she was in Hebrew school three years ago. There was a boy in her class, Barry, who used to sit behind her and tease her sometimes, although it was never mean.

During Rabbi Greenbaum's ten-minute cigarette break, Barry had tugged on her ponytail, prompting Leah to whirl around from her institutional desk and conjoining chair to see what Barry wanted. Holding up his notebook, Barry, a cutie with a dark Beatles mop, a long straight nose, and a mischievous glint in his brown eyes, had showed Leah the doodles he'd made during class. Usually, it was a character from a sci-fi movie that Leah could never figure out. But she was too bashful to admit her ignorance and, predictably, would gush over Barry's latest sketching, something not difficult to do considering he had obvious artistic talent.

There had also been another girl in the class, Debbie, an overdeveloped, towering, buxom brunette with a solid frame, who was blessed with mahogany-brown eyes she'd flutter ad nauseam. Leah wasn't sure if it was intentional, a trick pulled from a budding flirt's grab bag of wiles or an inadvertent tic. Still, that didn't prevent Debbie and Leah from forming a brief friendship. They'd met outside the Highland Hills' premises, where they'd both linger after school waiting for the bus that would squire them to their Hebrew school twice a week for their lessons. Hebrew school was on the other side of town, too far for them to walk and make it to class on time. And because Highland Hills let out while Irv and Dana were still working, Leah had no other choice but to take the bus.

Strangely enough, neither had known the other before, although they'd been vaguely aware of each other's existence through Sarah. This was before the camp fiasco.

"Oh yes, Leah," effused Debbie the first day they spoke, "I know who you are. You're Sarah's friend. She told me a lot about you. Glad to meet you!"

Leah had reciprocated the pleasantries. Although Debbie had seemed initially annoying with her fledgling coquette act, as well as intimidating with her precocious voluptuousness, Leah discovered they had a nice rapport aside from having some obvious commonalities that included age, religion, and suburban upbringing.

Their one glaring point of differences—Debbie's sexual experience, or rather her claims of sexual experience, versus Leah's nonexistent expertise in that area—was what ultimately drove them apart, as it had with Sarah.

"I've been to first base and second base a dozen times," Debbie bragged to Leah in the privacy of her bedroom one weekend. "How about you?"

Leah had almost choked. Her skin colored a bright shade

of scarlet. *Should I lie or tell her the truth?*

Truth won out.

"None," burbled Leah, her voice in its lowest possible octave.

"You're kidding," Debbie answered, her features freezing in a mask of utter stupefaction as if Leah had confessed, she was secretly controlled by aliens.

"No," reaffirmed Leah, shaking her head. "I'm a virgin. But then...aren't you as well? You haven't gone all the way."

"I don't want to have a baby at twelve," Debbie declared definitively, adding that she'd begun menstruating a year earlier. "But there are other things we can do, Leah, to make boys happy."

Leah gaped incredulously at her friend before she replied, "I can't do that. I have braces." The girl then pointed to the metal orthodontic handiwork that had been cemented on her teeth since the previous summer.

Debbie's jaw dropped. "I didn't mean that, silly!" she exclaimed. "I meant..." She stopped to make a masturbatory gesture with her hand. "You see?"

Debbie had then asked Leah who she thought was cute in Hebrew school. Straightaway, Barry popped into Leah's head. But because Leah was awkward and shy around boys and loath to reveal anything that could subject her to even more humiliation, she hemmed and hawed at saying Barry's name. She wouldn't have to, as Debbie beat her to it.

"I think Barry is hot." She paused to take in her friend's reaction. "Don't you?"

Leah equivocated. "Yeah...he's okay."

Debbie gawked at her friend, her full upper lip curling into a grin. "Can you keep a secret?" She sidled up close.

Leah nodded. On the outside, she tried valiantly to retain her composure and not let on that she had a small crush on Barry. But behind the veneer, Leah felt an ache tearing at the pit of her stomach, a physical manifestation of an intuitive hunch she would not like what Debbie was about to disclose. And she was right.

"I'm seeing Barry."

The lump in Leah's solar plexus tightened. "For how long?" Leah asked, catching her breath.

"Two weeks. Look," Debbie said, lifting her wrist to show Leah a slender silver bracelet. "He gave this to me."

Leah forced a smile, which appeared more like a depressed sneer and less a demonstration of empathic joy at a pal's blossoming romance.

And sure enough, the next time they were in Hebrew class, Barry had not tapped Leah on her upper back to check out his latest drawings during the break; rather, he'd strutted outside with a giggling Debbie in tow.

It's not as if anything was happening or would have happened. Leah had known that in her heart. She had no cause to think there was anything amorous sprouting underneath the surface of her past interactions with Barry. But it didn't matter—the heart and the mind were incompatible.

She had wondered, though, if Debbie might have already sensed her feelings toward Barry because no sooner did her pal spill the status of her relationship with Barry than she stopped calling. At first, Leah justified that she was perhaps too busy with Barry to phone. Yet when weeks without calling turned into months, the only thing that crossed her mind was an expression she'd purloined from a young-adult historical novel she'd read months before, a story about a fourteen-year-old lady-in-waiting in the court of Henry VIII, who competes with another for the affections of a handsome fifteen-year-old courtier: "a rival vanquished."

"Do you have any questions?"

Leah emerged from her fog to see Michelle peering down at the monologue lying face up on the desk.

"I love that monologue. Helena is one of my favorite characters. I've played her several times over the years." Michelle's dark eyes misted at the recall. "Brings back great memories."

"So, Helena likes a guy who likes her friend, and she doesn't understand why he prefers the other girl. She's just as pretty as her friend," said Leah. "That's what she's saying, right?"

Michelle nodded. "Yes. Very good. What else do you think

she's saying?"

Leah reread the monologue to herself. She stopped at the passage:

Things base and vile, holding no quantity,
Love can transpose to form and dignity.
Love looks not with the eyes but with the mind.
And therefore, is winged Cupid painted blind.

"Umm, ...she's also saying that love can make the ugliest things in the world look beautiful. It's, it's...deceiving. Love can deceive."

"Excellent. What else?"

Leah hesitated. "Uh, I'm not sure, but I think she's saying it's also...um..."

She searched her mental lexicon for the right adjective. "Fickle." Her eyes sparkled with exultation at finding the perfect word. "Love is also fickle because...this Demetrius guy used to like her. Then he met her friend Hermia and that changed. Now he likes Hermia and has forgotten all about Helena."

"Right," Michelle replied. "Okay, now recite the last stanza—that's the last group of lines. What is she saying there?"

Leah shot Michelle a perplexed expression.

"Yes, it's okay," responded Michelle. "You can read it aloud."

Leah combed the room and noticed that, aside from her and Michelle, everyone—other than Frank and the brawny jock, Derek, both busy conferring about Derek's monologue from *Julius Caesar*—had disappeared. She guessed that most of them were either in the hallway reading and discussing their scenes or outside in the windy sunshine with Downey running interference.

"You're right. It's not like there's much of an audience here anyway," Leah gibed.

She licked her chapped lips and recited the remaining lines:

I will go tell him of fair Hermia's flight.
Then to the wood will he to-morrow night

Pursue her, and for this intelligence
If I have thanks, it is a dear expense.
But herein mean I to enrich my pain,
To have his sight thither and back again.

Stumbling over "sight thither," Leah repeated the words again. When she finished, she looked up at Michelle, waiting for her to say something, anything.

"Very nice. Now...what do you think she's saying?"

"Well." Leah paused, rereading to herself the strange Shakespearean verse—*iambic pentameter*, her English teacher, Ms. Schroeder, had called it last year when they were studying *Romeo and Juliet*. "I think she's saying that Hermia has gone off with some other guy. Helena knows that, and even though she knows she shouldn't do it, she's going to tell Demetrius about it. It'll hurt her, but it'll also be worth it just to see Demetrius again and to have him thank her for telling him the truth about Hermia running off with that other guy. What's his name?"

"Lysander." Michelle's face was riven again by a wide grin. "Great! You got it. You should also read the entire play. I think you would enjoy it. It'll give the scene more context for you to work with. If not, you can always read the CliffsNotes."

Leah cackled at Michelle's suggestion, a sacrilege to every hard-working English teacher.

"Yes, I know. It's wrong," joked Michelle. "The acting gods will strike us dead for admitting we suggest that, but we don't have a choice sometimes, with you kids pressed for time with your full days at school and your homework."

Leaning down to a still-seated Leah, Michelle affected a mock whisper. "But if you ever tell anyone we suggest doing that, we'll deny, deny, deny!"

A terrible thought entered Leah's head. "Um...Michelle," she coughed out, swallowing the phlegm in her throat. "Am I going to have to memorize all of this?"

Even though Leah had a tenacious memory—one reason why she consistently scored so well on tests and was a straight-A student—she felt a surge of fear about this whole undertaking. Other than playing one of Abe Lincoln's sisters in a third-grade play, an acting exercise that was hardly cumbersome, considering the role had required her to do little more than squeeze out a *tee-hee-hee* at certain times and utter an insipid "Oh, Abe" at others, Leah was not an experienced thespian. She didn't want to flounder and make an ass of herself.

"Unfortunately, yes, you do." Michelle poured salve on the bad news. "But you will become so familiar with the monologue and your other scene by the time we're finished, you'll be able to do it in your sleep."

Leah gave a half-hearted nod of her head, her stomach sinking.

"What else is it? Are you worried your acting skills won't be up to snuff? I can tell from hearing you read aloud that you'll be fine," Michelle assured her.

Leah's lips tightened. "It's not so much that, although that does worry me. It's just that—"

She balked.

"Go on…"

Leah scoped out the room again to make sure it was safe. Derek and Frank were now gone. It was only her and Michelle. She drew in a long breath.

"Helena says she doesn't understand why that guy likes her friend more than her, considering she's as pretty as her friend. Well, that's just it. I'm not as pretty as anyone. I'm a laughing stock at school, or I was until—"

Her eyes welled up. Michelle placed a comforting hand on her right shoulder.

Leah continued, "I'm not beautiful like my mother. I never was. I'm just a brain. I don't know how I'll ever be able to even pretend!"

Despite her better efforts, tears streamed down Leah's cheeks. Even after she wiped them away with her hands, more trickled from her eyes.

"Hold on," entreated Michelle as she dashed to the front of the room where her purse was tossed on the floor. "I think I have a tissue in my bag."

She handled a slightly crumpled but unused Kleenex to

Leah, who hurriedly cleaned up the damp moisture on her face.

"Sorry," Leah uttered in a tiny quaver of a voice, the used tissue clenched within her fist.

"Don't be." Michelle put her hand back on Leah's right shoulder and knelt to be closer to the sitting Leah. "I was once like you too," said the older woman. "When I was your age, I felt like the ugliest girl in the world. I used to be called 'ghost' because I was so pale and fair. I had, maybe, one or two friends. Then when I was in the tenth grade, my English teacher, Mrs. Rogers—she was a wonderful person—she invited me to speak to her after class. I was so scared, Leah! I didn't know what I'd done wrong."

Michelle hooted at the memory, then resumed her account. "She saw how nervous I was, and calmed me down: 'It's okay, Michelle. You didn't do anything wrong. You're not failing,'" she recalled with a throaty laugh. "Mrs. Rogers was also the head of the drama club and taught acting. Well, she told me she liked the way I recited the poems and plays we'd sometimes read aloud in class. She said I read with intelligence and sensitivity and asked whether I was interested in joining the drama club.

"My sophomore year was just beginning, and the club was starting up for the new school year. I had nothing to lose, so I said, 'Sure.' Leah, that changed my life. From then on, I got completely involved with the drama club. I auditioned for everything: children's plays, musicals—and I'm not much of a singer—and straight plays. Anything.

"And if I didn't get cast for a particular production, I did props, or I worked on costumes or I helped with painting flats. It didn't matter. I wanted to be involved and be with my new friends. Now, I'm not saying that's your destiny, nor should it be. Obviously, the circumstances that led you here are a lot different than what I faced when I was in school. This session is part of your sentence, I know that. But you can use this experience to build up your confidence so, that way, you won't...get into trouble again."

Leah's heart was pounding with fury and her eyes

narrowed.

Michelle's eyes dilated in alarm at Leah's visibly irate reaction. She opened her mouth like she knew she'd said the wrong thing and wanted to correct it, but it was too late.

"What was I supposed to *do*?" spat Leah. "Wait for her to beat the shit out of me, as if she and all the other kids at school hadn't humiliated me enough already? What do you know about being so ugly that when the teacher assigns a boy to sit next to you in homeroom, he starts screaming and complaining about having to sit next to the 'class dog'? This went on for twenty minutes; the teacher couldn't quiet him down! Almost everyone in class cheered him on. That happened. And that was nothing compared to what it was like every single day once Dede zeroed in on me at school."

Leah was now so livid with rage that even her neck glowed a bight shade of crimson. The mere thought of having to relive the nightmare of the past few years enflamed her so much she could barely contain the cauldron boiling inside her.

Vainly, Michelle labored to remedy her gaffe. "I'm sorry," she said humbly. "That must have been terrible."

Quite a few minutes passed before Leah could feel her racing heartbeat slowing down to its normal rate and the heaving in her stomach lessen. She looked sheepishly at Michelle, who was still mired in contrition for a wrong she hadn't meant to commit.

"I shouldn't have snapped at you like that, said Leah, apologetic. "That was so wrong of me. I know you're trying to help. It's just that ever since this whole thing started, I...I get so sensitive about everything. Someone says something, anything and I explode. I used to be this nice, quiet sweet little kid, if you can believe it..."

"You still are."

"No, I'm not. I haven't felt like myself for a long time. I'm not even sure I even know who I am anymore. You didn't say or do anything bad. It's me."

"Leah, I can't presume I know what goes on in your life. I only know the general stuff, not the details. What happened to you wasn't good. But you have a chance here for a do-over, to get some perspective on your actions and learn."

"From Shakespeare?" Leah raised her eyebrows, incredulous. "I mean, it's better than being in reform school but...." She shrugged her shoulders.

"We are such stuff as dreams are made on, and our little life is rounded with sleep," said Michelle, the corners of her lips curling into a smile, a shrewd gleam in her eyes.

Leah knitted her eyebrows.

"What?"

"It's a line from *The Tempest*. Also, Shakespeare. Did you ever read it?"

Leah shook her head.

"It's one of Shakespeare's later plays. It's about this magician, Prospero, who conjures up a storm so he can shipwreck his brother and a couple of other people on this island. I played Miranda, Prospero's daughter a couple of years ago."

Confused, Leah continued to gape at Michelle.

"What that line means, Leah, is that we are only here for a short while and it's up to us to decide what to do with the time we're given."

Michelle waited for Leah to absorb that.

"I added that bit about the time we've been given, that's my own interpretation, but it's something I believe in. Strongly. And you should, too."

Leah was about to answer when Michelle cut her off.

"Oops, we're five minutes over. You have to go," she said, staring at her watch. The time was 5:35 pm.

Leah hastily scooped up her books and notebook into her arms, the strap of her purse dangling from the tip of her right shoulder. She panicked, as she thought about Stu waiting outside in the car.

"Don't worry," said Michelle, noting Leah's anxiety about being late for her pick-up. "Blame me for talking too much."

After exchanging goodbyes, Leah made a beeline for the door but not before Michelle threw out some parting words, which temporarily derailed the girl's exit.

"By the way, you may not believe this or want to believe this...but you are very pretty."

A pained smile crossed over Leah's face as she looked at Michelle, acknowledged the compliment with a nod, then ran out like an Olympic sprinter heading toward the finish line.

Chapter 8

Leah was standing in front of her locker, unloading some of her books, when she felt someone touch her shoulder. A tsunami of terror swept through her entire body. Leah's heart leaped inside her chest, beating so loudly it embarrassed her, especially when she jerked her head around and saw the witness to her traumatized behavior was none other than Mr. Thomas, the school counselor.

"It's been a while… How's it going with you?" he asked.

Quickly, Leah averted her eyes from him and cast them downward, staring at the soles of her new black patent leather shoes, the newest "guilt gift" her mom had bought her on top of other similar purchases, like a brown satchel with fringes Leah had admired a month ago when they were at Kohl's. Her mother, racked with remorse for having "failed" her only daughter, was trying to make amends and atone for her maternal lapses with these presents.

"Okay…I guess," Leah responded cautiously.

"Sorry to scare you. I shouldn't have snuck up on you like that," he lamented, "considering what you've been through the last year. That was stupid of me, Leah. I apologize."

"I didn't, uh, expect it to be you," she responded, her quaking subsiding.

"Apparently not," he jested, trying to make light of the situation. "Would you have a few minutes today to come to my office? It's been a while since we talked, and I want to know how you're doing."

She agreed to his request, but once in his office wished she hadn't. Memories of her last meeting with Mr. Thomas nearly two months ago, before the blow-up with Dede, flashed in her head.

Holed up in his poky office after yet another round of harassment and name-calling, Leah focused on the sterile off-white walls plastered with photos of Spain and France. They looked remarkably similar to the generic travel posters at the local Triple-A where she'd gone with her parents a couple of summers ago before they'd taken her and Stu on vacation to Washington, DC, and Williamsburg.

"Do you know what a 'scapegoat' is?" Mr. Thomas asked.

Although anyone over twenty seemed ancient to Leah, she knew that Mr. Thomas, with his glasses and nerdy demeanor, couldn't be that old. Oh sure, he had a receding dark-blond hairline, but there were no discernible wrinkles on his face. Plus, he spoke with a lilt that made him sound young. This was unlike some of the older teachers, such as Leah's math teacher, the perpetually fatigued, prune-faced Mrs. Lancaster, whose palpable weariness was so ludicrous some students would joke, "She'll keel over and die in her next class!"

Shrinking into the institutional plastic chair, Leah shook her head. She glanced at her right hand, still clutching the tissue Mr. Thomas had given her when she'd stumbled into his office that day, her face streaming with the tears she'd been fighting to control.

"It's when someone is blamed for something, they're not responsible for," soothed Mr. Thomas in a voice so docile it almost lulled Leah to sleep.

Saying nothing, Leah dabbed at the residue of moisture still gathered around her eyes. She then blew her nose.

"It can also mean," he continued, scratching his chin, which was slightly whiskered with reddish-blond fuzz, "when someone is being unfairly targeted or picked on for no real reason other than... they're there." A pause ensued. "Do you understand what I'm saying?"

Leah nodded, then crumbled the tissue up before tossing it into the trash can sitting to the right of Mr. Thomas's mahogany laminate desk.

"Why are they going after *me*? I've done nothing to *them*."

A moment of silence prevailed as both Leah and Mr. Thomas stared impassively at one another, considering the question.

"Maybe that's the problem."

"I don't understand," said Leah, her eyes gazing

accusatorily at the school counselor.

"It means sometimes kids will go after someone not because there's anything wrong with that kid, but just because they know that kid won't fight back. That's what I mean by 'a scapegoat.'"

"I understand you're in the Shakespeare program. How's that going?"

The question jolted Leah back to the present.

"Sorry," she mumbled. "Um...the session, that's what they call it, is going okay. I've been assigned a monologue and a scene to work on. The guy who runs it—"

"Lee Downey," Mr. Thomas cut in.

The pupils of Leah's eyes enlarged with surprise.

"I'm familiar with him. We've had a number of students here that have gone through the program. It's a good one. I'm glad you're in it."

Truthfully, Mr. Thomas wasn't a bad sort. He had tried to help her, she knew that. But it had been ineffective and as irrational as it was, Leah had a difficult time forgiving him.

"It's all right," he said, resigned, not waiting for a reply. "I know I'm not your favorite person. I suppose, given how things went...I don't blame you."

"Is there anything else you'd like to ask me?" she asked in a dull monotone. "I have a test tomorrow in social studies I need to study for..."

There was no test, but she didn't care. Leah didn't want to talk about Shakespeare rehab, and she didn't want to talk to Mr. Thomas.

Thwarted, Mr. Thomas conceded defeat, his professional vivacity surrendering to gloom.

"Well, then, I won't keep you." He stood to open the door. "Stay in touch."

Because work period was still going on, Leah had some time to kill. She went to her locker where she unloaded the books she was carrying, then yanked her phone out of her bag and saw a text. It was from Kelly.

"How r u doing? Want to hang out later?"

Leah texted back: "K, but can't go out too long. English test tomorrow."

Actually, it was next week, and it was on grammar—a subject that Leah felt confident she would ace—but she still had doubts regarding how much she could trust her new chum. Other than the basic details of her life, the nature of her offense and details surrounding it, Leah knew very little about Kelly. Plus, based on Leah's checkered history, she couldn't help but be suspicious when it came to anyone wanting to befriend her. Why was Kelly, a girl who seemed at first so cranky and ornery to her and everyone else at the session, so interested in being chummy with her? Other than their current criminal status as juvies, they had little in common.

"Neither can I. I also have school tomorrow. LOL."

She saw another text from Kelly.

"Pick you up at 7?"

"K."

A pause followed, then another text appeared.

"Cool! I'll see you then."

Responding with a smile emoji, Leah stuffed her phone back into her bag, grabbed her science textbook and iPad and was on her way to class when she barged into Ms. Evers.

"Oh, I'm so sorry! I didn't see you," Leah cried out.

The gym teacher laughed. "No need to apologize. I should have seen you coming." Leaning in, she asked, "So, how are you?"

Unlike the other adults in school, Leah wasn't as resentful toward Ms. Evers as the other teachers. But she was guarded whenever they would speak post-arrest. The reason was simple: Although she appreciated Ms. Evers for telling off Dede that time after their fight and for her support after that mess, Leah couldn't forget that Ms. Evers was still in the enemy camp—another teacher who had done nothing while Leah was being hounded and harassed. This gave their interactions a sliver of unease that Leah doubted would ever go away. Interestingly, Ms. Evers never brought it up.

"I'm okay," said Leah. "The program is weird, but I guess it's better than being in reform school."

Ms. Evers's grin evaporated, her countenance turning more

solemn. Her usual ascetic plain features looked softer today, no doubt rendered so by the new blonde streaks rippling throughout her short light-brown hair. Under the fluorescent lighting, the highlights practically glistened.

"Well, that's good," she chirped back. "It's a process, Leah. A one-day-at-a-time process, but you'll get through it."

Saying nothing, Leah conveyed skepticism through her facial expression and body posture.

"No, really," insisted Ms. Evers. "There were other kids who were far more hardcore than you, Leah. I mean far more hardcore. But they did that program, they came out, and have done well since then. Truly."

* * *

Leah licked the vanilla ice cream dripping off the cone.

"You do that so...daintily," teased Kelly as she tackled her strawberry sundae, topped off by a generous dollop of whipped cream.

It had been ten minutes since Kelly picked up Leah from her house. Now they were lolling on a bench in front of Carvel, the ice cream chain, at dusk. Though it was April, the weather was abnormally warm and humid that day.

With some of the vanilla still in her mouth, Leah's cheeks reddened. Her lips pursed as she tried to squelch the peal of laughter threatening to dislodge from her mouth and eject a confectionary mess.

"I've been called that before— 'dainty.' My mother calls me that. Or 'ethereal,' which I looked up and it means the same. My third-grade teacher said I was 'refined.' That was before the braces, before I turned 12 and started looking gross. I think it's a polite way of not saying I look weak or a pushover. I wish I looked tougher." Her tongue licked at more of the vanilla, which was melting in the heat. After she swallowed, Leah completed her thought aloud. "Like you."

Kelly's aquamarine eyes widened in shock. "Are you kidding me? You think I'm tough?"

"Aren't you?"

"*No!*" she avowed, placing undue emphasis on the word, which she repeated for extra effect. "No way!"

Leah glanced at Kelly. Although the girl wore a smile on her face, the edges of her lips, faintly smudged with the ice cream, were taut with tension. Her new friend seemed irked.

"I'm sorry I said that. It's just that you seem—" Leah paused, licking what was left of the ice cream. "Formidable!" she abruptly exclaimed, almost jumping off the bench. Two weeks ago, her English teacher had the class learn new words for the weekly vocabulary lesson. That word had reminded her of Kelly. "That's it. 'Formidable.' That's you."

"I know what that word means," Kelly answered between finishing off the sundae. "Intimidating. Daunting. Indomitable."

She got up from the bench and tossed the plastic tray into the garbage can.

Leah's eyes followed her stride, imposing with every step. *Yes, formidable.*

Sitting next to Leah, Kelly pulled out a pack of cigarettes. She put one in her mouth and was about to light it with a match she'd picked up from a bar at a Chinese restaurant before she suddenly turned to Leah.

"Do you want one?"

Leah shook her head.

Kelly lit the cigarette, inhaled, and then blew a jet of smoke into the air. "I know, I know." She waved her hands. "It's an awful habit, but I'm down to only five a day."

The tone of her voice dropped. Her striking features, which could look hard when she was upset, relaxed.

"I'm not formidable. Not at all. I know I have a short fuse; I think I get it from my father. He used to scream so much. We were all relieved when he finally left. My mother, she's a sweet person, never raises her voice. I think she lets people take advantage of her. That will never happen to me."

Kelly took another drag from the cigarette, and this time the smoke blew out from her flared nostrils.

"Leah, what do you want to do when you graduate from high school?"

"First, I have to get there," she responded with a wry grin, her eyes flashing irony.

Kelly slapped her head, her cigarette still clenched between the forefinger and middle finger of her right hand. "I keep forgetting you're still in junior high. You seem older."

"Two years younger than you," Leah offered.

"Yeah," said Kelly. She took another puff from the cigarette, which was down to the stub, then threw it on the ground, extinguishing it with her sneaker. "Seriously, do you have any thoughts about what you might like to do?"

Leah shrugged. "I don't know. I'm not sure. I don't want to get stuck doing something I hate."

"I don't blame you." Kelly gazed out into the distance with such undisguised yearning. "You won't believe this," she said in a voice above a whisper. "But I want to be a doctor. I want to go to medical school."

Leah was so surprised her eyes nearly popped out of their sockets. "Really?"

"I know," Kelly said, twisting her mouth into a configuration that was neither a grin nor a frown. "Me, a doctor. But it's true. I guess you didn't know that about me."

"How are you in science?"

"It's my best subject. That and math."

"Interesting," Leah tried to conceal her surprise but couldn't. She never would have guessed Kelly had a bent for those two subjects. She certainly didn't give off the vibe of being a geek.

"Yeah, believe it or not, when I apply myself, I can be a good student, especially when it comes to math and science. You know, I got over a seven hundred on the math portion of the SATs. My English wasn't as high, but it was in the six hundreds."

"That's great," Leah responded, impressed.

She knew all about the SATs through Stu, who'd boned up for weeks a few months ago before taking his first stab at them. Stu wouldn't tell Leah when she pressed him for the results. Instead, he told her with a coy smirk, "I did okay, sis. *Very* okay."

"What's your GPA?" Leah cringed at herself for asking such a loaded question.

But Kelly responded nonchalantly. "About a B or B-minus. I could get straight A's easily. I'm not bragging. I know I'm smart. But sometimes it's hard for me to focus and stay still."

"Do you have, um...AAD?"

Kelly smiled like she wanted to snicker but held it back. "It's ADD," she corrected gently without condescension. "And, yes, I have it."

"Don't you have to take drugs to...control it?"

"Yes. I used to take them, but then I stopped."

"Why?"

"They were making me feel foggy. My mind never felt clear when I was taking them. I remember calling the doctor to complain about how they were making me feel like a zombie. He told me I needed to get used to it. I listened to that crap for another month before Mom told me to stop taking them. I flushed them down the toilet, and that was that."

"Did it get worse—your ADD?"

Kelly made a "so-so" gesture with her fingers. "Not really. No, that's not true. Yeah, sometimes, but most of the time I do feel 'level'—that's what my old shrink called it. But I need to regulate it. My mother took me to a naturopath to do that."

"A what?"

"A naturopath. That's a doctor who prescribes natural remedies. He checked my blood and my pulse. He prescribed a whole boatload of vitamins for me to take. Here they are."

Kelly opened her large purse to reveal a cornucopia of vitamin bottles. There must have been a half dozen.

Leah gasped. "Oh my god! Do you take them all?"

"Well, one at a time," Kelly said drolly. "Yeah, they've been making me feel better. But I have to take about eight of them a day; otherwise, I could flip out. It's a pain, but I want to get my life back on track. I want to improve my grades. If they're not good enough to get into Rutgers, I may try my luck at Passaic Community, work my ass off for two years there, get straight A's, and then transfer."

"Is there an area in medicine you're interested in?"

Kelly was on the verge of answering, then she stopped. She was gaping at whatever or whoever was behind Leah, which caused the latter to spin around.

"Hi, girls."

It was Jake.

Leah was so flustered by his appearance she was tongue-tied. Mercifully, Kelly took over, asking the obvious question.

"Hey, stranger," she teased, narrowing her eyes. "What are you doing here? Aren't you from...um, I'm sorry, where are you from again?"

She was evidently half kidding, and Jake chuckled, the puckish glint in his green eyes growing more prominent.

"Mah*wah.*" He inflected the last syllable as if to make sure both would remember where he was from. "And I go to James Madison." He paused to see if that would sink in and jar their memories of when he mentioned it at the session.

"Oh yeah," Kelly retorted. "What are you doing here then? Mahwah's...about twenty minutes away. If there's no traffic."

"My aunt and uncle live here. I was visiting them and my little cousin. My uncle was taking me back. He drove past Carvel, asked me if I wanted ice cream. I did. So here I am." Picking up the combative baton, Jake hurled it back to the ring. "What about you?" he asked in a challenging tone. "Aren't you from...where is it again?"

Leah was silent as she observed Kelly and Jake sparring, her focus fluctuating between them as if watching a tennis match between two opponents jockeying for the upper hand.

Jake's insolence clearly irritated Kelly, and her blue-green eyes grew darker while her lips puckered into a hybrid smirk and scowl.

"Ho-Ho-Kus," she reminded him in a vaguely reproving manner. "I go to Townsquare."

"Oh yeah, I forgot," he answered with an acerbic bite. "How could I forget?"

Knowing Kelly had a short temper, Leah deflected the conversation to an innocuous topic that had no chance of progressing into a heated altercation. "Did you read our scene?"

Ignoring Kelly, Jake turned toward Leah. His face brightened, the impish gleam in his emerald eyes becoming ever more pronounced and twinkling like they had when Leah had first seen him in the courtroom.

"Yeah, I like it. I like it a lot. I think it'll be fun working on it with you. What do you think?"

There was a forwardness to his behavior that unsettled Leah, although she couldn't fathom the reason for her discomfort.

"Um, I think it's going to be...o-o-o-kay," she stuttered. "I just don't know why I'm playing your mother."

"Are you *kidding*? That's a great part. She's somebody's mother *and* somebody's lover. Yesterday I watched the movie on YouTube. Gertrude rocks," he continued. "Ophelia is a sucky role. What a mindless loser."

Jake punctuated his dismissal of one of Shakespeare's classic female roles by mildly nudging Leah's right shoulder. This time, the physical contact from a boy didn't cause her to blush like it had in sleepaway camp a few years before, forever tainting her friendship with Sarah. But the touch did unnerve her. And, as much as she didn't want to admit it to herself, it also excited her as well.

"Anyway, girls, I've got to go," Jake said, pointing to the Carvel counter inside the store where the line, unlike ten minutes earlier, was dwindling. "I have to order. My uncle is waiting for me."

Leah scanned the abating crowd for signs of a middle-aged man with a probable resemblance to Jake. Kelly expressed no such interest as she pored over e-mails on her phone.

"No, he's in the car. Over there." Jake pointed to an old black Mustang idling in a small parking lot near the ice cream shop. Leah's eyes fell on a middle-aged man with short, receding salt and pepper hair, sitting in the driver's seat, his hands gripped on the steering wheel.

"See you tomorrow, girls. Nice to see you, Leah."

Again, he tapped Leah on the shoulder, bowed his head slightly to an unappreciative Kelly, and with a jaunty gait, briskly slid through Carvel's doors to place his order.

Leah and Kelly said nothing as they watched the back of his figure disappear from the store with an ice cream soda and then dash to the car where his impatient uncle was revving up the engine.

Kelly rubbed her eyes, then fished out car keys from her purse. "Let's go."

In the car, the silence between the two girls was earsplitting. Kelly broke the lull.

"You're a virgin, right?"

Though stunned at the boldness of the question, Leah coughed up a candid reply. "Yes."

Another fraught pause followed.

"Do you have any experience with guys?"

"No," said Leah. "I'm not exactly what guys want."

Kelly shook her head definitively as she drove. "That's not true. You're a cute girl. I don't care what those jerks at school tell you. You are."

Leah's brown eyes lit up. First Michelle at the session, and now Kelly. It was the second time in a week someone had complimented her looks. Was this strange synchronicity or a whimsical planetary alignment at work?

Leah hadn't believed Michelle when she'd said it—she was surely just trying to be nice. However, Kelly's honesty had a harsh bluntness to it, an unpolished edge that made Leah feel like she wasn't being duped.

"Thank you," murmured Leah.

Kelly nodded. "I know I haven't known you that long, Leah, and maybe I shouldn't say anything, but...be careful of that guy.

"Jake?"

"Yes. He likes you, I can tell. But he seems really...off."

Chapter 9

"Now, everyone, I want you all to walk in a circle, but get up on the tip of your toes and keep your backs arched," ordered Frank, the charismatic, ugly-appealing movement instructor, to his underage charges. "Good. Now move as if you're part of the Tudor court. Henry VIII is present, and you want to be on your best behavior to impress this temperamental, fickle monarch. Don't give him a chance to chop your head off."

Leah's physical coordination wasn't conducive to doing these concurrent movements. She could get up on the tip of her toes and strut around like a royal peacock, yet she was too spastic to arch her back at the same time.

"No, Leah!" said Frank, alarmed. "That's not it. On the tip of your toes. Yes. Good. Arch your back. No, no, no."

He stopped Leah and positioned himself behind her.

"Okay, now arch your back and walk on the tip of your toes—and remember you're part of the Tudor court!" he commanded, removing his arms from her shoulder blades.

Leah still floundered...miserably.

"No, Leah, that's not it! Arch your back! No! Now you're walking like an old lady!"

The comment elicited a peal of giggles among the others, including Kelly, who apparently, unlike Leah, had the physical suppleness to master the exercise.

When her effort didn't produce the desired outcome, Frank, with the elasticity and languid ease of a human pretzel, demonstrated by throwing his front pelvis as forward as anatomically possible while arching his back, as if emulating an ostrich.

Leah tried one more time, but it was hopeless.

His hands flailing in the air, Frank despaired before resigning himself to a muted chuckle. "Well, I applaud your effort."

After the movement class, as with the previous week, each person was either paired off with one of their scene partners or, in Leah's case, teamed up with her only scene partner—Jake.

Frank was working with them while Downey and Michelle split their coaching among the others. Most of their peers were in the hallway or outside where the weather was relatively mild for a late-April day. Leah and Jake opted to stay inside the classroom.

Even though Frank assured Jake that some of Hamlet's excessively verbose monologue—where he brutally reprimands his mother Gertrude for her various follies—would be edited down for time purposes, Jake still stumbled over a mass of words and expressions, such as "tristful visage," which didn't exactly fall trippingly off his tongue.

"What do you think Hamlet is feeling?" asked Frank.

"He's pissed at his mother," responded Jake, the forefinger of his right hand rubbing his upper lip and his thumb scratching his chin, showing the silhouette of incoming whiskers. "He's angry at her for marrying his uncle, whom he thinks killed his brother, Hamlet's father."

Jake paused before beaming a smile at Leah and then Frank. "I saw the movie. The one with Mel Gibson. It's really good."

Frank laughed, his well-toned arms crossing over the white T-shirt that accentuated his sculpted muscles. "We won't be getting as intense as that film."

"So, I won't be dry-humping my mother?" Jake asked with a disheartened expression.

Leah made a face, then snorted with disdain.

"That won't happen here," said Frank, reassuring Leah. "We do something like that, and our program will be shut down forever. So, the answer is no."

"That's too bad," countered Jake, lifting his brows as he adjusted his glasses.

Gaping disgustedly at him, Leah snorted again, this time with far more auditory gusto than before.

Frank, wanting to change the subject, settled his bulging brown eyes on her. "Leah, you've been fairly silent. What are your thoughts on the scene? What do you think is going on in

Gertrude's mind while Hamlet is telling her off like this?"

Leah pondered for a moment before responding with an air of diffidence, her words dripping slowly and tentatively out of her mouth like tiny globs. "She thinks he's going crazy. He just killed that old guy who was eavesdropping—"

"Polonius," corrected Frank.

"Yeah, Polonius. He was hiding behind the curtain and Hamlet stabbed him," Leah synopsized, buying for time as she tried to frame a passable answer.

"Yes, we know that, but what are your general thoughts on what Gertrude is feeling?"

"Um...she's confused by his behavior. She doesn't know why he's losing it like this," she said, scrunching her forehead. "But was it that weird for royal in-laws to marry each other after their husbands or wives died? That happened quite a lot in the Bible. When does this take place?"

"That's a very good point. The play takes place around the late Middle Ages, in the fifteenth century. In Elsinore, Denmark. It's not so much that Claudius, Hamlet's uncle, marries Gertrude after Hamlet's father dies. The issue here are the sinister circumstances that led to that union. You saw the movie," Frank said, gesturing to Jake, who nodded his head. "And you," he continued, pointing to Leah, "do you know the play?"

"I saw the movie too, on TV. And bought the CliffsNotes," muttered Leah timidly.

"Did you finish reading it?"

She shook her head.

"All right, so do you know about the part when Hamlet's father appears to Hamlet as a ghost to tell his son what really happened to him, and how his brother conspired to murder him, seize his throne, and marry his wife, Hamlet's mother?"

"Well, Gertrude doesn't know that. She thinks her husband died naturally; he was poisoned, right?" Cocking her right brow, Leah gazed directly at Frank, who nodded at her. "Maybe she was always kind of hot for her brother-in-law." She shrugged.

Straightening out her slumping posture in the seat, Leah

massaged the lower curve of her back that was still a little sore from the movement class.

"Hmm, you're not that far off at all," said Frank with a gallant bow of his head as Jake mimed handclapping.

Great. Something I've done right!

"We don't have much time left, but what I want both of you to do is to work on your scenes—not only this one but your other scenes—over the next few weeks before we start blocking—"

Both Jake and Leah shot Frank a perplexed look at the word "blocking."

"I'm sorry. 'Blocking' is when we put movement into scenes. Lee, um, Mr. Downey, will begin directing, and Michelle will help as well."

Leah raised her hand. It was a silly gesture, she conceded, considering Frank was only speaking to the two of them and not the entire group.

"Yes?"

"So, we should start memorizing?"

"Well, not right away. But yes, if you can get off book—um, 'off book' means memorizing the script—sooner rather than later, that would be very helpful.

"And both of you, I strongly urge you to read the plays that contain your assigned scenes. Read the whole thing. I'm not saying this to be a pain and to burden you both with more work in addition to your regular homework. I'm saying this because it will give your scenes greater context and meaning if you've read the entire play, not just a fragment. And yes, CliffsNotes and movies can be good shortcuts—but most of the time they don't tell the entire story."

* * *

After the session was dismissed for the day, Leah pulled out her phone. She saw a text from Stu.

"I'm running a little late due to practice. Should be there in ten."

Leah sighed and sulked as she waited outside. Since Leah's

sentencing, her brother had been tasked with the duty of dropping her off at the space and then picking her up two hours later when class was finished. Because their parents were still working, there was no one else but Stu to act as the de facto car service, as Leah was two years away from taking driver's education, which was compulsory in the state of New Jersey.

She texted back: "K, I'll be here."

"Need a drive back?"

She glanced up and saw a smiling Kelly toying with her car keys.

Ever since Kelly had replaced her meds with that vitamin regimen, she was less contentious and combative with Downey and the others in the session. Still, she did have her moments when she was prone to being what Irv would've called a "sourpuss." Right now, was not one of them.

"No, I'm okay. My brother is coming for me," said Leah, her attention piqued at Kelly's buoyancy. "You seem happy today. You finally like working on Shakespeare?"

The smile vanished but not the flicker in her eyes. "No, it still sucks," she said, still clanging her keys. She sidled up close to Leah and lowered her voice. "But Derek is really cool."

Perhaps it was serendipity, but the boy whose name had just passed Kelly's lips strode out of the building.

"Hey!" He winked at her. "It was kind of fun today."

Kelly beamed back. "Yeah, it was."

His eyes locking with Kelly's, Derek sauntered to his car, an old Honda. Opening the driver's seat, he yelled out to her, "See you next time."

"Remember the rules," Leah warned her friend under her breath as they watched Derek tool away in his car.

Kelly rolled her eyes, discharging a scornful harrumph, but not before saying in a low voice so only Leah could hear, "Oh, look who's coming..."

With his knapsack strapped to his back, Jake moseyed out of the building with a lilt to his step as if he were weightless.

"Hello, girls," he said as he approached the two, the irises of his green eyes turning a slate gray as they took Kelly in with guarded curiosity before moving on to Leah and filtering back to their natural hue.

He was about to say something to Leah when a loud and discordant car horn rang out. They all looked at the source of the noise. It was originating from a black Ford SUV idling in the parking lot outside the building.

An older man who didn't look like Jake's uncle was behind the driver's wheel. With thinning white hair dotting his scalp and glasses on a nose that resembled Jake's ski-slope beak, the man was noticeably skittish and restless. He honked the horn again, this time letting go of the wheel with one hand to wave Jake into the car and away from those pesky girls.

Jake held up his right hand, waving five fingers to the man, who nodded back, frowning. "Is that your dad?" asked Leah.

"Yeah, not exactly patient, is he?"

Leah laughed. "No."

"We should get together to go over our lines. I'll text you," he said to Leah, dashing into the waiting vehicle.

Immediately after Jake jumped into the front passenger seat of his father's SUV, his dad sped off like a NASCAR superstar.

"What was that about the rules?" Kelly coyly winked at Leah, who was staring at the skid marks on the road left by Mr. Miller's car.

Luckily, at that moment, Stu, driving his red Fiat—which was Dad's old car before he'd given it to Stu after he got his license—loomed in the near distance. Leah was happy to see her brother, as it saved her from responding to Kelly.

Opening the door, Leah jumped into the passenger seat and waved back at Kelly, who reciprocated with a half-hearted flourish of her hand.

"Remember what I said," Kelly shouted so loud that everyone in New Jersey and the surrounding states could hear before turning on her heels and walking to her car.

Raising his eyebrows, Stu was taken aback at the vehemence of Kelly's admonition to his sister. "What was that about?"

Leah shook her head, feigning ignorance. "It's nothing."

"So, what do you do? You...act?" Stu narrowed his dark eyes, glancing at both his sister and the road as he pulled out of the parking lot.

"Well, sort of. That, and we do movement work and speech. We discuss the scenes we've been assigned. I think that's called 'text analysis.' And other stuff. It's interesting."

"Okay...but is it...helping?"

"Helping what?"

"You know, *helping*. You've been through a lot, kid. Is it making things better for you? Isn't that the whole goal of this thing?"

Leah shrugged. "I don't know. I guess it gets us off the streets and keeps us occupied." She paused. "And out of jail. Doing Shakespeare isn't too bad when you think of the alternative, Stu."

"By the way, that girl, your former friend," he said, emphasizing "former" for effect. "What's her name? You used to hang out with her all the time."

"Evelyn?"

"Yeah, she came to the house earlier, looking for you. I came home to change and take a quick shower before picking you up. When I opened the door, I was in a towel—literally."

"She must have loved that."

"I know you're mad at her. I don't blame you. But maybe...you should call her up, listen to her..." And then he added with unapologetic irony, "Then blow her off forever. Fuck that bitch!"

Leah laughed at that. Still...she supposed he did have a point.

Chapter 10

"So, what do you want to tell me, other than you're sorry?" said Leah to Evelyn in between bites of her tuna-fish sandwich.

After Stu had told Leah about Evelyn coming to see her, Leah had unblocked Evelyn from her iPhone and texted her.

"U came by to see me?"

"Yeah, want to meet for lunch tomorrow? The cafeteria? At noon?"

"R you sure you want to be seen with the class outcast?"

Leah couldn't help herself.

For two minutes, there'd been no answer until the following text materialized.

"I'll live." Another text from Evelyn surfaced. "Thanks for meeting me."

Leah had texted back: "Sure, tomorrow then." She'd stared a few more minutes at her phone to brace herself for another text from Evelyn. *Nothing.*

Now it was the next day, and they sat at the farthermost section of the cafeteria, the hinterlands, or the back area at the left overlooking the window. It was Leah's favorite section, which she silently designated as "in exile."

"Is this okay or do you want to sit closer to everyone?"

It's not just for my protection, but yours.

"No, it's cool. It's better...so I can really talk to you."

"Okay, it's your funeral."

Leah tried not to be so antagonistic toward Evelyn, but it was hard. Stu was right. It took guts for her to knock on the door, seeking to hash things out with her. She wasn't Sarah, that was for sure.

"Sorry, I shouldn't have said that." Leah grimaced. "I guess I suffer from...what do they call it? Oh yeah, 'lack of impulse control.'"

"That's okay," said Evelyn, munching on a hamburger. "I deserve it."

The silence between them intensified. Nothing was heard except overlapping sounds of chewing and swallowing.

Evelyn broke the lull. "I shouldn't have stayed away from you that time. That was so stupid and mean of me. You were always such a good friend. Like the sister I never had."

Leah remembered three years ago when they were in the sixth grade and Evelyn's parents were breaking up, the constant stream of texts and phone calls from Evelyn.

"I'm probably bugging you, but I don't know who else I can talk to," despaired Evelyn the night her father moved out of the home he shared with her and mother. Although Evelyn was talking to a child psychologist to help her get used to her parents breaking up, the girl was a jumble of emotions. She found it difficult to confide in the psychologist who was a stranger. Who better to talk to during that rough time than Leah?

For so long, Leah took it as a *fait accompli* that, if anyone was friends with her, it was because they couldn't find anyone better to be friends with. Given her recent history, it was a knee-jerk visceral reaction. But Evelyn, until recently, was different; she was special, like family.

"You don't have to say that or feel like you have to say it," Leah insisted in a tremulous voice.

Evelyn held Leah with a firm stare. She put her burger down. "I want to say it. You may not believe this because it's coming from me, but I'm so sorry I hurt you the way I did."

Leah felt her cheeks heat up. She tried to fight the tears forming in her eyes. So, she averted them from Evelyn, directing her focus toward the window. It was a rainy day and especially windy, judging by how hard the trees were swaying.

It was no use; despite her better efforts, a tear fell down her face, and she quickly brushed it away.

"Okay," rasped Leah, her voice reduced to a throaty purr as breakers of emotion rose and ebbed inside her throat. Even her stomach was convulsing in knots.

Evelyn's unwavering gaze remained on Leah. Both girls had stopped eating, food relegated to a minor concern.

"I guess," Leah continued, her voice still a rough croak as

she took a long breath to regain her composure and push out as much air as possible from her esophagus so she could sound like herself again and not like someone with emphysema, "this means I'll have to...unblock you from Facebook, Twitter, and Instagram."

Evelyn's jaw dropped, and her eyes flew open in shock until she met Leah's gaze. She and Leah burst into gales of laughter so infectious and raw, the kids at the other tables swiveled their bodies to look at them.

Noticing they were drawing attention, Leah signaled the horde's interest to Evelyn with her right hand. The motion caused Evelyn to rotate in her seat and take heed of the onlookers, her face still engulfed in laughter. She nodded at one table of girls before she turned back in her seat toward Leah. Shaking her head, her hilarity subsumed by a massive grin, Evelyn removed her glasses, rubbed them with one of the extra napkins, then put them back on her nose again.

"They are such jerks," she said, her smile fading. "But they don't pick on you anymore, I've noticed."

"No, they're petrified of me," Leah answered, taking a sip of her Diet Coke.

"Actually, I can't tell you how many of the other kids told me they wanted to thank you for finally getting rid of Dede. She had it coming. Look at her little slaves. They're lost without her."

Evelyn pointed to the table where Dede's minions sat glaring unceasingly at her and Leah while munching on pizza and potato chips. "Nobody misses her except them."

"I wish...I wish the other kids would tell me that," Leah admitted.

"They can't," said Evelyn. "They feel bad for what happened to you. And..." Evelyn cast her eyes down on her empty plate. "Responsible."

"Well, some of them did join Dede's Facebook page," Leah said bitterly.

"Yeah, some of them did. But not everyone, Leah. There are still people here who know you're a nice kid, and you didn't deserve that. Most of us have known you since forever. Then

Dede moved here a few years ago. She was a psycho; everyone knew that. Even all the teachers."

"A lot of good that did," Leah retorted. No sooner did she say that did Leah felt guilty about making that bitchy jab. "Sorry."

"No, you have every right to be pissed. We all failed you."

A brief pause followed.

Hesitating, Evelyn bit her upper lip.

"Umm...so...how's Shakespeare rehab going?"

The bell rang, signifying lunch was over.

After both girls bussed their trays, Evelyn sought Leah's reassurance. "So, are we friends again? Can I call and text you?"

"Yes," said Leah, and she meant it.

Yet she would never forget. How could she? Trust had been broken. It would take a while, if ever, for that delicate tissue of confidence between them to be mended. Until then, a truce was in effect.

* * *

Later that night after finishing her homework, Leah got into her pajamas. She thought about reading the Helena monologue yet again. Instead, she turned on her TV and flipped to MTV to watch a reality TV show involving wives of superstar athletes. Then she heard a ping from her phone, which was charging next to the TV.

Dragging herself from the bed, she shuffled over to her phone and picked it up. There was a text from Jake: "Want to get together this weekend to go over our scene?"

She gaped at the message, unsure of how to answer. She mulled it over for a minute, then texted back: "Yeah, that would be okay."

"Cool!"

Immediately, Leah chided herself for her impulsiveness.

That was stupid. I should have played hard to get. I shouldn't have replied so fast.

The self-incrimination reached a summit when a

realization dawned on her.

Why am I getting so nervous about this? It's not like it's a date.

She would be up the entire night, pondering if it was.

Chapter 11

At first, when Leah told her parents after breakfast that she had an appointment—it was *not* a date—to go over her lines from Shakespeare rehab with Jake, they were worried.

"You think this is a good idea?" asked Dana. "Didn't you say one of the rules of this program is no dating?"

Leah almost lost her temper.

"We're *not* dating. We're not even friends. I don't know him that well, and I'm not sure I want to. But I do want to know my lines. If I don't do the work, I'm going to jail."

"You're not going to jail!" contended Irv after swigging down his black coffee. "That's not happening. Nobody's going to jail. Jerry assured us of that."

He eyed Dana for backup.

"Your daddy can drive you to this boy's home in Mahwah," Dana said. "Then he'll pick you up when you're done. I don't like this boy driving you back home. Will his parents be there?"

"Great. My free day and I'm playing chauffeur!" joked Irv.

"Yes, his parents will be there," answered Leah. In truth, she had no idea, but she wanted to pacify her mother. Then she added, "He doesn't drive yet. He's sixteen."

* * *

When Leah rang the door at Jake's house, her dad's car was idling across the street. He was waiting until someone—an adult—opened the door. Once that transpired, Leah knew he would hurry off to a local diner and have another cup of coffee while reading the news on his iPad. That was part of her father's Saturday routine.

Leah pursed her lips as the doorknob turned. A slim man of medium height with thinning white hair stood in the doorway. Leah recognized the man as the same one who'd picked Jake up from the session—his father, Martin. Behind him was

Jake.

Leah turned around to wave at her father, who then sped away.

"Nice to meet you, Leah," said Mr. Miller. Turning to his son, he said, "Well, I'm off to Home Depot."

This worried Leah. *So, I am going to be alone with Jake?* She had no cause to think anything would go awry, but she couldn't remember the last time she had been left alone with a boy around her age who wasn't her brother.

Before bolting from the premises, Mr. Miller took Jake aside. He spoke quietly, but Leah could still hear him. "You remember what I told you?"

"Yeah, Dad," answered a mildly irritated Jake, his eyes glazing over. "I know, I know."

"Good," his father responded.

Mr. Miller then left the house, leaping into his blue SUV and driving away with such breakneck velocity Leah could hear the tires rumbling rough against the asphalt road. Leah stood there, uncertain of what to say.

"My father wanted to remind me that my mother needs to take her pills at two o'clock, just in case he's not back by then," Jake explained.

Jake's candor startled her.

"I'm sorry. That's more than you needed to know. TMI, and all that. But you seem like you'd understand."

"Where's your mother?" Leah asked, scouring the hallway, which led into a kitchen and a dining room.

"Outside gardening. She'd come and say hello, but...she gets nervous sometimes when new people come to the house."

He walked into the kitchen, inviting Leah to tag along. With his right hand, he motioned for her to glimpse through one of the windows at the petite figure of a middle-aged woman, her long, wavy auburn hair pulled back in a braid. Working with a mini spade, her hands covered in gloves, she was replanting geraniums in time for their late-spring bloom.

Jake knocked on the glass window, causing his mom to look up. Seeing Jake, she flashed a radiant smile. Her son reciprocated and pointed his right hand toward Leah.

His mother's smile evaporated, but she acknowledged the girl's presence with a diplomatic bow of her head. Leah returned the favor with a polite smile that showed no teeth. After this exchange, Jake's mother, Donna, resumed the replanting.

"My mother. As soon as it gets to be spring, even if it's cold out, she basically moves outside. Everyday."

"She doesn't work?"

"She used to."

A fraught silence followed as both stared at one another.

"Let's get started, then," said Leah, clearing her throat.

* * *

"What have I done, that thou darest wag thy tongue in noise so rude against me?" With each line recited from memory, Leah felt a sense of accomplishment.

No stumbling yet. So far, so good.

She sat there waiting for Jake to say Hamlet's next line. He was taking a while, and she could tell he was trying very hard not to peek at the copy of the scene lying face down on the kitchen table. His features compressed as he closed his eyes.

"Um...uh...okay, I got it, um, 'such an act that,' ugh." He swallowed the breath he was inhaling, then heaved it out. "Oh yeah, 'blurs the grace'...shit." He sighed, his eyes still shut. He opened one eye while keeping the other closed.

Leah marveled at the optical dexterity that enabled Jake to do this.

During those suspended moments when Jake was at a temporary loss for what his next line was, Leah couldn't help but notice the kitchen's décor: peach walls with a few simple paintings of flowers and fruits adorning them for good measure, offset by loads of modern accouterments—two coffee makers, a microwave, a granite countertop (also peach), a stainless-steel sink, and above it, a clock that looked indistinguishable from other clocks one would typically find at a home-furnishings retailer.

"Leah, what's the next line?" Jake prompted.

She peeked at the side. "'That blurs the grace and blush of

modesty, calls virtue hypocrite, takes off the rose from the fair forehead of an innocent love...'" Leah read to Jake, whose face was clenched like a fist as he closed his eyes in concentration.

"Okay, okay, I think I got it now," he responded with avid glee, both his eyes shooting open.

Because the scene hadn't been blocked yet by Downey, they didn't bother to get up on their feet, rehearsing their movement and going full throttle. Except for Jake faltering over a few words and lines here and there—not surprising, given his character's proclivity for morose verbosity—they were finally able to get through the scene without any more snags.

"You didn't stumble once!" Jake said, his face aglow with admiration. "Wow. You must have a photographic memory."

"I don't think so," she said, almost blushing. "I mean, everyone says that, but it's not true. If I need to memorize something, I just read and reread it to death. I've been rereading this scene a lot—this, and the monologue I've been assigned. That's the secret to my so-called photographic memory."

Jake laughed, his sparkling gaze never leaving Leah's face.

Befuddled, Leah wrinkled her forehead. "Um...did I say something funny?"

Despite fading from the lower part of his face, the smile lingered in Jake's eyes.

"I'm sorry. I didn't mean to be rude. It's just that...the face you made when you mentioned your photographic memory..." He let out a giggle once more, then put his right hand up to his mouth as if to clog it from further tactless outpourings of glee.

A little confused, Leah changed the subject. "How's the scene going with Rob?"

"Really good. He's not a bad kid once you get to know him. He's nice and quiet. Kind of like...you."

"I talk...sometimes."

"When? Seriously."

Leah bit her upper lip as she thought back to the sessions. "How about the time I asked Downey why I was being assigned to play someone's mother?"

"A fifteen-year-old could be a mother," said Jake with a shrug. "It was not socially unacceptable during Hamlet's time; now it's weird and trailer-trashish, but not then. I've read a lot about the royalty in the Medieval and Renaissance periods. If you were in court back then, Leah, you'd be very busy cranking out one baby after another. You'd be on your third one by now, I'm sure."

Leah chuckled. Her newly transformed face spurred Jake to light up even more.

"You see, I made you laugh. You never do, and you never smile."

"Not true," she replied, still grinning. "I'm doing it now. And I think I smiled yesterday for one second. It was when I saw it was three o'clock and Friday was over. Yippee!"

Leah twirled the forefinger of her right hand in a spiral. A current of laughter burst from her yet again, with Jake joining in.

Then without provocation or notice, Jake leaned toward Leah and gave her a quick peck on the lips. The kiss stunned Leah into silence. The joy that previously illuminated her soft features disappeared, replaced by a grimness that made the light in Jake's eyes disappear.

"Why did you do that?" she flared, her eyes burning with rage.

"I'm sorry." He threw his hands in the air. "But you looked so cute and happy…I wanted to kiss you. I've wanted to ever since I saw you in the courtroom."

Leaping to her feet, Leah pulled out her phone from her satchel. "I'm going to text my father to pick me up."

"I'm sorry, I really am," he said quickly. "I didn't mean anything. I like you, I do."

A cynical thought entered Leah's head. "This isn't part of some bet you made with Rob, is it?"

Jake gaped, dumbstruck, at Leah. "No!" he insisted, standing. "Why would you think that? Did someone do that to you?" he probed.

She shut her eyes. "Not quite," she said, casting her eyes downward. "But they might as well have."

"I'm not exactly Mr. Popular either," he added, an unmistakable note of bitterness seeping into his voice. "But you know that already."

Without broaching the offense that had landed Jake in court the day he and Leah first saw each other, Leah decided to defuse the situation by repeating one of Tully's warnings.

"She said 'no dating,' remember? I don't want to get into trouble. It would kill my parents if I flunked out of this program and got sent to a reform school."

"Yeah, I know. The rules. That was stupid of me," he agreed.

Leah glanced for a second at the unsent text message on her phone. Making no movement to send the digital SOS, she took a lengthy breather and composed her frazzled thoughts. What came out of her mouth astonished her; it was as if she had no control over her power of speech like she had a kind of Tourette's syndrome minus the utterance of obscenities.

"I think we should hold off on anything until, um, the program is over. I think that would be good."

Startled, Jake's eyes flickered as his head jerked back slightly.

"Yeah," he replied. "That's cool. And you're right. We should wait until we're done. Believe it or not, I don't want to get into trouble either."

"Good, but you know," Leah added, with a tinge of bashfulness, "I'm not, uh...committing! Yeah, that's it. I'm not committing to anything. It's just that if we want to get...involved, we should do it after." Cautiously, she extended her right hand to Jake. "Deal?"

An impish grin appeared on his face. "Deal!" he declared, shaking Leah's hand.

* * *

That night as Leah lay in bed, a groundswell of nervousness and excitement was still flooding her senses thanks to Jake's unexpected kiss. It replayed over and over in her head, along with their resolution not to pursue anything until

Shakespeare rehab was finished.

To get her mind off Jake, she clicked on her TV. Impatiently, she surfed from one channel to another, hoping to find something that would distract her. Nothing. Sighing, she grabbed her phone from the top of her bureau and texted Evelyn. She may as well make good use of their rapprochement.

"Guess what? I got kissed by a boy."

Chapter 12

Maybe it was because she had been rejected so early and consistently by so many of her peers, but Leah always felt like a real rube when it came to sex. While other girls her age were hooking up on some apps with the agile speed of champion athletes, Leah sublimated whatever callow hormonal urges she experienced with her imagination, supplemented by a semi-regular consumption of novels her mother's generation would've characterized as "smut."

Leah had found most of these trash novels from the eighties and nineties, authored by the likes of Danielle Steel or Judith Krantz, in a cardboard box in the garage. She guessed they were her mother's, which she'd no doubt read in between so-called serious works like Vasari's *Lives of the Artists* for college.

Leah loved these pulpy dime-store abominations. It made her feel like her mother, so impeccably groomed and well mannered, was an abject mortal just like her, one who could easily be seduced by the peanut-crunching crowd into surrendering herself to the lowest common denominator in taste.

Given how negative Kelly was about Jake, Leah decided not to confide in her new friend about the latest boy development. She didn't know Kelly well enough to trust that this tidbit wouldn't spread to the ears of Downey or, god forbid, Tully. *That's all I need.*

Honestly, she found Kelly's hostility toward Jake to be a bit inexplicable, if unsettling. To rationalize this weird antipathy, she chalked it up to Kelly's anger-management problems. Still, its reality always made Leah wonder when and how soon Kelly would turn on her.

On the other hand, Evelyn was not going to tell anyone—or at least anyone who had the influence and reach to disseminate it through the school. And, even if she did, who would care? Jake wasn't a student at Highland.

Like Leah, Evelyn was still a virgin. But unlike Leah, Evelyn had some experience with boys, having already had a boy-friend—Chuckie. She'd started going steady with him when they were in the fifth grade. Like her, Chuckie had worn glasses and loved science fiction. He and Evelyn discovered their mutual love of *Star Wars* when they were assigned to sit next to each other in social studies class.

To officially begin their relationship, Chuckie had given Evelyn an old charm bracelet of his mother's, which Evelyn kept hidden in her jewelry chest at home rather than risk exposure by wearing it. From what Evelyn used to tell Leah, their prepubescent romance was basically a chaste affair, defined by hours of conversation talking about Luke Skywalker and Princess Leia, and some occasional hugs and kisses that were mostly innocuous, tongue-free pecks and fumbling for Evelyn's bra, whose snaps Chuckie was too clumsy and frustrated by to unlatch.

The relationship had gone on for almost two years until Chuckie informed Evelyn that he and his family were moving to Phoenix that summer after seventh grade. His father, an architect, had landed a job as a managing partner at a firm there. The next day, Evelyn had ridden her bicycle to Chuckie's house, dropping off a sealed envelope for him in his family's mailbox. Inside, was the bracelet he'd given her when they'd first started their innocent courtship.

With the bracelet, she'd left a handwritten note. *To a great kid. Lots of good luck in Phoenix. I will always remember you. Yours, Evelyn.* She told Leah she'd been too shy to write "love" before her name, but Evelyn reckoned Chuckie would get the idea.

A day later, while she and Leah were having lunch in the cafeteria, two years before the entire Dede mess blew up and briefly upended their friendship, Chuckie interrupted them, asking to speak to Evelyn privately. It was an indiscreet move that shocked both Evelyn and Leah, who knew about their secret romance but was sworn to secrecy.

Evelyn agreed, even though Leah could see in her face she was nervous. A relationship she had taken pains to conceal, as neither party wanted to be targeted for ridicule by their oh-so-cool and sexually sophisticated classmates, was being laid bare for all to see.

The two had gone outside together. Even though it was a sweleringly hot June day, a casual summer breeze made the heat bearable. From his pocket, Chuckie had pulled out an envelope, the same one Evelyn had used to leave the bracelet and her note in his mailbox.

"This is for you," he said as he took out the bracelet and held it in his hand. "I want you to have this. Always. I asked my mom if I could let you have it forever, and she said yes. So, it's yours, Evelyn," he insisted, his doughy features animated by the beating noontime sun.

Evelyn's hand shook as Chuckie tenderly slipped the trinket into the envelope. When Evelyn returned to the cafeteria, Chuckie having absconded for his math class, Leah was still at the same table, waiting for her. There she was treated to a smattering of applause and giggles.

A boy from her homeroom rushed up to her. "I didn't know you and Chuckie were together," he said. "Good for you both for being in the closet about it, unlike all the loudmouths here."

The epilogue to the relationship was predictably bittersweet: two weeks after school let out for the summer, Chuckie and his family moved. Right before they left, Evelyn had dinner with Chuckie's family at an Outback Steakhouse.

"We want you to visit us if you can," cooed Chuckie's mom. "You can stay with us. I'll talk to your parents if you want."

Unfortunately, the old cliché about absence and the heart didn't apply in this instance. Although Chuckie and Evelyn did stay in touch that summer, texting, e-mailing, and sometimes calling each day, she began hearing less from him after the school year began. In an e-mail to her and not a call, Chuckie explained his laxness in keeping in touch with her was due to his adjusting to a new environment, homework, and other activities, such as a science-fiction club he'd joined at school. By Halloween, communication between the former grade-school sweethearts was almost down to nil. She did get a Christmas card and text from Chuckie, which she reciprocated, but it was clear he'd moved on literally and figuratively, so Evelyn did as well. "You'll find someone better, someday," Leah assured her.

Now, it was Leah's turn to spill all the details about *her* first romantic tryst. If a single kiss could even be called that. "Did you like it?" Evelyn asked Leah when she was finished recounting the story.

They were sitting outside on a bench devouring their lunches, forgoing the din and lack of circulation in the cafeteria for the soothing May breeze. The weather was perfect—high sixties, not too hot or cold.

"The kiss?"

Evelyn nodded.

Leah removed her light-purple windbreaker, rolling it into a heap next to her as Evelyn did the same; only, the outer garment she took off was an old, ratty yellow sweater that had holes and missing buttons she liked to wear. Leah advised her pal to throw it out, which invited an uncharacteristic reaction from Evelyn: she'd raised her voice and told Leah in no uncertain terms that the sweater was all she had left of her beloved Nana, who'd died two years before at eighty-five. Rightfully chastened, Leah never brought up the sweater again.

"It was...okay. Kind of nothing, really."

"I thought the same thing with Chuckie."

"Did he ever French you?"

Evelyn let loose a laugh that sounded more like a cackle. "Chuckie, are you kidding? I think he was too scared. One time, I tried to put my tongue in his mouth when we were kissing, and he wouldn't even open it."

Leah reflected on this as her eyes followed a squirrel scaling a tree fifty feet away. "We truly are pathetic, aren't we?" she mused. "Everyone here is screwing up a storm, and we still can't get past first base."

"I like being a virgin," said Evelyn with a shrug, breaking the momentary lull that developed following Leah's bleak commentary on their sorry carnal state of affairs.

Leah diverted her vision from the rodent back to her demure pal. "Really?"

"Yes, really. When I lose my virginity, I want it to be to someone I love and someone who loves me."

Leah deliberated. "Suppose you're thirty-five when you finally fall in love with someone? What then?"

Evelyn pursed her lips for a second, then answered, "Then I'll be a thirty-five-year-old virgin."

* * *

Later that day, Leah reported for session.

Downey kicked off the late afternoon's proceedings by announcing he would start blocking monologues before moving on to scenes. "We have about five weeks to go; can you believe it? Before you know it, you'll be done."

The loaded comment elicited a spate of "Thank gods," "Yeahs," and some clapping.

Without thinking, Leah, who was seated between Tiffany and Kelly like normal, looked over to Jake, whom she hadn't seen or spoken to since their kiss. He was in his usual spot too, a corner nook.

Jake's eyes were rigidly ahead, watching Downey. Either he was casually oblivious to Leah or making a conscious effort to ignore her.

That's strange. Quickly and as unobtrusively as possible, she shifted her gaze from Jake back to Downey, but not before she met Kelly's prying eyes, which seemed to receive her with an amalgam of curiosity and wonder. *Hmm. What's with her? Whatever...*

"For the next half hour to forty-five minutes, depending on how long I'll need, I'll be working with Tiffany, then Leah. And if I have time left over, I'll also work with you, Derek. Then we'll call it a day and resume next time. As you can see, it's only me today—Michelle and Frank are in rehearsals for a show. But they will be back next session.

"This doesn't mean that the rest of you will get to slack off today. Sorry. No can do. We don't have enough time for that. Tiffany, please put that away! What did Ms. Tully say the first day about texting?"

Downey's admonition to Tiffany had a stridency to it that rattled the teens out of their late-afternoon lethargy.

"Good," he said after Tiffany grumpily obeyed his order. "Now, let's begin."

* * *

Huddled together, Jake and Rob slumped on the hallway's cold floors, quietly reciting their lines with each other. Both boys had their sides sprawled upside down on the floor so neither could steal a glimpse at their next line. It didn't help. No sooner would Jake congratulate himself for remembering the next round of lines than Rob would stumble and falter. Or the other way around. Leah tried not to giggle as she listened.

"Shit," said Rob, turning over the side to peek at his next line. "What do I say next?"

Since he refused to wear glasses, Rob had to squint at the xeroxed copy.

"Okay." He turned the side over again, then resumed the next line. "One that was a woman, sir; but, rest her soul, she's dead."

It was the scene between Hamlet and a gravedigger, identified only in the play as the First Clown. The two engage in banter until Hamlet discovers the grave that the First Clown is digging is for Hamlet's beloved Ophelia.

Leah, sitting on the floor opposite Jake and Rob, was only pretending to study her Helena monologue, so she couldn't help but notice when Jake's emotionally impenetrable eyes fell on her. His inscrutability flustered her. *Did I do something wrong?*

Stung by his indifference, Leah gathered her things and marched outside, where she saw Kelly and Derek sitting very close to one another, laughing. Leah was hit with a pang of jealousy. She knew it was stupid for her to feel this way...yet she did.

She was about to pivot and walk right back into the building when Kelly called out to her.

"Hey, Leah! Where ya going?"

"Um," she said shyly, pointing to the door. "Back inside, I guess."

"Nah, come over here," Kelly beckoned, waving her hand excitedly. Leah complied.

Kelly's exuberant delight disappeared when she saw Leah's face. "What's wrong?"

Sensing it was his cue to leave, Derek intoned, "Later, girls," in a thick, husky baritone as he adjusted his knapsack and scuttled away.

As he moved off, Kelly's eyes followed the contours of Derek's fine physique retreating into the building.

"Damn that Tully and her stupid rules," gushed an admiring Kelly, her lips coiling into a lustful grin.

"Yeah, he's hot," said Leah, exuding apathy.

Kelly drawled sarcastically, "You sound thrilled."

"I'm tired."

A skilled multitasker, Kelly took out her phone and began scanning her Facebook feed while continuing the conversation with Leah.

"How did it go on Saturday?"

The question provoked consternation from Leah.

When did I tell her about Saturday?

To ascertain this, Leah played dumb.

"What do you mean, Saturday?"

Rolling her eyes, Kelly fixed her attention on Leah.

"Saturday! Remember, you told me you were going to Jake's to go over your lines?

"I did?"

"Yes. You don't remember telling me *this*? You texted me last week about it."

Oh damn. She's right.

Feeling guilty—though she didn't know why—Leah replied, "I completely forgot I'd told you. I wasn't sure if I was going to go because..."

"He's weird?" Kelly jumped in, deadpan, as she resumed scanning her Facebook feed.

"Yeah. Well, I did."

"How did that go?" Kelly asked, her face remaining

impassive.

"Okay, I guess..." Leah paused, biting her lip.

Unfortunately, Kelly picked up on the nuance in the hesitation. "*Yeah?*"

"Well..."

Kelly lifted her eyes from her phone and stared at Leah, annoyed. "Leah, if there's something you want to say, then just say it!"

"Promise me you won't tell anyone?" Leah pleaded, lowering her voice.

Even though she had initially resolved not to tell Kelly about the kiss, due to the girl's hostility toward Jake—not to mention Leah's misgivings about Kelly's overall trustworthiness—Leah couldn't help it. Her excitement over this latest turn of events suspended her power of reason.

"Yes, yes. I promise."

"He kissed me," Leah blurted out.

"Hmmm?" The irritation in Kelly's voice dissipated. She smirked as her eyes flickered. "Yeah, I knew he liked you. So...what happened afterward?"

"Nothing.

"How was it? Do you like him?"

"I don't know."

Leah cast her eyes on the ground. They detoured to a tiny colony of ants forming underneath a branch, a castoff from one of the towering trees adjacent to the building.

"This wasn't the first time you've been kissed, was it?" asked Kelly.

"Yes...it was," muttered Leah.

Eyes bugging out, Kelly stared at her.

"Hmm. Well, if you need advice on sex, just ask me."

"Kelly!" Leah leaned forward to Kelly but not before she cased the surroundings to make sure no one else was eavesdropping on their conversation. "It was just a teeny tiny little kiss. That's it. Might not happen again."

"Sure, it will. You don't know men."

Frustrated, Leah shook her head. "I give up."

Kelly persisted. "If you ever get to that point where you want to go all the way with him, I'll help you. I lost my virginity when I was twelve, so I'm an old hand when it comes to this. One thing, though, buy condoms because you can't depend on the boy to do it for you. They never do. They always depend on the girl for birth control. It's not fair, but there you go."

She deliberated some more on this topic. "You can also go to a clinic. Because we're in Jersey, thank god, you can get whatever you need without your parents knowing about it."

"Did you hear what I said? I'm not going to have sex," Leah protested. "I'm not going to see him like that. And if we ever date, it won't happen while we're in session. I don't want to get into trouble. I already told him that."

"How did he take it?"

"He seemed fine about it. But—" Leah glanced down again, her features twisting into a grimace.

"But...but what?" Kelly grilled.

"Today was the first day I've seen him since last Saturday. That's three days. He didn't even say hi to me. He *ignored* me."

"Probably because you blew him off."

"I told him we should wait until this is over and then if we're interested, we can see each other."

"That's very mature of you and sensible. But, Leah, boys are dogs. When they want it, they want it. And if they don't get it, they growl and bite."

Insulted, Leah glared at Kelly. "Or maybe he does really like me but wants to hide how he feels so he and I won't get into trouble? How about *that?*"

Kelly looked taken aback by Leah's sass. "You don't have to get all huffy," she said, her eyes rerouting from Leah to an SUV driving slowly past the building. "I'm sorry if I offended you."

There was a disingenuous tone to Kelly's apology that made Leah think she didn't mean it at all. Leah pulled out her phone to check the time. 4:15 p.m. She groaned. *An hour and fifteen more minutes of this?*

Bewildered by Kelly's rudeness over the latest occurrence in Leah's nascent romantic life—*you would think a friend would be happy for another friend*—Leah was on the verge of confronting her about it when Tiffany appeared in the door-way. She waved Leah over.

Thank god.

"Looks like I'm next," she said to Kelly, who barely acknowl-edged Leah taking her leave, choosing instead to surf her various social media sites with a semi-glower.

* * *

That night, after Leah finished reading a section of *Modern American History* for her social studies class, she heard a ping on her phone. She picked it up and saw a text from Kelly.

"Sorry if I upset you earlier. My mom always tells me I don't have a filter. Doesn't help I'm on the rag and my cramps are killing me. I forgot to take my pills too."

Leah texted back: "No, it wasn't you. I was being too sensi-tive."

The little dots appeared on Leah's phone, showing that Kelly was working on a text. Finally, the message unspooled on her screen: "I think you should see Jake."

Leah laughed, texting back: "Well, I'm going to have to. We do have a scene."

"That's not what I mean."

"I don't want to get in trouble."

"How would Tully find out about it? She hasn't been to the sessions in a while. She's gone."

"Downey is her eyes and ears."

"She won't find out. Just keep quiet about it. Remember when I told you I had a friend who was in this program? She was seeing the guy she was doing a scene with, and Tully never found out about it."

"I didn't know that."

"There are a lot of things you don't know."

No sooner did Kelly stop texting her than Leah got a mes-sage from the boy himself. *Wow. He must have cyber telepathy!*

"Sorry I didn't talk to you earlier. Had a lot on my mind. Also, Rob and I need to go over our lines. He's still having problems memorizing."

Leah gulped.

Be cool. Don't show him how nervous he makes you. And don't answer him too fast. Slow down. Let him wait!

To keep him at bay, Leah looked at her other e-mails. She saw one from Evelyn, who'd sent her a link to an article on People.com about Taylor Swift.

Clicking on the link, Leah tried to read the piece, which was nothing more than fluff on Taylor's new mansion in Nashville, and how she had everything painted in her favorite color, pink. This included the twenty bedrooms to accommodate her circle of friends, who would come over twice a week for pajama parties. Leah made a face. *Isn't she getting a little old for that?*

She read on. Taylor was describing a state-of-the-art twenty-four-track recording studio she'd had built in her home. From now on, all her albums would be recorded there. No more extended excursions to Los Angeles unless she had to attend premieres or visit agents or movie star pals.

Leah studied the gallery of photos showing Taylor's new palatial abode. The pink was so overpowering it looked stupid. Only a gold chandelier in the center of the foyer, coupled with a few white walls, offset the profusion of pink.

She exhaled, then picked up the phone and saw the text from Jake.

"I was wondering what was going on," she typed.

"Do you want to go over our lines? Maybe on Saturday again?"

"K," she typed back hastily before her mind could process her action.

As soon as she sent the text, regret made her stomach sick. Even though Jake had promised he would honor her request not to hit on her anymore—at least not until they were done with the program, and only if there were genuine mutual interest—she was beset with worry she'd made a mistake. She didn't know Jake, so how could she trust him?

Then it dawned on her what the motivator here was, and it wasn't a desire to go off book. She was fearful that if she weren't amenable to Jake's overtures, he would stop pursuing her. And she would never experience what it was like to date a boy, to be in a couple, to be wanted. She was an outcast for so long that as a result she had no experience with boys and envied girls who did.

She had no faith that there would be others like Jake in the future.

This could be my only shot. Not just going out with someone but also with sex. Then where would that leave me? The living embodiment of her worst nightmare: the middle-aged virgin.

A fate more wretched than being bullied to death by the likes of Dede and her disciples.

Chapter 13

The arrangement was the same as the previous Saturday: Irv would drop Leah off at Jake's house, and then after she was finished, she'd text her father to pick her up.

"If I don't see a car in the driveway, then you're not going in," her father declared as he drove his white Impala near the corner street leading to Jake's house.

Leah groaned. "Dad, we're only going over *lines*. I was assigned to do a scene with him. We need to memorize, or we won't be able to complete the program. And if I fail Shakespeare rehab, then I'll have to go back to court. You don't want that, do you?"

"That's not going to happen. I just don't want anything to happen to you. I should have done a better job of protecting you from those monsters."

"Dad, forget about it, please!"

When they turned the corner and saw a blue SUV in the driveway at Jake's house, which Leah confirmed was the car belonging to Mr. Miller, she sensed her dad's relief. Still, his hands were tense on the steering wheel, his eyes anxiously glued on the door of the Miller house.

After Leah exited the car, her dad honked the horn.

What now?

Leah trotted to the window of the driver's seat. Irv rolled it down.

"You forgot to say goodbye!"

Leah sighed. "Goodbye."

A triumphant smile emerged on Irv's face. Age and the ravages of his recent illness had exacted a toll on him, making him seem far older than his chronological years. From the car dividing Leah and her father, the dark circles under Irv's eyes looked more pronounced than usual and the laugh lines that ordinarily flanked them were now engulfed in deep wrinkles. His forehead, cheeks, and the corners of his mouth were similarly corrugated and creased.

Excited and nervous, Leah walked up to Jake's house. When the door opened, it was Jake's mother who appeared. Leah was momentarily startled as if she were seeing an apparition. Based on what Jake had told her about his mother's favorite pastime, she'd expected her to be outside hoeing and planting away.

Remembering her father was idling in his car, Leah turned around and waved to him. With his left hand on the wheel, he waved back at his daughter before vanishing into the distance.

With an awl in her hands, which were covered in gardening gloves, Donna welcomed Leah at the door.

"Good afternoon," said Donna softly. "I'm sorry about this," she gestured to the implement in her hand and the gloves. "I'm about to go to the garden. The gladiolas need replanting."

She turned her head and yelled so hard she was practically shrieking, "Jake! Your friend is here!"

The shrillness of her voice, so different from the way she'd spoken seconds ago, unnerved Leah.

"I apologize," said Donna, reverting to her former tone. "What's your name again?"

"Leah."

"Oh yes." She turned around again and then let out another piercing, full-throated yell. "Jake! Leah is here!"

"Yeah, yeah," mumbled Jake as he trudged down the stairs and headed toward the doorway where Leah stood with his mother.

Wearing jeans and a white cotton scoop-necked long-sleeved shirt, Jake broke into a grin and tucked his hands into his pockets as he took in his guest.

"Maybe you should both rehearse in the basement? It's quiet down there," Donna whispered to Jake as if Leah wasn't present and couldn't hear. "No distractions."

"No. Dad said he's going to go down there and paint the table by the bar," he shot back.

Donna contorted her lips in displeasure. "I don't know why. We never use it."

Jake opened his mouth like he was about to jump to his

father's defense, but something held him back. "We'll work in the kitchen," he said definitively.

Inwardly, Leah breathed a sigh of relief. Motioning Leah to follow him up the stairs, Jake pointed her to the same seat she'd sat in the last time she was in the house.

As his mother exited toward the backyard, she yelled out, "Do either of you want lemonade? I can make a fresh batch."

Jake cast a tentative glance at Leah. "Do you want anything?"

She shook her head.

"No, Mom, that's fine."

"What about some cookies? I think we still have some Entenmann's chocolate chip cookies. They're delicious."

Jake sighed, but not loudly enough for his mother to hear. "No, nothing."

"Well, I'll be out in the garden if you need me."

No sooner did they start to work on their lines than they heard a most unpleasant racket coming from outside—a lawnmower.

"Oh shit," exclaimed Jake. Jumping out of the chair, he raced to the window and let out another sigh. He clasped his face in his hands, shaking his head. "I don't believe it. She knows we're working here."

"Maybe she can do it later or tomorrow," said Leah, yelling above the cacophony.

Jake shook his head. The noise was so deafening at this point that Leah could only make out what Jake was saying by reading his lips.

"She won't do it later or another day because she wants to do it right now."

"Is there another room where we can go work on our lines— one with noise-proof walls?"

As soon as Leah asked this question, she knew instinctively she'd goofed big time.

Jake nodded. "Yes, my room. It's the quietest room in the house. The walls are sound-insulated." He turned to leave the kitchen and she swallowed hard as she stood up to follow him.

Talk about walking into the fire. I asked for it, didn't I?

She thought of ways she could disentangle herself from a situation that could get dicey. Nothing was forthcoming. Part of her hoped it would all turn out innocent, while the other part was curious about the possibilities of what could transpire within the sanctum of Jake's room.

Jake led Leah to his room at the end of the hall. It was a complete contrast to the décor of the rest of the house, with all the peach, the stainless steel, and the tasteful paintings.

Leah's eyes popped out. She had never seen anything quite like it.

"I know," Jake said, observing her reaction. "It's a bit much. My parents hate it. Well, my mom does, but my dad says it's important that I'm able to express myself, not have my spirit broken and all that other crap," he said, standing vigil in the center of his room.

"No, it's cool. I mean, really cool," faltered Leah as she scrutinized the room. "Really different." Painted black and purple with splashes of white, Jake's room was a tribute to the power of individual eclectic expression. Between the shocking juxtaposition of lurid colors were posters of characters from various fantasy blockbusters interspersed with those of exotic locales like Sri Lanka.

There was also a photo here and there of a younger Jake dressed as Legolas from *Lord of the Rings*, complete with a bow and arrow and a slinky, long blond-haired wig. Leah wasn't sure if it was for Halloween or some geek fantasy convention. Still, it was eye-opening to see Jake in fun mode, clearly enjoying himself away from the session.

Only Jake's peach bureau and desk, no doubt picked by the same person who determined the color scheme for the rest of the house, adhered to an aesthetic of normality.

Unlike Evelyn and other kids her age, Leah wasn't a huge fan of the fantasy genre. Sure, she'd seen a few films in the *Harry Potter* franchise, read the *Lord of the Rings* trilogy, watched all the movies and took in some of HBO's *Game of Thrones*. But she did it mostly out of a need to fit in with everyone else.

Leah's quiet, earnest, and erudite demeanor gave many

adults and kids the impression she was some kind of precocious intellectual; in truth, her palate wasn't as sophisticated
nor fanciful as her peers. Where they were drawn toward the
world of dragons and extraterrestrial goblins, she preferred a
steady menu of reality TV.

Not wishing to touch upon the fantasy references, Leah
broached another topic for conversation, which also seemed
obvious to her.

"Have you been there?" she asked, pointing to the poster of
Sri Lanka.

It offered a panoramic view of a craggy mountain topped by
a sky dotted with fleecy mushroom clouds and a burst of yellow.

Jake chuckled. "No. I thought it was a cool poster and I put
it up. My uncle Jeff gave it to me. He's a pilot for United. He's
been everywhere in the world."

Both looked at the poster.

"I'd love to go there," he continued. "I want to go everywhere. See the world."

"You want to be a pilot?"

"I dunno. Maybe." A mischievous glimmer sparkled from
his green eyes as his lips curled into an askew grin. "Or maybe
a drug dealer."

Leah broke into a lopsided smile, nearly mirroring Jake's.
"Okay," she responded flippantly.

Jake pulled out the chair behind his desk and motioned
Leah to sit. He lowered himself onto his bed in a movement
that could only be described as a languid swoon. Silence descended as both looked at one another.

"Where's the farthest you've traveled?" asked Leah, shat-
tering the fraught pause.

Jake shook his head, and his smile disappeared. "LA and
Orlando..." He let out a long sigh. "I've never been out of the
country."

"I've been overseas," Leah said. "Several times."

"Oh yeah?" asked Jake, his interest piqued and his green
eyes ever more luminous.

"Uh-huh. London, Paris, Amsterdam, Prague, and all over

Italy. My mother's a big art fan. She loves to go to museums and see all these famous paintings. She studied art history in college."

"Really?" noted Jake, sounding impressed.

"Yeah. That's how she and my dad met. He had room for an extra class—he was studying accounting—so he took this class on modern art. He sat next to my mom on the first day. Didn't know who she was except he thought she was hot. Then when the professor showed that Andy Warhol Campbell's Soup Can painting on this slide screen, dad wrote in mom's notebook, 'Why is this considered art when I can go across the street to buy this?'"

She giggled nervously while Jake smiled at her, saying nothing.

"Do you know who Andy Warhol was?"

He shook his head, a wide grin still etched on his face.

"He was big in the sixties, in the New York underground. Very avant-garde. He looked like death warmed over; he had this straight white hair that was like straw—I think it was a wig. Mom has a few books on him. He was from Pittsburgh."

Leah was babbling; she always did that when she got nervous, and the more Jake smiled at her, the more uncomfortable she'd got. Her hands were beginning to sweat.

Sunlight was streaming through the window opposite the bed, filling the room with lots of unfiltered illumination. It was so bright that Leah thought about making a lame joke about sunblock but refrained from doing so.

"And Israel. You've asked me where else I've traveled. We've been to Israel a couple of times. The last time was five years ago."

Jake nodded, his eyes and grin fixed on Leah as she prattled on.

"That's nice. You're very worldly," he said, not a trace of sarcasm affecting his voice, although Leah thought she heard a tinge of sadness.

"You're Jewish, right?" he asked.

The question wasn't couched in any negative context but posed in a straightforward, matter-of-fact manner.

"Yeah." She paused. "And you?"

"We're Methodists. We rarely go to church. Dad calls it a 'country club.'"

"Do you celebrate the holidays?"

"Yeah. Christmas and Easter. Mom loves Easter. I think it's because of the spring. Time to garden, you know."

Upon uttering that quip, he let out a bitter chortle. His smile faded.

"I hope you don't mind me asking but, your mom...um..."

Before Leah could finish asking the question, Jake replied without missing a beat.

"She has anxiety. She takes Xanax and some other drugs."

An awkward silence followed.

Jake continued, "She used to work in advertising in New York. Was a vice president. But then, after she had me—it took her and Dad a long time to get pregnant—she started not feeling well and getting panic attacks."

"I'm sorry about that."

"It's okay. She's doing better now. Gardening helps relax her. Dad always says that."

"My dad has cancer. Well, he had cancer." No sooner did Leah speak than she wanted to take it back. "Sorry, TMI," she said, embarrassed and regretful she was revealing too much already.

He doesn't need to hear this. He barely knows me.

"No, that's fine."

"He found out he had cancer two years ago." Why was she still talking? Something had come over her and she couldn't stop. "It was early stage, which was good. I mean, it's not good he had cancer, but it was good it was caught early. Like his doctors said. He had chemo. Lost a lot of weight. But he got better. He *is* better."

"That's good."

Jake eyes shone with warmth as he contemplated Leah, who was growing increasingly jittery under his observance.

"Uh...is there something on my face?"

"You're very smart," he said, aflame with admiration.

"Not really," she answered with a self-deprecating snicker.

"I think so. I noticed that when I first saw you."

"In court? Oh yeah, that was my finest moment. What a genius," she retorted sarcastically, shuddering in disgust.

"It wasn't mine either," he countered in a measured voice as he stared intensely at her.

Her hands were *really* sweating now. She cleared her throat.

"I think we should run lines," said Leah, changing the subject. "Don't you?"

"Why do you do that?" queried Jake, his voice remaining level. He kept his stare unflinching.

Leah squirmed. "Do what?"

"Change the subject. We were having a nice conversation. A real conversation too. Talking about serious stuff. I complimented you and then you want to run lines."

"Isn't that why I'm here? You do want to get off book, right? You want to complete the program, don't you? I sure as hell do."

"You don't have to get so testy," he answered firmly.

He grabbed the sides sprawled upside down on his night table and glanced at them before tossing them back onto the table.

Now it was all business, a perfunctory—albeit necessary—matter for both teens to wrestle with before moving on to the next step in their journey through Shakespeare rehab.

Forty minutes later, Irv picked up Leah, who had been waiting outside Jake's house for ten minutes until he arrived. He would have gotten there earlier, but he had been at ShopRite buying milk and some much-needed perishables when Leah had texted him.

"I thought you would stay longer like last time?" he quizzed his daughter, inspecting her face, which now had a sphinxlike expression.

"No," she grumbled under her breath. "No reason for that."

Chapter 14

"So, how did it go with you and...what's his name? Jay?"

"Jake. It didn't. It's not going anywhere. I think I'll join you in being a thirty-five-year-old virgin."

Leah and Evelyn were in a park taking a leisurely stroll around the duck pond at its center. It was six thirty p.m. Because it was now mid-May, the days were getting longer. The sun wouldn't set for another hour, so both girls were free to frolic in the dusky sunshine.

Because Leah hadn't seen Evelyn that day at lunch, Leah texted her friend asking if she wanted to hang out at the park after school. At six p.m. sharp, Leah moseyed over to Evelyn's house, which was a ten-minute walk from hers. On foot, they proceeded to the park, another short distance from them.

"No, I take that back," said Leah, irritated with herself. "I'm going to be a hundred-and-one-year-old virgin. Does that suck or what? And by that time, will I care? Will anyone care? I probably won't even know I'm still alive."

Evelyn laughed.

"You're too hard on yourself. Why do you need to sleep with someone right now anyway? We're fifteen. Chuckie and I never went that far, and I'm glad we didn't."

"I know, I know. You want to wait for love. But suppose that doesn't happen, Evelyn—then what?"

"You're just anxious because this boy made a pass at you. And you think time is waltzing by and you're never going to get the chance again."

Leah stopped walking and turned to Evelyn. "Do you think I want to use Jake?" she asked with deep earnestness.

Evelyn let out an ironic howl, flinging her hands in the air. "You tell me, Leah!"

"I don't know. I like him—and I don't. I'm not sure, you know," fretted Leah. "I just... don't know how I should behave. I've never *been* in a situation like this! And then there's the little fact, which I might have mentioned before, that dating another person at Shakespeare rehab is against the rules."

"So, don't do anything," Evelyn urged her frazzled friend.

Still frozen in her tracks, Leah spun her head from Evelyn to take in the pastoral spring tableau: a covey of ducks was either wading in the water or quacking on the grounds, foraging for food amid the thicket of weeds and dirt.

"What's it like to have a boyfriend?" Leah asked wistfully as she and Evelyn resumed their stroll.

"Um, I don't know." Evelyn hesitated. "I guess it feels like having a good friend, but it's someone who likes you even more than a good friend, so they want to kiss you and hug you and—"

"And go all the way," interjected Leah.

"Maybe. But that didn't happen with me and Chuckie. I'm sorry—he now likes to be called Chuck. He said that in his last e-mail to me months ago," she said coasting off tangent, with noticeable tartness. Getting back to the subject, Evelyn regained her erstwhile mellow manner. "We mostly kissed and talked about *Star Wars*. We were hardly Romeo and Juliet."

"But you *had* a boyfriend," emphasized Leah.

"Yeah...but it wasn't about sex."

Leah was on the verge of responding when she heard a ping from her phone. Yanking it from the pocket of her pants, she saw a text from Kelly: "What r u doing?"

Furrowing her brows, Leah eyeballed the text, mulling over if she should answer pronto or wait until she got home.

"Is that from him?" asked Evelyn.

Leah shook her head. "No. It's a girl from Shakespeare rehab."

She continued to ponder the message.

"Hold on," Leah said to Evelyn before sending a text to Kelly.

"I'm in the park with a friend," she texted Kelly. "Can we talk later?"

"Yeah, sure," Kelly texted back. "I'm going out for a while, but I'll be back after nine."

"Cool. Later then." Leah tucked her phone away and carried on walking and talking with Evelyn.

After Leah returned home a little while later, she sent Kelly a few texts. She heard nothing, then followed up with a phone call that went straight to voice mail.

"Hey, I'm home and done with school stuff if you want to still talk," she said, leaving a message.

She waited ten minutes, then fifteen, which swelled to a half hour. Shrugging, Leah turned on the TV with her remote. It was on Bravo. The opening credits of *The Real Housewives of Beverly Hills* were playing. Leah had already seen this episode, but she kept it on, figuring she would soon be distracted by a text or call from Kelly.

Fifteen minutes in, as she was watching two pampered middle-aged women engage in a food fight at an upscale restaurant, she heard a ping coming from her phone.

She was ready to type back, "What took you so long?" but stopped once she saw the text was from Jake.

"I'm still having problems with my lines. Big surprise, lol! Do you have time on Saturday? Sorry, I'm being a pest."

Her heartbeat picked up at that. Reflecting on her next move, she paused, then texted back.

"No, you're not. Sorry, I'm such a..." She sighed, typing, "killjoy."

"LMAO! That's hilarious! That was one of my grandfather's favorite words. He used to call my dad that all the time."

Leah laughed a little, her shoulders relaxing.

She agreed to meet up with Jake at his house the following Saturday, but not before being assailed with a flurry of doubts.

Maybe this is a bad idea. Maybe I should stop seeing him. But why should I? We're not doing anything wrong. It's totally innocent.

Maybe that *is the problem*, she mused cynically.

* * *

That Saturday, Stu dropped her off at Jake's house. Irv and Dana had left early that day to attend a college friend's afternoon wedding in Albany. Fortuitous or not, Jake's parents were also not home.

"They're at—you'll never guess!" Jake quipped, smirking when Leah inquired as to his folks' whereabouts. "Home Depot! Shocking, huh? They're looking at tiles for the bathroom. Then they're off to Costco. The fun never stops at Chez Miller. I love my folks, but they're drips. No"—he broke into a mischievous grin— "they're killjoys!"

"Sorry about that," said Leah, her cheeks reddening. "I guess I can be a real dope."

"Stop apologizing!" he said, frowning. "You need to stop that."

From her zebra-striped purse, a Michael Kors knockoff Dana had bought her at Marshalls a month ago, Leah dragged out the crumpled sides from their *Hamlet* scene.

Jake sized up the wrinkled sheets of paper Leah was now clutching. "What time do you need to get back?"

"Um, I have some time today. My parents are out." Leah cursed herself for revealing that bit of information. *I really have a big mouth.*

Jake's hands dug deep into his pockets. "Okay, then...let's get started."

Three hours later, Stu picked her up from Jake's.

"Thought you'd lost your phone, kid," he teased as he backed out of the Miller driveway, one hand on the wheel and the other on a cup of Starbucks coffee. "How did it go this time?"

Leah didn't answer.

"Must have gone well because you were there for a while."

Silence reigned on the ride back home.

It was only when Stu drove into their garage and turned off the ignition that Leah finally volunteered a response— "It was okay"—before dashing to her room.

Her parents were still not home, which relieved her to no end. Locking her door, she sent a text to Kelly.

"Are you around? I need to talk to you."

Chapter 15

"I don't understand," said Kelly in between copious licks of a chocolate ice cream cone. "Did you or did you not do it?"

Glancing quickly and nervously around, Leah shushed her.

"Don't be so loud. Somebody could hear," she admonished, slowly eating her scoop of vanilla ice cream.

Both were outside Carvel, seated on the same bench as the last time they'd been there, when they'd run into Jake. Save for an elderly woman at the register accompanied by a grand-daughter or aide, the crowds were not forthcoming on this weekend afternoon.

Maybe everyone's still asleep.

"Who can hear?" Kelly wisecracked.

It was much warmer today—eighty-five degrees—than the typical May day. The lack of humidity, fusing with an invigor-ating spring breeze, made the heat bearable enough for both teens to sit alfresco under the sun.

After Leah had sent Kelly the loaded text earlier—a message that Kelly hadn't answered until Sunday morning—Leah had asked if they could meet at Carvel in town.

"Yeah, sure," Kelly had texted back, adding: "...what is this about?????"

"I'll tell you. Can you pick me up at about one?"

At the scheduled time, Kelly had picked Leah up. Although Irv and Dana were still groggy from coming home late the night before, they both were alert enough to express chagrin over Leah meeting up with that girl from "that group" they would rather not spend too much time thinking about, because it reminded them all too well of how Leah landed in there.

"She wants to talk to me about her scene," Leah had told them, devising a specious excuse for her confab with Kelly.

Jeez, don't they want me to have friends other than Evelyn?

"Okay," Irv had clucked, poring over the newspaper and a steaming cup of coffee as Dana did likewise. "Just be careful," he cautioned.

Leah had rolled her eyes, grateful to escape her parents and their prying once Kelly honked the horn.

Now, outside of Carvel, she moved her spoon around in her ice cream. "I'm not sure," Leah said to Kelly in a whisper.

"What?"

"I said I'm not sure," she answered, raising her voice, irritated.

With her tongue continuing to lap up the ice cream, Kelly gaped at Leah, her incredulity increasing by the minute.

"What do you mean *you're not sure*? Seriously, the first time I did it, I knew. I mean, it wasn't great. There were no fireworks. But I was pretty sure."

Tense silence fell between them.

"Did you have sex or didn't you?" asked a frustrated Kelly.

Leah winced at Kelly's lack of discretion.

"Will you please be quiet?" she entreated, scanning for possible eavesdroppers.

The elderly woman and her young companion were gone. No one was present other than the two teens.

The irony of Leah's rebuke prompted Kelly to let out a hearty guffaw, which she then squelched by finishing off the ice cream cone.

"You're paranoid, you know that?"

Still holding the plastic cup with the vanilla ice cream, which was melting into soup, Leah stared at the messy confection, then looked at her friend.

"I'm not sure."

Kelly raised an eyebrow. "What? Did you not take sex ed in school? Do you need yours truly to explain to you the basics of the human mating process?"

"Very funny."

Leah recounted the particulars of that eventful Saturday afternoon, which left her brooding over this conundrum.

After they'd started working on their lines, Jake had stumbled a few more times. Rather than curse, he'd smiled at Leah, causing her to laugh sympathetically until a cloak of silence fell between them. They'd stared at one another.

"I don't know what alien force possessed me, but...without even thinking, I leaned forward and kissed him on his lips. It was a bad kiss. More like a peck, but...I needed to get my point across...I guess."

Kelly's eyes bulged out, almost leaping out of their sockets. "*What?*"

"Well, I was thinking, really thinking, Kelly, suppose this is my last shot at romance? It could be! No one has ever hit on me before, expressed any interest or desire to kiss me or do anything further. Suppose *this is it*? And I don't get my next opportunity until I'm thirty-five? What then?"

"So, you jumped him?"

"Yeah. Kind of," she admitted, thinking back.

* * *

After Leah had kissed Jake, he had frozen in utter stupefaction.

"But I thought you wanted to wait until the program was over," he said slowly. "You didn't want to get into trouble and..."

His voice trailed off; he looked dumbstruck by Leah's boldness. And a little bit impressed too.

Leah's normally pale visage colored with embarrassment.

"I'm so sorry! That was so stupid of me. Just idiotic. I shouldn't have done that," she rued, her face plunging into gloom.

"No, no, no," he countered. "You're on the right track. I like that. I like that a lot."

He pulled her back into a tender and sweet kiss, which grew into necking, then heavy petting. For Leah, this was entrée into a new, rarefied world, one that had previously excluded her. Because of her dearth of experience, she gave Jake, who seemed a little more adept at this than her, the right-of-way when it came to plotting the next carnal moves.

Leah resolved to go for broke: she wanted to see what the big deal was about, and if Jake was her vehicle for that knowledge, then so be it.

As she flopped back onto the bed, Jake glided on top of her. They continued to make out intensely. Not only was it the first time anyone had *really* kissed her, but it marked the first time a boy had put his tongue in her mouth. The sensation seemed odd to Leah, reminding her of a hissing snake in heat she'd seen on a documentary on the Animal Channel.

The lip-lock was accompanied by lots of expected groping. Reaching underneath Leah's shirt, a scoop-neck baby-blue cotton tee, he fumbled a few times as he searched for her bra.

Leah wondered if she should just unlatch it herself to make it easier for Jake, then decided against it. Maybe it wasn't the proper protocol for her to do this; maybe that was something the boy should do.

After three attempts, he got it open. However, he didn't try to remove it, leaving it to Leah to do the honors. Unsure what to do next, Leah kept her unfastened bra on, as well as her blouse.

He halted.

"I think you need to take off your pants," he said after a few overwrought moments. Then he faltered. "Unless you'd rather not. That's okay too."

Leah hesitated. "I don't know. I've never done anything like this before. Have you?"

"Yeah," he murmured in a voice so low Leah had to strain to hear. "It was one time, though. With this girl Kara. And we didn't know what we were doing. Not that I'm an expert now."

Without further prompting, Leah removed her black jeans and threw them on the floor. Getting off the bed, Jake picked up the pants and draped them on the chair.

He eyeballed the top drawer of his bureau. "Should I get a condom?"

Leah's breath quickened as her nervousness peaked. "Umm—umm...ye-ye-yeah...I—I—I guess," she stammered.

To emphasize her newly committed resolve, she threw in another "yes," this time in a clear voice without any wavering.

Opening the drawer, which creaked as it pulled out from its hinges, Jake scavenged through myriad items, searching for the prophylactic.

Leah's stomach flipped over. She could feel her determination to lose her virginity fading. *Maybe this wasn't a good idea. Maybe I should jump off this bed and text Stu to pick me up. There's still time. I think.*

The vacillation disappeared when she saw Jake rip the plastic wrapping off the condom.

* * *

"Does it get better the more you do it?" Leah asked Kelly, biting her lip after she finished relaying the details of what had transpired between her and Jake.

"Yeah. The first time always sucks, no pun intended. Well, so then you and he did it, right?"

"I guess. It felt…strange."

Kelly shot her friend a curious look. "Leah, I don't mean to speak to you like you're a moron, but…was there…um…penetration?"

"Yeah, for about a second."

Kelly broke into nervous giggles. "That was the same for me the first time I did it. It got better, and it will get better. Even if you don't do it with him again. The next time will be much better. Trust me." Still contemplating, Kelly added, "Do you like him, at least?"

"Yeah," said Leah, reflecting. "I do, I do."

"You sure?" Kelly asked, raising an eyebrow.

Leah stared at the white goo—formerly a scoop of vanilla ice cream—swirling in a tiny pool in her plastic plate. Making a face, she sashayed over to the corner of the street and tossed the dessert detritus into the garbage can before strutting back to the bench.

"I don't know. I think he's cute. He has super nice eyes and he seems intelligent, but…" She shrugged.

"Did you use protection?"

"Oh yeah!" Leah's head bobbed up and down. Then her forehead creased in worry. "They work, don't they?"

"Usually." She clapped Leah on the shoulder. "Now you're a woman! Welcome to the ranks, Ms. Friedman!"

Leah smiled a little. As gauche as it may have been for her to admit this to Kelly, she felt a perverse sense of pride that she had gotten rid of this albatross she'd feared would shadow her the rest of her life. If she never had sex again, at least this onus of virginity would be permanently removed. She could hold her head aloft, relieved she was on the same footing as her peers. Sure, they might be more experienced, more adept at it than she and Jake, but at least she had tasted the fruit and could spend the remainder of her days knowing that.

* * *

The next session had been postponed to Wednesday; Palisades Shakespeare was having a dress rehearsal for *Measure for Measure*, which Michelle and Frank were performing in and Downey was directing. Tully sent texts to everyone informing them of the change in plans. Leah was looking forward to the Wednesday session: Downey was going to block her and Jake's scene and then discuss costumes with them. This meant the end was drawing near. But even more important, she would see Jake again.

After she got home on Saturday, she thought it might be odd seeing Jake again after what had happened between them. Except for an "Are you okay?" text he'd sent shortly after they fooled around, to which she'd replied, "Fine," she hadn't heard from him since. Maybe her terse response had irked him?

But isn't that what she wanted? To get rid of her virginity and use him to do so? If so, mission accomplished.

It was only after she met up with Kelly the next day, she got a big surprise: another text from Jake.

"I've decided. You're the coolest girl on the planet."

She was so surprised and stunned she stared at the message for five minutes before answering.

"LOL. Really?" Then she texted before she could stop herself. "I thought I did something wrong. I'm so bad at this whole thing."

"No, you're not. You're the coolest girl on the planet."

She saw little dots forming on her phone. Another message unspooled.

"I wanted to text you yesterday what I thought but I guess I was afraid."

"Of what?"

"What you would think."

"That makes two of us."

Leah waited for the next message. When none appeared, she berated herself. *I shouldn't have written that. Maybe I revealed too much.*

Then her phone rang. Her eyes jarred open. It was from Jake.

"Yes?" she answered, slightly apprehensive but also delighted.

"You are coolness incarnate!"

Leah laughed.

"What does that mean?"

"I stole that line that from a book I'm reading now. It's awesome. It's about a group of scientists trying to colonize Jupiter after one of them says it's habitable. I'll bring it in when I see you next week. You'd love it!"

"Umm. Don't hate me but...I don't like sci-fi or fantasy or stuff set in the future. I'm boring, I know."

A pause followed.

Great. I turned him off. Me and my big mouth.

"Hmm. Okay. What do you like?"

Leah revealed the truth about her addiction to reality TV and her new-found love of smutty novels.

"Are you horrified? Be honest."

"Nope. Wanna laugh? I used to love wrestling. I even had wrestler dolls."

This time when Leah chuckled, Jake joined in.

"I think you win in the pathetic contest."

"Wanna hear something even worse?"

"Yeah?"

"Up until two years ago, my father used to take me to wrestling shows. I even have a photo of myself, an autographed photo, Leah, of me and Hulk Hogan. It used to be one of my prized possessions."

Leah howled, then stopped as a thought raced into her head.

"Wait, I don't remember seeing that in your room."

"I used to have it on my wall, but I took it down when I got over wrestling. Hold on."

A few seconds later, Jake texted Leah the photo in question: Hulk Hogan with his arm around a very young and pudgy Jake, whose smile was so broad it practically took over his entire face.

"Very dweeby, don't you think?"

"Yes, but so cute."

If not for school, the texts and calls would have been non-stop. At one point, they were on the phone watching an episode of *Real Housewives of Beverly Hills* together. It was a rerun, which Leah had seen so many times before, but Jake never watched it. He was curious why his girlfriend, which he was now calling Leah, was so fascinated with this show. Leah was giving him the lowdown:

"The tall blonde with the big hair is married to this old guy. He's about forty years older than her. And she always gets into catfights with this other blonde who speaks with a fake English accent..."

"How do you know it's fake?"

"She's from Connecticut."

Leah knew it was hard for Jake to watch a show he found as appealing as going to the dentist. But he was doing it for her, and she would return the favor by reading that book he was talking about. She couldn't wait for Wednesday to come already!

Her excitement mounted as Tuesday dissolved into Wednesday and she headed to the session. Opening the door to the space where they'd been meeting the past few weeks, Leah was accosted by Tully. Her arms were folded, and her face conveyed a sternness that disturbed Leah. And judging by her restless, impatient stance, it was clear Tully had been waiting for her.

"Leah, I need to speak with you."

Leah was too perplexed to offer any replies other than a banal, "Okay."

Tully escorted her off to a small, private room at the end of the hall. Walking past the session room, Leah saw the door was shut. She heard a babble of voices; the clearest one she recognized belonged to Downey.

"Um, shouldn't I be in there?" Leah wavered her right hand with an upraised thumb pointing to the session room.

"It's fine. Mr. Downey knows," Tully answered sharply.

The room's door was slightly ajar. Tully pushed it open completely with one hand, and with the other, she motioned for Leah to follow her in. When Leah was inside, Tully closed the door. A hush of ominous silence reigned for a minute.

"I'm sorry to tell you this, Leah, but...you've been suspended from the program."

Chapter 16

All the warmth drained from Leah's face. "What?" She gasped. "*Why?*"

"Jake Miller. We've received information that he and you have entered a sexual relationship, and as I stated during the orientation and warned all of you, that's against the rules and will result in suspension from the program."

Leah's heartbeat picked up, her mind racing for understanding. *How could they know—?* Anger swept through Leah as only one person's name surfaced in her head.

Kelly!

She must have told. It had to be her—Evelyn only knew about the kiss, and she'd never met Tully or anyone else from the program. It had to be Kelly. *But...why?*

"It's a lie," Leah flared. "Not true. I barely know him!"

Despite her protests, Tully was unmoved.

"The good news is that your suspension and Jake's is temporary, pending further investigation," she said with cold officiousness. "We've alerted your lawyer, Mr. Adamson. He knows the situation and is cooperating. Judge O'Reilly is aware of the situation. Do you have any questions?"

"Yes," piped back a perturbed Leah. "When will I know if I'm back in the program? We're only a few weeks away from the end. Mr. Downey needs to block my scene with Jake, then we have to rehearse more, and make sure we know what—"

Tully interrupted. "Not too long. You should know by the end of the week."

Leah nodded slowly, her mouth edged in pain. "Do the other kids know? And what's going to happen if...I can't come back? What will happen to me?"

"They don't know anything. We told them nothing, and that will remain the case, even if this suspension becomes permanent. It's none of their business. As for what will happen to your case if you don't finish the program, we don't know yet. Mr. Adamson will keep you and your family informed of the situation, I'm sure."

"Does Jake know? Is he here?"

"No, he's not here, but he does know. We were able to get in touch with his lawyer a half hour ago."

"What am I going to tell my parents?" Leah cried.

Miraculously, Tully's obdurate by-the-book demeanor softened. "It'll be okay. It'll work itself out. It always does."

"I don't want to go to jail."

Leah's heart was beating so loudly she was surprised Tully didn't comment on it.

Maybe she's hearing it and doesn't care.

"That may not happen. Each case is different."

"But I was told...you said—"

"Again, each case is different."

She waited for Leah to collect herself.

"Any other questions?" This time Tully's tone was far gentler.

The shock abating, Leah shook her head. Hoisting her purse from the floor, she grabbed her phone from the inside pocket and was about to text Stu if he was around so he could pick her up when Tully stopped her. Leah tried to steady her hands, which were shaking.

"Leah, it'll be fine—whatever happens," Tully mollified her, lightly tapping her on the shoulder.

"Sure!" Leah snarked back. "That's easy for *you* to say."

She exited the building holding her phone. After finally collecting herself, she texted Stu and paced on the sidewalk as she waited to hear back.

"I'm coming—stay right there," he texted back.

Leah pursed her lips.

Where would I go? Jupiter?

Ten minutes later, Stu and his red Fiat materialized. Leah slumped against the wall of the building. She was despondent at the thought of seeing her parents and telling them the truth. She repeatedly reprimanded herself for her role in this debacle: her gung-ho desire to go all the way with a boy she liked but hardly knew because she thought it might be her only chance at having sex—and her stupid trust in Kelly.

She wondered about Jake, what he must think of her.

Me and my big mouth.

Or maybe not. Maybe he'll think Tully's a good guesser.

Yeah, right. Lie some more to yourself, Leah.

Kelly's betrayal made no sense to Leah. Why on earth would she tell Tully about what had happened between her and Jake? Why? Did she secretly like Jake and wanted Leah out of the way so she could have him to herself? No way! If anything, she'd made it abundantly clear she disliked him and viewed him as a loser not worthy of her time or attention.

I wouldn't be surprised if she's been seeing Derek on the sly—with the way she looks at him and smiles every time he's around. Talk about transparent.

What did Kelly get out of this? Was this some sort of diversionary maneuver to get Tully off her scent regarding her and Derek?

As Leah slogged guilt-ridden toward the car, she noticed her brother had a stricken expression that was unusual for Stu.

He looks like he's lost his best friend. Maybe he and Julie broke up?

Leah opened the door to the front passenger seat, then slammed it shut as she threw her bag and books onto the floor.

"Easy," Stu chided.

"Sorry," Leah mumbled.

A beat passed.

"So how pissed are Mom and Dad at me?"

"Dad's in the hospital," Stu said in a low voice.

She froze. "What did you say?"

He raised his volume, repeating what he said.

Leah's face turned ashen.

"What happened?"

"They're not sure. He's taking tests and then they'll know what's wrong with him."

A horrifying thought entered Leah's brain. "The cancer came back, didn't it?" she whimpered. "Mom told me he was cured."

"Leah, we don't know. He's in Hackensack. We're going there now. Mom and Dad wanted me to take you there. Also, that lawyer, Daddy's friend—

"Jerry."

"Yeah, Jerry. He's there. He was visiting Dad before and they were talking about your case. Dad wants you to speak to that guy so he can straighten out this mess, that's what they called it, this mess you're in."

Guilt and fear tore at Leah. *I did this. I'm responsible.*

"Was it because"—she choked up— "of me? Did hearing about what happened with me make Dad sick?"

"No," said Stu gently. "Mom says he hasn't been feeling well the past few days, and today when he was at work, he got some kind of attack, I guess, and they called an ambulance."

"I read that stress is the underlying cause, the root of all diseases," retorted Leah.

Stu took a long breath, then sighed.

"Leah, you're not the reason why Dad is in the hospital."

"Right," she answered sarcastically. She looked out the window and swallowed hard against the lump in her throat.

* * *

Stu pulled into the parking lot of Hackensack University Medical Center. Leah hated this place. Not just because it was where people got sick and died, but because it was so huge and unwieldy, she always felt trapped in a maze every time she was there.

She remembered how weak and listless Irv was when he'd returned home after chemo; how much weight he lost, so much that it looked like he'd lost a third of his regular body mass; and how often Dana would help him stand up whenever he wanted to get up and go anywhere—outside, to the bathroom, or even to take a book off the shelf in the den.

"Mom says Dad is in the cardiology unit," said Stu, glancing at a text from Dana.

Leah furrowed her eyebrows.

Cardiology? Doesn't that have something to do with the

heart?

Leah got queasy as she followed her brother through the swinging doors at the entrance, then to the front desk to get visitor passes. She proceeded to trail after Stu as they walked through a massively long and lumbering hallway searching for an elevator. At last, they found one, at the end of another long and lumbering hallway.

Leah's unease shot up after she and Stu walked into the room and saw their father hooked up to machines with so many tubes, he looked like something out of a science-fiction movie. Only, those movies were fake, and this was real.

The corners of Irv's eyes creased as his children walked in. Dana was standing beside the bed holding his hand, while Leah's lawyer, Jerry Adamson, was sitting in a chair.

"Give your father a kiss," ordered their mother. Amid a network of interconnecting tubes and catheters, Irv hugged Leah and Stu separately, an effort he strained to make through gritted teeth.

"I'm sorry," Leah uttered, her eyes locking with her dad's; his sparkling hazel-gray eyes were now leaden.

He motioned Leah closer to him while Dana and Stu pulled back.

His left hand, below where an IV tube was inserted into the vein of his arm, rubbed Leah's hand. "Don't worry. Jerry will straighten out everything."

He raised his voice, "Won't you, Jer?"

With a forced smile, Adamson leaned in from his chair, nodding.

"This whole thing has been a misunderstanding," Irv continued. "Hasn't it?" His voice grew weak and strained the more he spoke.

Leah's mother stepped in. "Honey, you need to rest. Jerry will talk to Leah, and he'll take care of everything."

"Listen to your wife, my friend," urged Adamson.

"Leah, Jerry is going to take you to his office and then he'll drop you off home. Stu, you can go home, too," said Dana. "It's fine. I'll be home later."

Apprehensive, Leah froze.

"It's okay," Irv murmured, his voice fading. "I'll be fine. Just a little thing with the heart. I'll be good as new in a few days. Don't worry."

Now that her father's health issues had returned to the fore, Leah's problems seemed so secondary, so unimportant. She no longer cared about Shakespeare rehab or Jake or Kelly's betrayal or the kids at school. All she cared about was her father getting better.

I don't want him to die.

As Adamson drove Leah to his office to discuss her case, it didn't matter how much he kept assuring her that Irv would improve in a few days, that he'd had a minor heart attack that could have been a lot worse had the ambulance not gotten to his office in time. Her father's mortality was uppermost in her mind.

After parking in the underground garage, Leah and her lawyer walked through what seemed like a cinder-block tunnel until they reached the elevator. Inside, Adamson pressed the button for the second floor.

"Leah, listen to me. I've known your father for a long time. Since before you were born. He's a trooper. And I think you are too. We must clear this thing up with the Shakespeare program. I have a few ideas—"

"Who cares," said Leah under her breath.

"What?"

The elevator jerked open.

Leah walked out, this time speaking louder so Adamson could hear. "Who cares."

Putting his hand on her shoulder, Adamson stopped her before they could enter his office.

"What do you mean, 'who cares'? How about your parents and your brother? And I may be the lawyer for hire here, but how about me? I've known you since you were a baby. There are people who care about you. I'm sure you know that deep down inside. Leah, you have to start seeing yourself the way people who love you see you."

Leah's eyes were focused on the floor. Scrunching her lips, she remained silent.

"If you don't care about yourself, fine. Do it for your father, then. Think of him."

A combination of guilt and worry twisted in her gut as she thought about her father. All her life he had been her biggest cheerleader, her beacon. And this was how she would repay him? By blowing up her case?

She lifted her downcast gaze to face her lawyer, then nodded.

"Okay, you're right. Let's do it, then."

Chapter 17

"Leah, do you know what 'client confidentiality' is?"

Leah wriggled in her seat. "Um…is that, um, when someone who's accused of a crime tells their lawyer they really did it and the lawyer can't use it against them?"

Adamson broke into a grin. "I knew you were bright. Your father always tells me how smart you are."

"Not true, sir," muttered Leah. "I used to watch a lot of *Law & Order*. I remember a few episodes where they talked about that."

"Well, you're right, and it's 'Jerry,' not 'sir.' My father is 'sir,' not me. I'll invoke client confidentiality here and ask you to tell me the truth. It will not be used against you, but I need to know before I proceed further. How much of this, you and that boy, is true? I was a kid once too, so I know all about raging hormones and all that."

Leah darted her eyes from Jerry and cast them at the mountain of unfiled briefs piling up in the out-box tray on his desk. It was a small, cramped space, an unmitigated mess buried in an avalanche of briefs, affidavits, and other assorted legal documents. Not that the rest of the office was an architectural masterpiece; aside from a copy machine, a small fridge, a watercooler, and two desks—one for the secretary and the other for the paralegal—two dull paintings, a generic blurry seascape and a vase full of flowers, adorned the walls that were painted a nonthreatening taupe.

"You won't tell my father?"

"Absolutely not."

Reluctantly, she pulled her gaze from the floor, guiding her eyes toward Jerry's blank face.

"Yeah…but it was only one time. That was it. Just once."

"Okay. Thanks for telling me the truth. I appreciate it. I'm almost ninety percent sure—no, make that eighty-five percent sure—that you'll be able to return to the program and finish it. Tully is a wild card here. She's a real pill. She's been ruling that program with an iron fist since it began. I don't know why the judge gave her so much power. But, ultimately, it's the judge who gets to decide whether you'll be readmitted to the program. Honestly, other than Tully sometimes acting like a loose cannon, I don't think you're going to have a big problem here. They all like you—Downey, the others from this theater troupe, and even Tully, believe it or not. She was quite surprised about this charge leveled against you. Me, I think the no-dating rule is so dumb and unrealistic, given you're all a bunch of teenagers and that's what kids do. I wouldn't doubt there've been many others who've broken this rule since Tully instituted it. Maybe someone right now in the program other than you."

Leah's thoughts zeroed in on Kelly. "Who squealed on me? Was it Kelly? Do you know?"

"I wasn't told the source of the information, other than it was someone else in the program with you. I'm assuming this girl Kelly is a person whom you confided in about you and Miller, correct?"

"Yes," replied Leah dully. "I thought she was my friend. Can you believe it? I don't understand why she did this."

The more she meditated on Kelly's betrayal, the angrier Leah got.

"It's not like she's this saint herself. I think she's been messing around with this guy Derek, another kid in the program. I'm almost sure of it, but I can't prove it."

"Of course not, unless you have a CIA-level surveillance system installed in her bedroom."

Bewildered, Leah stared at Jerry.

"A lame joke, I apologize," he replied, abashed. "Very inappropriate of me." He modulated his flippancy to a serious tone. "Listen, I'll talk to the judge tomorrow morning, and hopefully we'll know by the end of the week if you'll be readmitted. In the meantime, I strongly urge you to cease communication with this girl. She's not your friend. Stay away from Miller too. He's also on suspension, as you know. He'll probably return to the program like you. But if, and when, that happens, I advise you as your attorney to not resume your previous relationship with him. Once the session's over, that's another story. Your personal life is none of my business as long as it doesn't impinge upon the program's rules."

Leah nodded, distracted. Her thoughts drifted back to her father again, lying in that hospital bed hooked up to all those machines.

Her worry must've been showing on her face because Jerry said gently, "It'll be fine. Your dad, your case, this Shakespeare program. It will all blow over. Trust me on this."

* * *

In accordance with Leah's suspension from Shakespeare rehab, her mom imposed a curfew on her. Her dad was still in the hospital. He was getting a stent, a tiny tube doctors would insert into a blocked artery to keep it open. Leah looked it up on Google after she asked her mom when her father was coming home.

"Just another day or two, honey," her mother had told her after Leah gawked at her in disbelief. "It's a pretty minor procedure—very common nowadays."

Leah was to remain home at night, study, do homework, and not go out anywhere with anyone until the situation with her case was resolved. She could only venture out one night a week and with a friend approved by her parents—which meant Dana, now that Irv was indisposed. Translated into the vernacular, Leah knew this included only Evelyn, and not Kelly or anyone else in the program.

That didn't stop her from trying to ascertain why Kelly had ratted her out.

Seriously, what did she gain from doing this? Was it pure malice?

Leah had assumed they were friends, confidantes. She had reached out to Kelly because she needed advice from someone around her age who wasn't a virgin—and that ruled out Evelyn.

And...this was how Kelly repaid her? By running to Tully and repeating verbatim everything she'd told her in confidence? It made no sense.

After completing her English homework, she began studying for her social studies test on the Civil War. She'd dived headfirst into homework immediately after dinner to get her mind off her suspension. But it was difficult. In between poring over the details of the Emancipation Proclamation, Lincoln's executive order that freed all slaves in the Confederate states, Leah's mind kept reverting to Kelly. Jerry's warning notwithstanding, Leah couldn't help it; she texted Kelly. She had nothing to lose at this point. And what was Kelly going to do? Run to Tully and Downey?

"I need to speak to you. Please call me."

That elicited no response. A half hour later, Leah texted her again.

"Did you tell Tully about me and Jake? Why?"

She stared at the text for a minute, then again, an hour later. Nothing but her last message. Impulsively, she wrote another text, then pressed send.

"I thought we were friends."

The unresponsiveness on Kelly's end was as infuriating as it was baffling.

She picked up her phone and dialed Kelly's number. Predictably, the call went straight to voice mail.

Leah contemplated hanging up. It was clear Kelly was blowing her off, which to Leah was an obvious manifestation of her guilt. But after hearing Kelly's prerecorded announcement—"I'm not here right now. Leave a message and I'll get back to you."—Leah felt defiant and defensive. She left a message, affecting an upbeat cadence. She didn't want Kelly to know the scope and breadth of her fury, as that would give her friend-turned-foe power.

"Hi, Kelly. It's me, Leah. I want to talk to you about what happened. I know you told Tully about me and Jake. I doubt Jake told anyone. Why did you do it? Please let me know. If you don't want to talk to me or text me, then I would appreciate it if you e-mailed me. Thanks."

Radio silence.

She knew she shouldn't have left that message or sent

those texts to Kelly, as it would leave an electronic trail of evidence that Kelly could use to prove Leah's guilt. But Leah was too fired up with rage to think rationally. Plus, she was still on emotional overload from her father's situation.

Leah clicked her text app to see if she had any texts from Jake. She hadn't heard anything from him since this whole thing had blown up. Most likely, he hated her for having such a big mouth.

Again, as with Kelly, emotion trumped reason. And again, she was indifferent to the consequences. *What's he going to do? He's in the same boat as me.*

"I'm so sorry. I really am," she texted him.

She typed another message: "I spoke to my lawyer. He says they'll probably let us go back to the program. That bitch Tully just wanted to make an example of us, teach everyone a lesson. Stupid. I hope you don't hate me. I thought Kelly was my friend. She told on us."

Also, radio silence.

Leah groaned, turned on the TV, and surfed various channels before switching to Bravo. Nothing from the *Housewives* franchise was on, so she clicked it off.

She switched off the light on her bureau next to her bed, then closed her eyes, preparing for slumber. An hour passed, and she was still wide-awake. Frustrated, she turned the light back on and resumed reading a trashy paperback Evelyn had lent her. It was dog-eared on the page where she'd left off.

The story was genuinely dopey, about a woman who's abducted by aliens and falls in love with the strapping son of the commander after they spirit her away to their secret lair on Mars. Evelyn had insisted she read this, as she said the sex scenes were hot.

There was certainly a lot of panting and ogling going on. But, so far, it was kind of chaste. *Maybe the steamy parts happen later?*

After an hour of reading, Leah finally fell asleep.

Chapter 18

From the moment Leah went off to buy tampons, she sensed it wasn't a good idea. Of course, she needed tampons—that wasn't the problem. The problem was what happened while in pursuit of that item.

It was right after dinner. Stu was home and not at Julie's. Thanks to her curfew, Leah pondered asking Stu if he could go to the local CVS to pick up tampons for her. But she suspected he would adamantly refuse and squawk about it, a vehement overreaction that all people of the male persuasion seemed to express at the mere mention of feminine hygiene products.

Her mother wasn't home, though—she was at the hospital visiting her father. Dana had gone there straight from work, texting both Leah and Stu that she'd be back later in the evening and instructing them to heat up the leftover spaghetti and meatballs from the night before.

With her mother away, Leah rifled through the bathroom cabinet in her parents' bedroom, looking to see if Dana had any extras lying around. Nothing.

To preempt any possibility of Leah slipping serpentine out of the house, Dana had been quick to follow up her text with a warning: "I may not be there, but I have eyes and ears."

Ah, that's why Stu's here. He's Mom's squealer.

Truthfully, her brother's newfound informant status didn't bother Leah all that much. She had no plans to venture out and party 'til dawn. Instead, she asked Stu if he could drive her to the pharmacy chain, located at a pedestrian mall in the middle of the town—not that far away from her house, but not that close either to where she could walk.

Stu dropped her off at the drugstore and insisted he'd wait for her in the car.

"You don't want to come in?"

"No, thanks," Stu said emphatically, making a disgusted face. "I'm going to call Julie."

Leah snickered to herself.

She would never understand why boys were so squeamish about tampons. *How stupid. Do they expect us to ask them for their help putting it in?*

As soon as Leah entered CVS, she made a beeline for the aisle with the sanitary napkins and tampons. She was about to grab her favorite brand when she heard a voice, *that voice,* which she'd hoped she would never hear again. A voice that made her whole body freeze up in panic.

"Well, look who's here," said Dede.

Right away, out of self-preservation—a finely honed instinct of survival that impelled her to protect herself from harm even if it led to her arrest—Leah scanned the premises to see if there were any other people around; perhaps their presence might be enough to deter her worst enemy from making a scene. But save for a yawning cashier, who looked like she was only a few years older than Leah, and an older male customer who was haggling with the pharmacist about the price of his Lipitor pills on the other end, the store was practically empty. For a CVS, it was uncharacteristically not busy; then again, it was still dinnertime.

Slowly, Leah turned around.

She almost didn't recognize her. It had been nearly three months since their brawl, the seminal fight that had turned Leah into a delinquent and gotten Dede kicked out of school. Dede's long, straight, lustrous blonde hair, the hair Leah envied and wished she had instead of her rat's nest, was cut into a closely shorn bob. Dede had lost so much weight she appeared emaciated and frail—her washed-out jeans were hanging off her legs, and those mean cobalt-blue eyes that had held Leah hostage with their laser glares were nearly eclipsed by a pair of cheap glasses. Only a semblance of her trademark sneer remained.

The change in Dede's appearance both rattled and heartened Leah.

"What are you doing here?" blurted out Leah.

"Same reason you're here."

"You're not supposed to come near me. That's an order of

the court—"

"You mean you're not supposed to come near me!" Dede interrupted, spitting out the words. "You psycho bitch. You tried to kill me."

Leah snorted; she couldn't help it. "Talk about pot meeting kettle! You harassed me for months, humiliated me in front of everyone, then threatened me! If there's anyone who's a psycho bitch, it sure as hell isn't me."

Without thinking, Leah advanced a step toward Dede, which caused the girl to flinch and back away.

She's scared of me! A rush of power flooded Leah's veins.

"Get away from me, you sick freak," snapped Dede. "I was in the hospital and then kicked out of school because of you."

"Oh, poor you," Leah mocked. "Yeah, you did nothing. You got what you should have gotten a long time ago. You know what your nickname was at school? It was 'public nuisance number one.' I can't tell you how many kids and teachers have come up to me thanking me for what I did—which was ridding them of you."

Leah was lying about the part with the teachers, but she didn't care. She had the upper hand over her biggest tormentor, and damn, she was going to milk the shift in this power dynamic for all it was worth.

"You're lying!"

"No, I'm not. Ask any teacher." Leah pulled out her iPhone from her back pocket. "Call them now. Do it!" she said, thrusting the phone at Dede.

Dede stared at the phone as if she was contemplating calling the school—not a practical idea, considering it was seven at night and no one was left in the office—then shook her head, grabbing the package of tampons from the shelf and grumbling, "No one is at the school right now."

Dede was about to storm off when Leah stepped in front of her.

"Get the fuck out of my way!" Dede snarled.

"Ladies, is there a problem here?"

A middle-aged man of average height and features, wearing a CVS name tag that identified him as "Ralph," busted up the altercation.

"I was minding my own business trying to buy tampons when she," said Dede, pointing to Leah, "came at me."

"You're such a liar. And a coward. That's why you went after me—isn't it, Dede? Because you thought I was weak. I wouldn't fight back. What a tough girl you are," said Leah, goading her.

Ralph turned to Leah. "Miss, I have to ask you to leave. You're disturbing the other customers."

Dede's sneer turned into a cackle.

"Me?" responded Leah. "What about her? She started it."

"Did not!"

"Did too."

In between them, refereeing, Ralph warned, "I'm giving you both a minute to vacate the store; otherwise I'm calling the police."

It was like sticking a pin into a balloon. Hearing the word "police," Leah deflated and fell silent.

She'd lost it once because of Dede and was currently paying the consequences. She wasn't going to lose it again.

"I'm sorry," said Leah, sheepish, her voice returning to a normal conversational level. "I'll leave."

"Good. Take a hike, loser," scoffed Dede, a smile forming on her lips.

Like a boxer, Leah verged on issuing a final blow to her opponent, one that would pulverize Dede and help Leah score a knockdown for this match. In the end, she decided against it and walked out of the store, hearing the mingling ruckus of Dede's shrill cursing and Ralph's ultimatums behind her.

Leah exhaled her frustration, shaking her head. *I shouldn't have let her get to me.*

"Hey, what took you so long?" Stu was holding his phone. Leah guessed he'd been texting Julie.

Leah slunk into the passenger seat.

"I almost got into a shitload of trouble, Stu. Don't tell Mom and Dad. I ran into Dede."

Stu's eyes widened in alarm.

"That little bitch who was picking on you?"

Leah nodded, keyed up. Seeing Dede again had injected her with an adrenaline she dismissed as nervous energy.

"Nothing happened," she said, answering the question on Stu's face. "But I won't deny it. Seeing her again---it just pissed me off. You know what was funny, though? She was scared of me. Me! Can you believe it? How's that for a turnaround."

"I'm glad it didn't get out of hand, because that would have sucked for you," said Stu as he drove toward another pharmacy so Leah could purchase her much-needed tampons.

"You know what else?" continued Leah, out of breath. "She seemed so pathetic. Until the old Dede came out, I actually felt sorry for her."

Chapter 19

Irv was back home. His presence—replete with a cane, as he was still too weak to walk on his own—brought Leah immense relief. However, guilt festered at her like an infected sore. Despite her mother's and brother's repeated denials, Leah couldn't quiet the fear that her problems, compounded by the suspension from the Shakespeare program, had intensified her father's stress, which led to his heart attack.

She resolved to make it up to Irv by doing whatever needed to be done to get reinstated into the program.

She was still shaken from the run-in with Dede, whom Leah now saw through a different lens. She still hated Dede—that didn't change. Only now Leah was open to trying to understand Dede. What motivates one kid to target another? Yeah, it was a twisted power play and certainly going after someone as weak and defenseless as Leah seemed to achieve that. But it was also fun for Dede. She was having a whale of a good time at another person's expense.

I'm not perfect. God knows I'm no saint. But I will never understand how anyone can do that to another.

Other than hearing she was an only child with parents who were much older than what you'd expect them to be considering Dede was fifteen, the circumstances of her family life were veiled in mystery. Trying to create a psychological profile on her, the kind Leah saw cops on TV shows routinely make on perps, was impossible because she knew so little about Dede.

If the circumstances had been different, could they have been friends or, at least, enjoyed a civil rapport? Given Dede's tendency toward cruelty, probably not.

Leah's foremost priority, if she wanted a chance at a decent future and to not end up another statistic, another Dede, was to get back into Shakespeare rehab.

She also wanted to make things right with Jake, if that was possible.

Anxiety, paralyzing and all-enveloping, plagued Leah as

she waited to hear her fate. Would she get the green light to resume and complete the program? Or would she be hauled back to court, hoping and praying for the judge to be merciful and not have her incarcerated? Jerry assured her that wouldn't happen, as did her mother and ailing dad. Yet the possibility terrified her.

She'd gladly do community service. Pick up the trash from Highland Hills and the neighboring towns. Clean the toilets in the municipal buildings, and in her school and other schools. Work with the homeless, ladle out soup, find and distribute blankets. If she had to do this for the next twenty years to fulfill her probation and finish out her sentence, that would be fine. Anything would be preferable to jail or reform school.

In between classes and when she was on a break, whether work study or lunch, she'd whip out her phone and check for voice mails and texts. Other than her mother or father checking in with her to see if she was fine, there was nothing. *Nada.* What did her grandmother say in Yiddish? *Gornisht?* Yeah, that too.

By the time Friday and her last class of the day, biology, rolled around, she'd relinquished all hope of hearing anything. It had been five days since her suspension and her meeting with Jerry.

What is going on? Maybe something went wrong?

Her period was making her feel especially cranky; now she had cramps and no Midol on her. Then again, that did provide the proverbial silver lining to her angst: she was definitely not a mother, not that she doubted it, considering Jake had used a condom and more than that, she wasn't even sure if he'd completed the act or they'd done it the right way, whatever that was.

What a crummy week this is, she opined as she rushed into the bathroom, opened the stall, and changed her tampon. She had five minutes to spare before her next class when Mr. Fisher would drone nasally on the infinite wonders of photosynthesis and spontaneous generation. Often it was a trial by endurance to sit there in class, pretend to listen with rapt attention, and not descend into deep Rip Van Winkle-like sleep.

After Leah left the bathroom stall, her heart fluttered at the sound of a familiar ping.

Usually, her phone was on vibrate when she was in school. All the kids had to do that or turn their phones off. No texting, Facebooking, tweeting, or posting anything on Instagram; those were the rules. Social media was off-limits unless they were on a break or in between classes. If they were caught checking their phones, they'd be asked to leave class. If they did it a second or third time, they'd face suspension. Because of her current predicament, Leah immediately turned her phone back on now during any breaks.

She saw a text from her lawyer: "Call me right now!"

Hyperventilating, she texted back: "Can't. I have class now."

She waited a minute for his response. When none came, she picked up her books and threw the strap of her purse around her shoulder, racing out of the bathroom.

As she headed into class, she heard another ping. *Damn.*

She unloaded her books onto her desk and pulled out her phone. Mr. Fisher was holding court at the podium in the front center of the classroom, a large blackboard and widescreen stretching behind him. He shot her a warning glance when he saw her reading the text Jerry had just fired back at her.

"Okay, pls call me after class then."

Putting it back on vibrate, she tucked her phone into her purse while offering the teacher a conciliatory purse of her lips.

When class was finished and the clarion bell rang for five minutes, ushering in the end of the day and week, Leah rushed out of the school and phoned her lawyer pronto. The time was 2:50 p.m.; Stu would be coming to pick her up in ten minutes.

Jerry put Leah on hold after explaining he was speaking to another client with whom he was going to court tomorrow. Would she mind waiting or did she want to call him back? She opted to wait, her nervousness escalating every minute as Muzak spilled into her ear.

"Sorry about that," said Jerry, resuming the conversation. "Here's the drill: I spoke to the judge. I have some good news and some bad news."

Leah groaned.

More bad news. Kill me now.

"Want to hear the good news?" said Jerry, a tone of forced gaiety in his voice.

"Sure," said Leah with a snort.

"The judge will probably let you back into the program, but—"

"What do you mean *probably*? You told me it would be fine, everything would blow over, it would work out," she said, parroting her lawyer's past words.

"Yes, and I think it will, but..." Jerry sighed. "Here's the bad news: the judge wants to speak to you first. He wants to know if you're sincere about wanting back into the program. He wants to hear it from you directly."

"Of course, I am! I don't want to go to a reform school!"

"No, Leah," reasoned Jerry. "That's not what he wants to hear. He wants to hear if you're genuinely remorseful."

For a second, Leah considered telling Jerry about Dede, then shook the thought away.

What would be the point? Nothing happened.

"When does the judge want to see me?"

"As soon as possible. He says there's not much time left in the session, so he would have to see you today."

"But when? I—I just got out of school and then there's dinner," Leah stammered. Another thought rushed into her head. She bowed her head when asking it. "Do my parents know about this? My father?"

"Yes..." he said softly. "They do."

"Great," she deadpanned, wiping her eyes. "Terrific."

Another thought entered her brain.

"Is Jake also going to speak to the judge?"

"Leah," continued Jerry in a pleading tone. "Take my advice. Don't concern yourself with anyone else right now but you. Tell the judge you want to finish the program, that you've learned from your past actions and want to make amends.

And hopefully, that'll be it."

* * *

"Miss Friedman, what do you have to say for yourself?" asked Judge O'Reilly. Behind his spectacles, he shot her a look that wasn't as benign as it was the first time she'd stood before him; now it was unsparing and merciless.

Leah gulped. Being back in the courtroom almost three months after her sentencing, her lawyer standing by her side and her parents sitting in the back pew like the last time, imbued her with an eerie sense of familiarity. What did they call this? Déjà vu?

She composed herself, hearing only the sounds of her heart palpitating and her stomach growling. She hadn't eaten dinner yet, as the court closed early on Friday—five pm, and it was now 4:45 pm. After Leah had finished the call with Jerry and Stu had picked her up from Highland Hills and taken her home, she'd changed her clothes to less casual, more appropriate courtroom attire—a plain black skirt and a blazer over a white cotton blouse—and left right away for the court with her parents.

As her mother drove, with her father in the passenger seat and Leah in the back, silence predominated. Both Dana and Leah hadn't wanted Irv to come, as they were worried about how his daughter's latest appearance in court would affect his health. But he'd insisted his duty was to support his daughter when she needed him the most.

Leah's hands had been shaking in the car; she even bit her nails, which she rarely did.

"I'm very sorry for...what happened, the misunderstanding that led to my suspension from the program," she said now, in the silence of the courtroom. "This whole thing has been a learning experience for me, sir, and I promise to make amends."

Sighing, the judge took off his glasses, rubbed the bridge of his nose, and then put his glasses back on.

"Miss Friedman, I would like to hear your own words and

not what your lawyer, Mr. Adamson, coached you to say," said the judge, his expression unflinching in its lack of emotion.

Leah exchanged glances with Jerry, who had a stricken expression on his face, as if exposed by the judge.

"I'm sorry, Your Honor, but I don't know what else to say," she answered, knitting her eyebrows together.

"Let me rephrase. As a condition of your probation, I sentenced you to the Garden State Bard Program with the understanding you would comply with the rules set forth by Ms. Tully and Mr. Downey. You have been accused of violating one of those rules. I understand from your attorney you say you are innocent, and your contention is supported by the fact that other than a highly dubious and prejudicial secondhand hearsay account, there is no tangible proof. Ordinarily, in a situation like this, I would simply order you and Mr. Miller, who was suspended along with you, to return to the program. But you stood in this courtroom nearly three months ago, Miss Friedman, expressing regret for the actions that led to your arrest. Do you still express regret, and more importantly, what would you do differently today that you did not do prior to your appearance in my courtroom almost three months ago?"

Leah took a lengthy pause to reflect on the judge's questions. Her hands were growing clammy at her sides, and she could feel sweat dripping down the back of her neck, too, even though it was cold in the courtroom.

I'm such an idiot.

She wasn't sure whether it was her father's health problems or her latest run-in with Dede that had made her finally wake up when it came to her recent poor decisions.

She shut her eyes, then opened them.

No more bull.

If that meant time in a reform school or detention facility, then so be it. It would be hard, but it wasn't like she was innocent. Yes, she had been targeted and persecuted by a bully, but fighting Dede and with a rock and a penknife, no less, had reduced Leah to the level of her former bully and look where that got her!

She cleared her throat, then answered: "To be honest, Your Honor, when I first came to this court, I had some regret but not a lot of it. I felt much of what I did was out of self-defense. But it got out of hand. Looking back, I don't think violence was the answer. I don't think it should ever be the answer. What I should have done was report the girl who was bothering me to the principal. And I should have told my parents. I was wrong to take matters into my own hands. I'm sorry for all the trouble I caused."

Leah saw the judge staring at her with a rapt, pensive look. She rapidly spun around and saw her parents sitting in the same pose as they had when she was first sentenced, their faces etched with worry and distress. They nodded at her. She turned back to face the judge.

"Please go on," he urged.

"I know I've made some really *bad* decisions this year," said Leah. "I also know I can't take them back—I have to live with the consequences. But I promise you, sir, um, Your Honor, that if you send me back to finish up the Shakespeare program, I will stay out of trouble and do better. I mean that. And if you don't, then I'll live with that. I probably deserve it."

She avoided glancing at Jerry; he leaned over to her and whispered, "It'll be okay."

Leah acknowledged his support with a minute shake of her head.

The judge's pensive expression remained. It unnerved Leah, as she couldn't tell which way he would rule—back in the program or reform school.

"Thank you, Miss Friedman, for that heartfelt statement," he said. "I appreciate your candor. By order of the court, you will return to the Shakespeare program on Monday..."

Leah's eyes glimmered with joy as a huge jack-o'-lantern grin overtook her face, and Jerry enthusiastically patted her on the shoulder.

"However, I do urge you to steer clear of anyone in the program who may be trying to make trouble for you. Also, please remember that all rehearsals of scenes should be done in a professional setting and only under the supervision of Mr.

Downey. Anything untoward or improper that does not fall under the guidelines of behavior acceptable for the program should be reported at once to Ms. Tully and Mr. Downey. Do I make myself clear, young lady?"

"Yes," said Leah, elated. She drew in a long, deep breath.

"Final judgment on this case is rendered," boomed the judge, slamming down his gavel.

Leah turned around. Her mother's face was luminous with rapture as if she'd undergone a religious experience. For a second, Dana looked like a human replica of one of those Madonna and child paintings from those museums she had often dragged her family to see.

It was a reaction shared by her father—sans the holy aura. He raised a clenched fist in the air, his other hand clutching his cane.

* * *

The following Monday, Leah was greeted warmly by nearly everyone at Shakespeare rehab, from Downey to Tiffany, who smiled and winked at her when she waltzed into the room. She was surprised when Derek waved an exuberant hello to her; clearly, he hadn't been corrupted by Kelly yet. Maybe he wasn't sleeping with Kelly as Leah had thought, or if he was, he wasn't susceptible to her influence other than what was between her legs.

As she made her reentrance, the only chill she felt in the air was from Kelly, who buried her eyes deep in her phone and pretended not to notice Leah's presence. Seeing her, Leah's stomach twisted with pangs of nausea, the bile surging inside her.

Leah searched the room for Jake, but he wasn't there. She wondered if he'd also had to appear before Judge O'Reilly to plead his case. Had he blundered while speaking up for himself? Or was there some legal snafu that accounted for his absence? If there was and he didn't return, would that mean the *Hamlet* scene was out and she'd have that one monologue? Or, would Downey scramble to put her into another scene last minute?

The prospect of Jake no longer being at the session sad-dened her. Yes, a natural actress she was not, and Jake's absence would help her heed her lawyer's warning to resist any physical contact, at least until the session was over. But she missed their exchanges, his incredible green eyes, his goofy sense of humor, his calling her the coolest girl on the planet and the fluttery sensation in her stomach she'd get whenever he was near her.

"Good to see you back, Leah!" Downey said in his smooth baritone as he kicked off the day's session. There were two remaining scenes—Kelly and Derek's from *Taming of the Shrew* and Leah and Jake's from *Hamlet*—which still needed to be blocked. Because Jake was not in that day, Downey ex-plained that he would work with Kelly and Derek; the others were to study and run through their scenes and monologues.

Rob stared at Leah, his mouth opening almost as if he wanted to ask her a question. Instead, he closed his lips and raised his hand.

"Yes?" responded Downey. "What is it?"

"I only have that one scene with Jake. Is he coming back?"

"Good question," answered Downey as he nodded at both Rob and Leah. "Yes. Jake will be back on Wednesday."

Leah's heart danced at the news of Jake's imminent return.

But will it matter if he doesn't want anything to do with me?

Downey continued, "You can rehearse your scene with him then. And I'll work with you both on the blocking for your scenes. I may cut it a little bit since we're crunched for time."

Because Leah felt like she knew her monologue so well she could recite it in a coma, and she was still on a high knowing Jake was returning, she ambled outside to enjoy the pleasant late-afternoon sun. She parked her rear on the ground, folding her legs into a lotus position while pushing her back against the building.

In one month, her ninth-grade year would be over, and a week later, so would Shakespeare rehab. Other than her re-maining term of probation, which consisted of her checking in with Tully and the court, she hoped the end of this program would be the precursor to closing a nasty chapter in her life.

She scrolled through her texts. The last one was from the night before, from Evelyn, asking if she'd finished that tawdry novel about the woman and the alien commander's son. "Not yet," Leah had texted back, adding: "Kind of slow, don't you think? Where's the smut?"

Maybe Evelyn thought that was a rhetorical question because she hadn't answered.

Leah hadn't told her about the run-in with Dede, nor did she tell her parents. Thinking it would exacerbate her father's stress, triggering a relapse of his heart condition or, god forbid, a recurrence of the cancer, she'd begged Stu to keep quiet about it too. Judging by her parents' lack of queries about "that awful girl," so far Stu was honoring his promise.

She was about to check the *Housewives* message board on Bravo when she saw Tiffany, brandishing her xeroxed monologue from *Merchant of Venice*, gliding like a swan out of the building.

Leah watched Tiffany with admiration and awe. She was a stunner. And it wasn't just because of her flawless symmetrical features and model-like height and slenderness. It was her innate aura and poise. Even the way she lit up a cigarette, which she was doing now, was steeped in nonpareil elegance and beauty.

I wish I could be more like that.

Leah sighed as she deflected her gaze from Tiffany and went back to her phone. Smoking a cigarette, Tiffany strolled toward Leah, sidling up next to her.

"Anything interesting?"

"No, same old boring stuff," Leah responded as she flipped through her old e-mails. The *Housewives* board was dead.

"How are you doing?"

Leah looked up, her lips contorted in a sardonic grin. "Great. Couldn't be better."

"That was some fucked-up shit. Seriously," said Tiffany.

The stream of profanities caused Leah to giggle, considering it was emanating from someone so impeccable she resembled a walking, talking porcelain doll.

"Did they tell you all what happened? Why we got suspended?"

"Not really. But we kind of figured it out," she said, carefully blowing the jet of smoke away from Leah. "I mean, it doesn't take a genius."

Finished with the cigarette, she tossed it to the ground, then stubbed it out with the heel of her silver-strapped sandal. Her eyes caromed from the remnant of the extinguished nicotine stick to Leah.

"Kelly said something, right?"

Startled, Leah eyeballed Tiffany. The complicity of silence and Leah's grave expression made Tiffany nod in understanding.

"Yeah. Has to be," Tiffany drawled. "Working with her has been nothing but a big pain in the ass. You know, I saw you once with her at H&M. I was with my mother. I hadn't been there since, well, you know, the shoplifting. Anyway, my mom and I were walking past H&M toward the shoe store when I saw you and Kelly browsing through the racks. I was like, 'What the hell?' I couldn't understand what you were doing with her."

"You should have said hello or gotten me away from her," said Leah, shaking her head. "I was so dumb. What I don't get, though, is why she told Tully about me and Jake. She's not interested in Jake. At least, I don't think so."

Tiffany shrugged. "Probably no good reason other than she enjoys being spiteful and mean. You saw how she behaved at the orientation."

"She was on the wrong meds. They got adjusted later."

"Bullshit. She's a bitch, pure and simple. That's why she yapped her mouth to Tully. It wasn't because she had an ulterior motive, or she even disliked you. She just likes to cause trouble. Makes her feel important, gives her a rush."

"Makes no sense to me."

"Sure doesn't—because you're normal, and so am I. Yeah, I know; we shouldn't talk because we were arrested, and we're here too. But deep down, we're okay. We are. We, well, I did a stupid thing. And you defended yourself."

"The court didn't agree," said Leah.

"The hell with that. Sometimes the law isn't always right. How about a person who steals food from a supermarket because he's starving, or he wants to feed his family and then he has no money to get a fancy lawyer, so he's sent to jail with serious hard-core criminals? How is the law right when it comes to that, Leah?"

Tiffany's impassioned tone made Leah wonder if she were talking from experience. *Did that example apply to a relative or friend of hers?*

Rather than risk Tiffany's wrath, Leah changed the subject. "You know Jake from school, right?"

"Oh yeah, that bomb was legendary," Tiffany smirked.

Leah twisted her mouth. "I always try to forget that."

"Hard not to. It was bogus. He used birdseed, not fertilizer like the terrorists. He wanted to scare those jerks."

"Did you see him get bullied? Was it...intense?"

Tiffany screwed up her lips. "Yeah, a few jocks harassed him. They always harass the geeks. Makes them feel important. Jake is right—at our school, they're gods, and the rest of us are nothing. But Jake, I don't know, he always seemed a bit different from the other geeks. Had a personality. We had this stupid talent show last year. Jake did card tricks, and guess what? He was good. He was the runner-up to this girl Emilia who sang opera."

Leah stared in astonishment at Tiffany. The revelation that Jake knew sleight-of-hand tricks intrigued her to no end.

"He never told me he could do card tricks!"

"Yeah. I knew this girl who kind of liked him. I think they may have gone out a couple of times. He used to always talk to her about magic. He likes that stuff a lot."

"Was her name Kara?"

"No, Janet."

Leah dropped the topic of Jake's love life, deciding it wasn't her business what had transpired before her, nor was it that relevant.

At that juncture, Downey appeared in the doorway, beckoning Leah and Tiffany to return to the room.

"Leah, why don't you sit over here?" Downey asked when they entered the room. He led Leah away from her usual seat next to Kelly to an empty seat up front—a sensible move, given the circumstances.

Leah was relieved and grateful to Downey. The idea of sitting next to her ex-pal nauseated her.

Downey explained to everyone in the session (minus Jake) how the final weeks of the program would proceed: after blocking the remaining scene that required it—Leah and Jake's—he would set up a running order for the performance in front of an invited audience. From there, they would rehearse everyone in that order. Frank and Michelle would pitch in, offering assistance when needed while timing all scenes and monologues to make sure they fit into the prescribed time parameters of forty-five minutes to an hour.

"And like any play we do at Palisades Shakespeare, all of you will be in costumes," added Downey.

A mingling of jubilation and anguish arose in the teen ranks.

Downey threw his hands up to appease the crowd. "It won't be so bad. Don't worry; they're not going to be as elaborate as they would be for our mainstage shows. Boys, you won't be in tights, and ladies, no corsets or fancy undergarments."

The disclaimer provoked a swell of applause.

"Thank you," he replied, his mouth crimping into a wide grin. "We've been at this for a while now. We know what we're doing. Do you think we'd torture you?"

"Yes!" boomed Derek drolly from his regular spot in the back row.

"Well, you're wrong," replied Downey, the smile still planted on his face. "We know why you're here. We never lose sight of that." Assuming a more subdued demeanor, he continued, "The costumes will be pulled from wardrobe we've used for past productions from our second stage, the playhouse, and unlike our mainstage, which has about five hundred ninety-nine seats, this theater only has a hundred and ninety-nine seats, so it's much smaller. Have any of you ever attended any of our productions there?"

No one raised a hand.

Unfazed, Downey forged on. "Any questions about the final weeks?"

He scrutinized the teens, who said nothing. A few glowered back in boredom and annoyance.

No sooner did Downey end the session than Leah bolted out of the room. She didn't want to risk any confrontation with Kelly, although, given her proximity, Leah knew this would be a singular and likely improbability.

Thankfully, Stu was already outside waiting for her.

Chapter 20

"Hi."

She saw him lingering outside the room, poring over his phone. The session would start in five minutes. Mostly everyone else who had arrived was inside, save for him.

He was sitting with his back curved against the wall, legs splayed out in front of him and reading a message board for fantasy genre fans; it was one on which he actively posted.

Jake looked up and gazed at Leah with sulkiness as if the simple act of acknowledging her presence was an insurmountable burden.

"Did you get my texts?"

His concentration meandered back to his phone.

Leah persisted. "How about my voice mails?"

Jake grunted something Leah could not understand.

"What did you say?" she asked, her voice rising in exasperation.

Again, he muttered an indecipherable reply.

"Okay, you're pissed," she said, losing her patience. "I get that. I'm sorry. I am. But even if you never want to talk to me again, we still have to work together for our scene. So, you'll have to live with it...and me for the next few weeks. Then you don't."

To emphasize her point, Leah made an "it's over" gesture with her hands.

Still sulking, Jake gradually lifted his lithe body from the floor, straightening his posture. He begrudgingly offered Leah an, "Okay," then trudged into the room with her in tow.

Leah glanced over at Kelly, who was looking at the two of them with unsparing scrutiny. However, as soon as Leah glared at Kelly, the latter retreated in defeat, diverting her focus to her phone and e-mails.

After ordering the teens to work on their own, Downey, as expected, spent the next forty-five minutes blocking Leah and Jake's scene. He had already cut the Polonius bit when

Hamlet catches Polonius, the father of his sweetheart Ophelia, eavesdropping on him and his mother behind a tapestry. Crazed, and out for revenge against his uncle Claudius for betraying and killing his father to become king and marry his mother, Hamlet snuffs out Polonius with a sword in a fit of madness while also viewing him as a spy for his uncle.

"That's too complicated," explained Downey, using a red pen to cross out that section with a large X. "It's a very gripping and scary scene. We've done Hamlet a lot at Palisades Shakespeare. Every time we do that scene, you can hear a pin drop in the theater. People become engrossed in what's happening. But we don't have enough time, so it's out."

Because Gertrude, Leah's role, didn't have as many lines as Hamlet, Downey left most of her part intact; instead, he went to town with Hamlet, excising chunks of lines he called "exposition."

When Jake issued a histrionic groan, the lines in Downey's forehead deepened. "Are you kidding? You want more lines? I thought you'd be happy."

"I memorized it all," the boy snarked.

"Well, next time you're cast as Hamlet, you can recite everything," deadpanned Downey. "But for our purposes, it has to be abbreviated; otherwise the entire performance will go over the acceptable time limit, and then I'll really get it."

Although she understood it on a rational level, Leah was stung by Jake's coldness. Yes, she wanted the program to be finished and to start the next phase in her life; yet she also didn't want Jake to hate her either.

* * *

For the next three weeks, Downey, with the help of Frank and Michelle, put everyone through the rigors of the rehearsal process. The running order had Leah's monologue second and her scene with Jake as the second to last. Leah was disappointed; she wanted both her performances to be grouped together to get them over with so she could relax.

For the last two weeks, the program moved to the

playhouse for rehearsal. When Leah and the others weren't up on deck, they were either on the sidelines observing the action or waiting for their cue. Throughout this process, Leah was successful in avoiding any unwanted close encounters with Kelly; however, that didn't stop each girl from throwing a dirty look at one another when they thought the other wasn't looking.

During this highly charged period, all the teens were asked to reserve the upcoming Saturday to go to the playhouse where Sandy, a stocky, effervescent redhead in her thirties, would measure them and pull costumes from wardrobe that might work. If need be, she'd make alterations.

For the Helena monologue, Sandy pulled several knee-length chiffon dresses for Leah to try on.

"No gowns?" Leah asked, disappointed.

"No, not for this. Gowns are too long and clunky to do quick changes. And because you have"—she scanned a sheet of paper— "this and the *Hamlet* scene at the end, you'll be wearing two different costumes. Gertrude is different from Helena, obviously. She's older, a mother and a queen, so what you'll wear as Helena won't work for Gertrude."

Leah tried on several dresses. Her favorite among them was sea blue with short, puffy sleeves and sequins dotting the collar. As she and Sandy sized it up in the mirror, Leah was especially entranced. The fabric was delicate, which worried Leah; still, she couldn't help but admire how beautiful it was.

"Oooh, this is so nice," Leah gushed.

Then they heard a rip. Their eyes dropped to the culprit: the sleeves, which were badly fraying at the ends.

Sandy ejected a sigh. "This is lovely but too fragile. We can't have you go out and do your monologue while the dress falls apart. Take it off. Put on the other one."

Leah squeezed herself into a pink dress ending just above the knee. It was snugger than the other one—not as loose, but not super tight either. Leah liked the tiny white beads embroidered into the bodice. She gawked at it in the mirror as Sandy studied it from the front, side, and back angles.

"Very nice." Sandy nodded, a wisp of a smile on her lips.

"This one fits you well. It's perfect for Helena. It has a youthful, free spirit that's right for the character. And Lee likes you guys to be simple and functional for your performances."

"I look like I'm going to a prom or someone's wedding."

"Yes, it's a bridesmaid's dress," said Sandy. "One of our actresses wore it for a wedding, and rather than have it hang in her closet, she brought it in afterward so we could use it."

Sandy touched the sleeves. "So, we'll go with this for Helena."

"What about shoes?"

"You can wear what you want, but make sure they have a heel. No sneakers or flip-flops, please. They don't have to be stilettos—one or two inches will be fine."

After Leah took off the dress, she handed it back to Sandy, who put it on a rack marked "Garden State Bard—June 2018." Dressed down to her white bra and underwear, Leah covered her torso with her arms, feeling very self-conscious; it was a quirk of modesty, considering they were both women.

"We've done *Hamlet* many times, and dressing Gertrude is trickier than Helena," remarked Sandy as she rifled through a wardrobe rack full of dark frocks, "even though we always have her wear black. She's basically in mourning because her husband died, yet she's also remarried and isn't exactly melancholy; she's getting it every night from Hamlet's uncle. Since she's having a good time, we don't want her to look too sad."

Sandy pulled out a silky black knee-length dress. The collar and short sleeves were made of lace and mesh.

"That also looks like something you'd wear to a wedding. A fancy wedding," commented Leah.

Sandy chuckled. "Yes. We used it last year for Gertrude. It was for a modern-dress production of *Hamlet*. The actress was a similar size to you, except maybe a few inches taller. It'll probably fit, but I bet I'll have to hem it."

She was right. Although the dress fit Leah well, giving her a sophisticated maturity conducive for playing someone's mother, it dragged on the length. With pins, Sandy marked it for alterations.

* * *

The final two weeks of the session also coincided with the end of Leah's turbulent ninth-grade year. Come September, Leah would enter the tenth grade. She'd be leaving the chaos of junior high behind for the unknown comfort of high school, where half of the incoming student body, pouring in from another local junior high, would not know her or her history. She'd be starting anew, a blank slate.

"I'm going to miss you, kid," said Ms. Evers after Leah asked her to sign her yearbook.

Leah cocked her eyebrows.

"No, honestly," affirmed her unflappable, soon-to-be-ex gym teacher. "I'll miss having someone around here who seemed more like an interested contemporary and less like a student."

The admission touched Leah, filling her with a twinge of guilt considering she still harbored a grudge toward all the grown-ups in school, including Ms. Evers, about their inaction regarding Dede. Maybe it was time to let it go.

"Thank you for supporting me, Ms. Evers," Leah answered.

"Well, of course," Ms. Evers piped back, her face infused with warmth. She edged closer to Leah, the flicker in her eyes gone.

"I know you were perhaps mad at me, everyone one of us, for not doing anything about Dede until it was too late. I understand that. If I had been in your situation, I would feel the same. I was wrong, all of my colleagues were, and I want to apologize."

A specter of tears dewed Leah's eyes. Speechless, the girl nodded at the teacher, whose expression brightened once she saw her student had forgiven her.

"You're a nice girl and good luck with everything. You deserve it."

For a moment, Leah thought about inviting Ms. Evers to the performance. Unfortunately, passes were limited to two per person—or at least that was the rule for the other kids in the program. For the adults, they, like the judge, could invite a slew of people, such as other members of the legal community. This included Leah's lawyer, Jerry Adamson, and through his intervention, Leah wangled one more pass for Stu.

Thank god the school year was over. It was a chapter she never wanted to revisit. Now all Leah wanted to do was get through the next two weeks and the performance as painlessly as possible.

Chapter 21

"Why did you do it? Why did you tattle on me and Jake to Tully?" asked Leah.

It was dress rehearsal, the night before the performance. All the teens were congregated for the final run-through and garbed in their costumes. They were on a break while Gordon, the millennial lighting director from Palisades Shakespeare, was reviewing some of the cues with Downey.

In her pink Helena costume, Leah had spotted Kelly in her *Taming of the Shrew* costume—a plain russet dress past the knee, minus farthingale, drawn at the waist and with ruffles at the edge of the short sleeves—walking outside to smoke a cigarette. She was with Derek, who was in full Petruchio regalia: a long purple hunting shirt, a black leather vest, black boots, and a cocked hat with a white feather sticking out of it.

Seeing them together, Leah had initially hesitated to confront her former friend. But with the performance tomorrow night and time so tight right now, when else could she do it? It was now or never.

As soon as Leah threw down the gauntlet, Derek was quick to make an exit, causing Kelly to emit a long groan as he disappeared back into the theater. Kelly continued to puff on her cigarette for a few seconds.

Finally, she spoke. "I dunno."

Leah narrowed her eyes. "What do you mean, you don't know? That's a lame explanation. I could have gotten kicked out of this program. I could have been sent to some jail for kids, a reform school—"

"That would never happen to *you*," Kelly interrupted, her voice pitched to a cold, dull octave. "Things like that would never happen to you. You're a good girl, right? You have a good family. A mom and dad who love you. A good brother. You go to a good school, get good grades. You're a nice girl."

"I got arrested!" Leah angrily protested.

"Yeah...but the thing is, Leah, you'll bounce back. Girls like you who have everything always do."

"*Everything?* I'm practically an outcast at school!"

"That won't last. You'll move on from this and do well. Be successful. Have a great life. And all because you were born lucky and you don't even realize it."

"That's why you tried to blow up my life...because you *resented* me?"

Leah had thought about saying the word "jealous" but had stopped herself; she couldn't imagine anyone feeling that way about her.

Kelly took another puff from the cigarette, then tossed it on the ground, stamping it out until it became nothing more than a muddle of ashes. She looked back at Leah, her lips pressed together tightly.

"You don't get it, do you?"

Leah shook her head.

"Yeah. Why would you? You have *everything.* It might not seem that way to you now, but believe me, you do. I've seen your house—it's a big one. I live in a crummy, run-down apartment with my mother and sister. We can't find my father anymore, and my mother is constantly struggling to pay the bills. Last week, we got an eviction notice from the landlord. We might be moving in with my aunt and uncle, whom I can't stand. My mother also hates them. They've always treated us like we're white trash because they have money and we don't."

She pivoted her eyes away from Leah, her focus lingering on the entrance of the playhouse, where minutes earlier Derek had gained sanctuary. She then dragged her gaze back to Leah.

"Leah, I don't dislike you at all. I do think you're a nice girl. Really. I was curious about someone like you. I was...what's the word? Intrigued. Yeah, intrigued. Right. I liked hanging out with you. I've never been friends with people like you. The people I know don't live in big houses and drive fancy cars and go on luxury vacations."

"We don't go on luxury vacations," Leah snapped.

Sure, they'd been to Europe a few times when she was younger. But these days vacations were a rarity for the

Friedman family thanks to the debt incurred from Irv's cancer battle, bills her parents had been trying to pay off the last few years. Leah didn't bother tallying her father's recent heart attack and hospitalization into the equation.

But why should she tell Kelly any of that? Or anything at all? That kind of information was reserved for real friends, people who genuinely cared about her, not two-faced, backstabbing phonies.

"We don't sail around the world on yachts," Leah continued. "My dad is a CPA, and my mom works for a nonprofit organization, which means they don't have a lot of money—in fact, with her job, she's always asking other people for money. They're not millionaires, far from it."

"They hide their poorness very well."

Leah gaped incredulously at Kelly, flabbergasted at her ex-chum's presumptuousness and its corollary, ignorance. Yet, there was a part of Leah that could not deny Kelly wasn't completely wrong. She did have advantages that Kelly did not have, such as a family that supported and loved her. Plus, stability and a roof over her head. She was luckier than Kelly. That still didn't give Kelly the right to try and trash Leah's life.

"So, you wanted to become friends with me because it was some socioeconomic experiment? Let's see how the privileged live. And while I do that, let me slowly work my way into this girl's life and then ruin it when she least expects it, huh?"

"It wasn't like that," maintained Kelly with a vehemence that stunned Leah. "I liked you. I did."

"Then why did you go behind my back and squeal about me and Jake to Tully? Why? He's so pissed at me I can kiss that relationship goodbye too. Thanks so much," Leah facetiously countered.

Shorn of her familiar bravado and bluster, Kelly's tough-girl façade withered for a moment. In the end, all she said was, "I don't know. I don't."

Leah wanted to scream into Kelly's face at ear-shattering decibels, *"I don't believe you. You're a liar! You know damned well why you did it. You're a psycho. No wonder your purse looks like a drugstore. You don't have AAD or ADD or whatever;*

you're just a vicious bitch who gets off on hurting other people. That's what this was about. Don't think I can't see it! You already admitted you were jealous of me because you thought I was rich!"

Instead, Leah fixed a prolonged, troubled stare at Kelly before walking away.

* * *

From the wings of the stage, Leah stole a sweeping glance across the theater rows to find her parents and Stu. After the second round of searching, her eyes alighted on them.

They were in the third row: Dana and Stu were chatting while poring over the makeshift playbill created for this performance. Sitting to the right of Dana was Irv. Although visibly on the mend—his complexion wasn't as sallow as it was before, and he'd gained a few pounds—he hobbled when he walked, relying on his cane, which he was now holding. He was engaged in a lively conversation with Jerry, who was sitting directly in the row behind him.

Leah's family had dropped her off earlier so she could make her six thirty call time at the playhouse. Even though the performance would start at eight p.m.—the traditional time for an evening performance—Downey wanted to gather all the kids first for a last-minute pep talk. Joining him for the wrap-up of this latest session of the Garden State Bard Program was Tully.

Leah bristled at the unedifying sight of the chief probation officer demurely dressed in a baggy peach-and-gray pantsuit that would've made Hillary Clinton proud. Maybe this reaction was immature and unreasonable on Leah's part—considering she was guilty of violating one of Tully's major program rules—but emotions and logic were never mutually exclusive.

"I want to tell you all we're proud of all of you," said Downey at the start of a speech whose inspiring, pontifical tenor would not have been out of place in a locker room before a big game. "This wasn't easy for you; I know that. Ms. Tully," he said, gesturing toward her, "knows that too. But you got through it all, and you will get through the next hour and you will do so beautifully. We have the utmost confidence and faith in you.

"Ms. Tully and I have seen hundreds of kids like you come through this program since it started fifteen years ago. So many of them thought they would never be able to do it, that they would never be able to get to this moment. But they did. And you will too. We know it. So, go out there and have fun. If you get stuck on a line, just say 'line' in character, and Ms. Tully will feed it to you. She'll be following the script the entire time you're onstage. Michelle, who will be here soon—she will be on the headset in the booth with me, calling the technical cues for our lighting and sound operators. We don't have a lot of them, as we try to make these performances as bare bones as possible—not only to make it easier for ourselves but for you guys as well.

"I'm really looking forward to seeing the performance," said Downey, beaming at all of them. "I've admired how hard you've all worked and grown since that first day. What you're doing is not easy. Most of the audience out there, the legal eagles and judges—they couldn't do it. But you can and you will. So, break a leg, everyone, and I will see you after the show."

A few of the teens, including Leah, burst into raucous applause. Although most were excited, they were also trepidatious. Leah could feel her heartbeat racing like a locomotive and her breath quickening. Like that first day in court.

Hearing footsteps on the flight of stairs, she looked up and saw Jake skulking in, attempting to be as unobtrusive as possible. Failing at that, he threaded his way to the greenroom, a purgatory for actors to wait to hear their cues.

Ensconced in the basement of the theater, the playhouse's greenroom was an unsightly rathole of a space—a "dump," as Leah's dad would call it—reeking of mildew and chock-full of dilapidated furniture that resembled relics from a great-grandma's attic. Leah sat her butt on a tan chair with ripped upholstery as Jake and Rob plopped down on a ragged brown couch that squeaked every time either boy moved. Tiffany swanned in and glided down on one of those junky chairs with such style and ineffable grace, she seemed ludicrously out of place amid the shabby ambiance.

Her balletic movements filled Leah with an envy that temporarily put her nervousness at bay. That evaporated when Kelly, accompanied by Derek, descended the stairs. Whatever running conversation the newcomers had been caught up in ceased as the two toured their surroundings and absorbed the reality of their situation. Inadvertently, Kelly and Leah exchanged fleeting glances; the latter stifled a pained groan, a reaction shared by her former friend. The stillness grew into a deafening, taut hush as a few others traipsed in.

The resounding quiet only increased Leah's stage fright. As she examined the faces of her peers and observed their body language, she could feel a contagion of fear spread throughout the space—it was that palpable and ponderous.

Maybe I should have swallowed one of my mother's Valiums.

An unexpected source—Rob—dissipated the tension.

"Good luck, everyone," he sweetly uttered, his thick-lidded eyes rotating to all the teens, who, up to that point, were acting more like they were facing the executioner's block than performing Shakespeare.

His benevolent words were greeted with a chorus of "You too."

Although the collective fear wasn't gone, it ebbed in intensity as relief flowed in.

Leah heard a clattering on the stairs as legs encased in knee-length black boots sans pantyhose, followed by a gossamer black shift dress, came into view. It was Michelle.

"Hey everyone," she said brightly. "We're here—at last. Can you believe it? I'm going to give you the lowdown of what to expect before the performance begins. Lee, uh, Mr. Downey, will give a short speech welcoming the audience, then Ms. Tully will follow. Then there'll be a delay of about five to ten minutes as we honor Judge O'Reilly, whom you all know..."

At the sound of the judge's name, Leah and the others nodded their heads.

"He's going to be honored, as he will be retiring next month. So, this is the last performance of the program for him as a sitting judge."

Michelle paused like she was expecting to hear titters or clucks of approval. None followed. She continued, "After Ms. Tully gives her remarks and the audience acknowledges the judge—he'll probably stand up and they'll applaud—we will wait a few minutes, dim the lights, and then the performance will begin. Tiffany, because you're the first one up, Ms. Tully will cue you, as I'll be in the booth with Mr. Downey. Ms. Tully will be on a headset listening to cues from me, although she will be backstage with all of you. So, everyone will get their entrance cues from Ms. Tully. Sound good?"

Swiftly, her eyes skimmed over everyone. "Great! Five minutes everyone," Michelle announced in the manner of a town crier. "Time to take your places backstage. Let's do it!"

In a flash, she vanished into the sanctum of the control booth located at the topmost point of the house, right above the last row of the theater.

* * *

After O'Reilly took his expected bow from his seat and the thunderous applause began to die down, Leah and a few of the other kids stole last-minute peeks at the audience before the performance. Leah saw Irv biting his nails while Dana and Stu, clutching their programs, whispered to each other. Not wishing to be spotted by them or anyone else, Leah crept stealthily back to the center of the backstage area, where she would wait with the others. But on her way there, she accidentally bumped into someone. Her throat tightened when she saw it was Jake.

They hadn't had a full-length conversation in weeks, other than forced pleasantries steeped in embarrassment of an intimacy that perhaps shouldn't have been. Or at least they should have waited until after the session. Just like Leah initially suggested.

But no, I had to rush things and act like I was in a contest. And for what? To prove I could be as cool as the other girls. And he seemed to like me a lot, too.

Jake had been poised and polite while he and Leah were rehearsing their scene with Downey. But his tangible unease with Leah when they were not rehearsing, his diligent avoidance of her company, and his nonexistent eye contact with her now were excruciatingly obvious.

Of all the actors, Jake was blessed with having the most mundane costume. He was attired in all black, wearing a turtleneck, slacks, and shoes. No quick changes for him, as he was only portraying one character: Hamlet.

Because Jake hadn't fled from her sight—the notion was counterproductive, given the confines of the space—Leah seized the opportunity to whisper to him, "Good luck, Jake." Then she added, mixing both candor and the balm of conciliation, "You'll be great. I know it. Maybe you should consider acting...I'm not kidding."

His green eyes glimmered as a tiny phantom of a smile ghosted his lips. "Really?"

"Yeah, definitely. You do a good job when you confront me in the scene and tell me I'm a slut and you're ashamed I'm your mother."

Jake let out a nervous giggle. "Thanks, Leah. Thanks so much."

Leah wasn't finished. "And you're amazing with Rob."

She signaled to Jake's other scene partner, standing a few feet away from them wedged in between Kelly and Derek.

Noticing Leah's acknowledgment, Rob, his arms locked over his chest, nodded at Leah, even though there was no way he could hear what she was saying to Jake.

Leaning closer to Jake, Leah said, "I think you're the best one in the group. I know that's not why we're here. But you are. I've thought that for a long while, but I didn't know if I should tell you or if you would believe me because...you know."

"I have been thinking about staying with it—acting, or something similar, I guess." He shrugged. "I do like it. I spoke to Mr. Downey about it last week, after you left. I might be working here for the summer as an apprentice, helping with props and working in production—stuff like that."

"That's so cool," Leah answered. Unthinkingly, she grazed Jake's arm with her right hand. Seconds later, she wished she hadn't done that. *What is with me?*

"I'm sorry for doing that, I'm—"

"No, that's fine. It is," he appeased.

"Good." *I hope you no longer hate me.*

Leah was about to say something else when a noise made both she and Jake jerk their heads around. Tiffany appeared to be embroiled in a fierce standoff with Tully.

"Tiffany, you're starting this in two minutes, so you have to go out there," pleaded Tully.

"I don't care. I won't do it," Tiffany insisted, shaking her head. "You can't make me."

Leah glanced at Jake and he back at her. It was odd to see Tiffany, ordinarily so cool and suffused with immoderate maturity and aplomb, acting like a petulant, scared child.

"Tiffany, just think how good it'll feel to finish it," said Tully, "something you've been working on for so—"

Tiffany shook her head, her lips contracting into a defiant pout.

Tully looked at her watch. "If you don't get out there when you're supposed to, I'm going to forcibly push you out," she threatened.

"I dare you to," parried Tiffany.

"Oh no?"

Michelle popped in from the booth to yell, "Places!" Tully touched her arm to stop her before she could leave again.

"Tiffany is not going on," Tully told Michelle, her face conveying a blend of disbelief and befuddlement.

"Tiffany, you're on in one minute," Michelle cajoled the girl, whose arms were ferociously interlocked over her chest.

Michelle sighed. Cupping her mouth so Tiffany wouldn't hear, Michelle whispered something to Tully.

"Don't worry," Tully reassured her. "You go back to the booth. I'll take care of this."

Bobbing her head up and down, Michelle retreated to the booth.

Not budging from her resolve, Tiffany offered a weak

solution, "Maybe Leah can go on instead...?"

"No!" responded Tully. "What is this, kindergarten? It's time and you're going out there now!"

"No, I'm not," countered Tiffany.

"Yes, you are!" persisted Tully. To prove her point, she pushed Tiffany with all her might onto the stage.

Leah gasped.

"Oh Christ," Jake snickered under his breath.

Others echoed his reaction in the form of strangled laughter. To squelch her guffaws, Kelly covered her mouth.

Leah stared at Tully with her jaw agape. "I can't believe you did that."

Tully dismissed it with a flap of her hand. "She's out there now, isn't she?" She snorted.

"That's not the point," Leah retorted.

She and all the other kids hurried to catch a glimpse of Tiffany on the stage. She was just catching her balance, straightening herself out to recover her poise. From the wings, Leah was riveted to Tiffany, wondering what she would do next. For a moment, it reminded her of the sensation you feel when you barge into the aftermath of a car accident in which the vehicle is smashed beyond recognition and the passengers trapped inside are either severely injured or dead. You know it's the morally correct instinct to pass the grisly scene, and yet morbid curiosity won't let you.

In the blanket of near darkness, save for the dim lights, Tiffany resembled a scared gazelle.

Come on, Tiffany, you can do it.

Leah felt her hands shaking. She was up next, and the more Leah watched Tiffany implode like this, the more her own nerves skyrocketed.

Tiffany looked out into the black amorphous mass that was the audience, craning her neck.

She must be trying to search for someone. Her mother, maybe, or someone else she loves?

Suddenly, Tiffany spun her head around to upstage left, sending a none-too-furtive glimpse at the wings. Her eyes were dilating. She was heaving, breaths spewing out in sharp, jagged spurts.

Leah could no longer watch. It was too painful. She tore her eyes away, seeking to focus on something mundane; in this instance, it was the legs of a backstage table.

Amid a staccato symphony of coughs, seat shuffling, paper rustling, and unwrapping of lozenges, the silence was blaring.

Her eyes still averted, Leah heard Tully, on book, prompting Tiffany.

"The quality of mercy is not strained..."

And out of nowhere, Tiffany jumped on the next lines, reciting them in full voice:

It droppeth as the gentle rain from heaven
Upon the place beneath: it is twice blest;
It blesseth him that gives and him that takes...

Unabated relief overcame Leah as she veered her eyes back to Tiffany.

Hooray! Thank god.

When Tiffany finished, there was no clapping. But Leah knew it wasn't because the audience was still traumatized at the sight of a young girl in the throes of stage fright; it was because, prior to the start of the show, Downey had requested the crowd to hold their applause until the performance was over.

Exiting stage left, Tiffany strode confidently into the wings and then backstage. A Cheshire-cat grin of satisfaction appeared on her comely countenance.

There Leah and the others lavished her with congratulatory hugs and kisses. Among her well-wishers was Tully.

"Nice job," she said. "You see, I told you, you could do it."

Trying to squelch a scowl, Tiffany's lips contorted into a synthetic grin. She stole away, rolling her eyes. Leah swore she heard Tiffany mutter, "Bitch," underneath her breath when Tully's back was turned, but she wasn't sure. She wouldn't blame her if she had.

Leah was now on deck. She waited for Tully, who was wearing a headset so she could hear Downey and Michelle in the booth calling the show, to give her the cue to enter the stage.

Just pretend it's your Bas Mitzvah and instead of having to recite the Haftorah, you're reciting Shakespeare. Same thing, kind of. Just in costume.

She took a few protracted breaths, inhaling and exhaling. Yet the more she did this, the more she was convinced she was hyperventilating.

"You'll be okay."

She pivoted her head to see Tully.

"If it gets bad, just visualize everyone in their underwear," Tully quipped.

This tired advice on conquering the fear of public speaking, a platitude enshrined in the pantheon of clichés, had no effect on Leah, who couldn't flex a muscle on her face. Terror froze her expression in place.

Tully shifted tactics, seeming to sense Leah was on the verge of a panic attack. "Don't worry. You know what you're doing." Then, as if she couldn't help herself, she tossed in a zinger. "If not, it's only an hour in your life, an hour you'll never have to repeat again. And then, it'll be over. Oh, by the way, you're on."

The first thing that popped into Leah's mind when she hit down center were the lights, which were so blinding she could feel her eyes blinking and squinting more than usual.

Attempting to transcend the optical convulsions, Leah drew a hearty swig of breath, inhaling and exhaling, then began.

Unfortunately, a minute into her speech when all was going well, she blanked.

Rather than surrender to panic, Leah ran the lines of the monologue in her head. Lines she'd drilled into her mental computer at home over the last twelve weeks, lines she'd recited to herself at school so only she could hear. Of course, the other kids at school no doubt thought she was crazy when they saw her in a preoccupied, almost hypnotic state, talking to herself in the hallway or at lunch by herself and not sitting with Evelyn. But then, after that imbroglio with Dede, they thought she was crazy anyway, so what they thought now was immaterial.

Before Tully could prompt her, Leah, snapping out of her stupor, leaped on her next lines. She was so grateful for the providential intervention that had jogged her memory, it made her want to say a blessing right there. Instead, Shakespeare would have to suffice.

Love can transpose to form and dignity.
Love looks not with the eyes, but with the mind,
And therefore, is winged Cupid painted blind.

Then she was done. Three minutes. One scene down, one more to go.

She remembered Downey's instructions: *Remain on the stage for five seconds, then exit; otherwise, you're going to break your neck and fall when it goes totally black. And that'll be a new set of problems for you.* As walking around in a brace or on crutches was not an uplifting alternative, Leah adhered to Downey's decree.

Backstage, she was greeted with the same round of congratulatory hugs previously showered on Tiffany. Only Kelly, standing like a figurine on the outskirts of the backstage area, was mute, although Leah thought she heard her ex-pal mouth, "Good job," under her breath.

Or maybe she was imagining that...

Before Leah could process any other stimuli, Sandy padded up to her. Leah's black dress for her *Hamlet* scene was folded over Sandy's arm.

Without warning, she reached for the zipper of Leah's Helena costume.

"What are you doing?" Leah screeched, an outburst that caused Tully to order her to be quiet.

Leah apologized, having forgotten where she was. Then she whispered to Sandy, "There are boys here."

It was an ironic statement, given her recent intimacy with Jake; still, that didn't mean she wanted everyone to see her practically naked. At her core, she was still a modest fifteen-year-old.

The light bulb went off over Sandy's head. "Oh right...okay. Let's go out to the hallway."

There was no zipper on the Gertrude costume, only buttons on the back. Leah's nervousness returned in full force as it seemed to take Sandy an eternity to fasten each button.

"Why did I pick this dress for you again?" Sandy joked. From her dresser's kit, she pulled out a lint roller, which she briskly moved up and down the sleeves, the front, and then the back of Leah's dress.

Onstage, Jake and Rob were already going through the paces of their Hamlet and First Clown scene. Leah was eager to watch; however, Sandy's fastidious ministrations were preventing that.

"Are you done yet?" Leah asked, impatient.

"There you go," replied Sandy as she finished fussing around the mesh collar of Leah's Gertrude dress. "Perfect."

Sandy's benign manner made Leah regret her testiness.

"Sorry, I—I—"

"Leah, it's okay. I've heard far worse than that. Trust me. Now go have fun."

Leah navigated the tiny throng comprised of her fellow juvies, who swarmed around an oblong prop table with an arsenal of emergency essentials: flashlights, batteries for the headsets, a tape measure, a screwdriver, and red spike tape, the latter used by the Palisade Shakespeare production assistants to mark where set pieces would go on the stage.

Only two scenes, Tiffany and Kelly's from *King Lear* and Leah's and Jake's *Hamlet*, were using set pieces. For *Lear*, the design was barebones and conceptual: two platforms on the side and, in the background, three red and black stone pieces, exactly what the Palisades Shakespeare had used for an experimental production of *Lear* two years earlier.

As for the *Hamlet* scene that took place in Gertrude's bedroom chamber, only a swivel chair would be used. Leah's Gertrude would sit in it while Jake's Hamlet, firing a volley of accusations, would circle her menacingly like an animal stalking its prey.

As Leah's delicate steps gingerly traversed into the backstage area, Tully jerked her head in Leah's direction, placing a finger to her lips.

Attired in a light lavender empire-waisted gown for her next and final scene in which she was playing Regan to Kelly's Goneril in *King Lear*, Tiffany was stretching her elongated neck from the wings to better see and hear the scene between the two boys unfolding.

Tiptoeing behind her, Leah whispered, "How are they doing?"

Tiffany hushed Leah, then softly voiced, "Really good," with a nod of her head. She moved slightly to make room for Leah to also watch.

Because of Rob's recurring anxiety bouts and other mental health issues, Tully had advised Downey to assign him only one scene. What Downey came up with was an ideal showcase: a humorous interlude—or "comedy relief" in theater parlance—in a dark melodrama. The highlight of the scene was the banter between Rob's gravedigger character and Jake's Hamlet. Rob held his own with a confidence and strength that enchanted his peers observing from the wings.

Watching him, Leah marveled that this boy was the same one who, three months earlier, had suffered a nervous breakdown when asked to speak about himself during the orientation process.

Noting the metamorphosis, Tully, lodging in next to Leah, pointed to Rob and effused, "That kid was a basket case a few months ago. Now look at him!" Then her attention switched to Jake. "Now, your friend is good, extremely good. He has talent. Most of our kids aren't like that. We don't expect them to be. But, Rob, he's the reason we do this."

After the scene, both boys were accorded a warm reception. Rob's face lit up with a pure, infectious happiness.

While the crowd fawned over Rob, Jake stood on the sidelines in an introspective haze reminiscent of his onstage character.

Leah sauntered over to him. She contemplated planting a kiss on his cheek to congratulate him, then stopped, thinking it maybe was not a good idea to convey any kind of physicality toward him, given their recent past.

"You were wonderful, so good," she said.

"Thanks. You were good too," he said with a smile. "You're good in front of people. You can act, too."

Leah chuckled at Jake's compliment. Now that she had

been sentenced to Shakespeare, there was one thing she was sure about—she would never go into theater. *No way.* She didn't like pretending to be other people, crawling into the skin of fictitious characters and feigning emotions and mannerisms that weren't hers. You would think after everything that had happened to her, the bullying, the name-calling, the ostracism, she would've relished playing anyone who wasn't herself. But she didn't...and the revelation puzzled and fascinated her.

Yet she also had to admit, she did like being center stage, speaking to an audience. If there was one benefit from this experience—other than it kept her out of jail—it was that.

"Not sure of that," she replied. Then, half-jokingly, she added, "Maybe I'll become a lawyer, and a kid from the Garden State Bard will be my client one day."

"Yeah," said Jake, stroking his chin. "I could see you doing that."

"Really? I was only kidding."

"No, definitely."

"Hmm," Leah gave this possible future vocation some thought, the idea flowering in her head. "Maybe. Wouldn't that be ironic?"

"Shhhh," shushed Tully. She then showed them the five-minute warning sign with her left hand.

Her nerves acting up again, Leah shot Jake a worried look.

"It'll be fine," he calmed her.

Except for Leah messing up one line and forgetting the next—a glitch that Jake remedied by diving in effortlessly with his lines—the scene went well. Jake was so captivating that Leah had no problems acting off him; she listened and reacted, with most of the lines (the ones she didn't mess up) pouring out of her organically.

As she reflected on the scene in hindsight, she guessed that was acting.

Jake also incorporated a few bits that were never in the direction. For instance, when Jake as Hamlet orbited Leah's Gertrude in the chair, he tenderly fondled her chin at one point before launching into a brutal tirade. The combined effect was so chilling that Leah could hear not a soul-stirring nor anyone with late-stage tuberculosis in the house.

Such an act that blurs the grace and blush of modesty,
Calls virtue hypocrite, takes off the rose
From the fair forehead of an innocent love
And sets a blister there, makes marriage-vows
As false as dicers' oaths.

Leah found Jake's recitation of Hamlet's lines when he's attacking his mother so memorable that weeks and months after the performance, they would reverberate throughout her head, becoming a kind of weird mantra. Of what, she wasn't sure. It wasn't so much that the words resonated with her, but she found Jake so entrancing to watch.

Despite Downey's preperformance request to hold any applause until each performance was over, a few people clapped and cheered at the end of the scene.

"Good job," said Kelly as Leah swished past her.

Kelly was waiting with Derek to start their scene, the last one in the performance. Hearing the compliment from a most unexpected source, Leah stopped and turned her face at a ninety-degree angle to Kelly.

"What did you say?" she questioned, confused.

"I said, 'Good job.'"

"Thank you," she murmured.

Tully then gave Kelly and Derek the cue to enter the stage. As Kelly was about to exit the wings, Leah wished her good luck, but she wasn't sure Kelly heard it.

"Can I talk to you for a second?" Jake whispered to Leah.

Leah looked quizzically at him before following Jake's hurried strides to the hallway.

"I just wanted to thank you for being so cool when things got crazy," said Jake in a gentle voice.

Leah wasn't sure whether he was joking or being earnest. "Really?"

"Yes, really! And, I also wanted to ask you if...you want to see a movie with me next week?"

Leah was dumbfounded. "But...I thought you didn't want to see me ever again because of what happened?"

Jake didn't answer; instead, he kissed her sweetly on the lips.

Leah's eyelids fluttered as he did this, and seeing this, Jake laughed.

"My eyes twitch sometimes...whenever I get tired or...excited," Leah spluttered. "Does it bother you?"

"No, not at all," he replied as he kissed her again. "I think it's cute." He paused. "You didn't answer my question," he teased.

"Uh," answered a dazed Leah. "What was it again?" Then her eyes popped open. "Oh yes, yes! I'll go to the movies with you. Yes!"

A radiant smile blazed across Leah's face.

They were about to kiss again when Tully's voice disrupted their bliss.

"Show is over! Everyone on stage."

Reluctantly extricating themselves from each other, Jake snatched Leah's hand to catch up with the others for the curtain call. Worry creased his young face. He stopped.

"Are you sure, you know, about...?" he asked, her hand still firmly gripped in his.

"Yes," she beamed. "Absolutely."

The thunderous ovation that greeted the two as they raced to the stage with the others flooded their senses. Leah eyes locked with those of her cheering parents and her brother flashing a thumbs-up sign to his sister. A smile so wide and infectious overtook Leah's face as she wondered if her family's hands and the rest of the audience would be red for days.

"We did it," Jake whispered to Leah, his voice scarcely heard above the roar of the applause.

"Yes, we did," she replied. Her eyes flitted from Jake to the audience and a future yawning before her.

Acknowledgements

Writing a book may seem like a solitary effort to outsiders but the reality belies that notion. It certainly applied with the development of "Sentenced to Shakespeare." In this context, I owe a special debt to the following: seasoned editor Elizabeth Zack, for her wise and judicious edits on the manuscript in its earlier incarnation; young adult novelist/editor Stephanie Diaz, for her role in helping me strengthen the teen feel in the story; and The Editorial Department's Karinya Funsett-Topping, for her brutally candid, tough-love critique, which forced me to kill my proverbial darlings and polish the narrative, moving it toward publication.

Also, special thanks should be extended to Michelle Hope for her copyediting acumen and to the beta readers who offered me their unfiltered thoughts on the manuscript throughout its gestation.

I'm especially grateful to Chris Fenwick of Sunbury Press for her patience in answering my unending questions and for shepherding the manuscript through the editorial and production process.

A deep and heartfelt thanks goes to the friends and family members who have never wavered in their support and encouragement of my creative efforts. I remain beholden to all of you. And, lastly, a big resounding thanks to my mother Esther for her love and unstinting belief in me always.

ABOUT THE AUTHOR

Iris Dorbian is a professional business and arts journalist whose credits include *Forbes, Wall Street Journal, Venture Capital Journal, Buyouts, Investopedia, DMNews, Jerusalem Report*, the *Forward, Playbill, Backstage, Theatermania, Live Design, Media Industry Newsletter* and *PR News*. She is the former editor-in-chief of *Stage Directions* magazine and author of "Great Producers: Visionaries of the American Theater," which was published by Allworth Press/Skyhorse Publishing in August 2008. Her personal essays have been published *in Blue Lyra Review, B O D Y, Embodied Effigies, Jewish Literary Journal, Diverse Voices Quarterly, Adanna Literary Journal, ThisSpace.org, Skirt!* and *Gothesque Magazine*. A New Jersey native, Iris has a master's degree in journalism from Columbia University.

www.ingramcontent.com/pod-product-compliance
Lightning Source LLC
Chambersburg PA
CBHW032116020726
47494CB00007BA/2096